"In this treat for Wester........................f his popular character Hewey Calloway. Kelton, who seems to have been writing Westerns forever, never missed a step in this dusty, noisy, completely absorbing adventure. Larry McMurtry might get lots of publicity and awards for his Westerns, but Kelton is just as fine a writer in this genre."   —*Booklist* on *Six Bits a Day*

"The keystones of his suspenseful, carefully drawn style can be found in these two early, previously published full-length novels. Both novels offer frontier excitement, suspense, a bit of mystery and romance, and plenty of flying fists and fast-shooting six-gun action. Kelton's first books are as good as his most recent work."
                    —*Publishers Weekly* on *Brush Country*

"Years of agricultural journalism have given Kelton's stories that ring of authenticity lacking in some Westerns"
                    —*True West Magazine*

"Once again, Kelton offers an exciting tale in which the bad guys are really bad and some of the good guys are, too. His characters are sharply defined, the historical background is vivid, and the gunplay can't be beat."   —*Publishers Weekly* on *Jericho's Road*

"Kelton creates a story rich in historical context, character development, and action."   —*The Houston Chronicle* on *Texas Vendetta*

"Kelton again lives up to his reputation as one of the finest and most prolific of today's Western authors."
                    —*The Abilene Reporter News* on *The Way of the Coyote*

"Award-winning writer Elmer Kelton—a star in the shrinking Western genre—totes you effortlessly to the post-Civil War Texas frontier, where white settlers were just learning to live with freed slaves, Comanches, and each other. . . . His characters, like Shannon, make mistakes, are far from perfect, and take life in stride."   —*The New York Post* on *Badger Boy*

"Elmer Kelton writes of early Texas with unerring authority. His knowledge of the state's history is complete, too—drawn from the lives of real people. . . . The fate of Texas is at hand, and Kelton will have readers eager to find out what happens."
                    —*Fort Worth Star-Telegram* on *The Buckskin Line*

ELMER KELTON

SIX BITS A DAY

A TOM DOHERTY ASSOCIATES BOOK
NEW YORK

This is a work of fiction. All the characters and events portrayed in this book are either products of the author's imagination or are used fictitiously.

SIX BITS A DAY

Copyright © 2005 by Elmer Kelton

A Forge Book
Published by Tom Doherty Associates, LLC
175 Fifth Avenue
New York, NY 10010

www.tor.com

Forge® is a registered trademark of Tom Doherty Associates, LLC.

ISBN-13: 978-0-765-34846-3
ISBN-10: 0-765-34846-2

First edition: November 2005
First mass market edition: October 2006

Printed in the United States of America

0 9 8 7 6 5 4 3 2 1

Dedicated to
RED STEAGALL, DON EDWARDS,
MICHAEL MARTIN MURPHEY, BAXTER BLACK,
WADDIE MITCHELL,
*and the many other poets and singers who work
to keep the cowboy spirit alive.*

SIX BITS
A DAY

ONE

Hewey Calloway's stomach growled like an angry bear. He had not been so hungry in all his twenty-two years. Yesterday he and his year-younger brother, Walter, had eaten their last chunk of hog belly. It was so fat that he had had to force it down. Now he would trade almost anything he owned for another piece of it, not that he owned much. Everything he had was either on his back or tied to his saddle.

Walter had been riding in moody silence. He pulled up beside Hewey after passing around the far side of a mesquite whose thorns threatened to reach out and grab him. He said, "Even the trees here try to tear off a strip of hide. How far do you reckon we've traveled?"

Hewey grunted. "A good ways." He wanted to keep a cheerful face, even if doubts were weighing on him.

Walter said, "We ain't seen a human bein' in two days, and no game bigger than a jackrabbit. My belly is flatter than a stove lid."

"Mine ain't no better."

There had been a few jackrabbits, and Hewey had shot at them with an old wooden-handled six-shooter he carried in his saddlebags. But he was no marksman. Each bullet kicked up dirt several feet from the target and set the rabbit into startled flight.

Walter said, "Some cowboys we are. I ain't got a pistol, and you'd just as well've left yours behind. I never saw such a poor shot."

Hewey tried not to appear testy. "Had you rather be choppin' cotton and sloppin' hogs? That's all we'd have if we went back to East Texas."

"Maybe we'd have a job and somethin' to eat."

Hewey saw one saving grace. "At least we're a long ways west of the cotton fields, and it's been a week since we've seen a hog."

The 1880s were nearing an end, and most Texas land still open for new settlement was in the semiarid western region beyond the Conchos. Short, sparse grass shared ground with desert plants such as greasewood and mesquite and a dozen kinds of thorny cactuses that lay in ambush for the careless or the unlucky.

Hewey and Walter's mother had died when they were boys. Over the next few years their restless father had led them in a fruitless circle from the East Texas blacklands to Oklahoma and Kansas, searching for an ideal home he would see only in his dreams. After his death the brothers had wandered about, laboring at whatever they could find to ward off the wolves that had been at the Calloway door as far back as Hewey could remember.

They struggled through a numbing variety of pick-and-shovel jobs before joining a trail outfit driving cattle to the Kansas railroad. Horseback work had fitted Hewey like kid gloves. Now, however, the trails north were mostly closed. Farms and barbed wire had blocked them off. Long cattle drives were being rendered unnecessary by the extension of railroads across Texas.

He had heard that large ranches were building up west of the farming country and needed men willing to work. He had no objection to work if he could do it in the saddle. Unlike Walter, he had never been able to fit his hands properly around a plow handle.

"Our luck is bound to change," he said. He usually accepted the vagaries of life without getting his underwear in a twist. "We'll find work out here somewhere."

Walter preferred a sparrow in the hand to a hawk on the wing. "If we don't starve to death first. I can imagine somebody findin' us five or ten years from now, two little dried-up husks layin' out on the prairie. Kind of like a pair of old corncobs with the shucks still on."

"The coyotes would chew us up long before that." Hewey toyed with the mental image. "I wish a coyote *would* show hisself. I'd eat him before he could eat me."

"Not if you had to shoot him."

The brothers had set out on this trip three weeks ago with hope and youthful high spirits. Like Pa, Hewey fantasized about the far hills and what might lie beyond. He envisioned a horseback life of freedom and adventure, excitement and glory. The trouble was that he was more than ten years too late to share the fighting against Comanches and Kiowas, and the buffalo were gone. Most of the famous outlaws were dead, too, like Billy the Kid and Sam Bass and Jesse James. So far as he could see, the cowboy life was about all that remained to him. He meant to carve out a piece of it somewhere in western Texas.

Walter did not share Hewey's longing for adventure. He was comfortable with what he could see and hear and touch. He would be content with a solid job where pay and meals came regularly, where tomorrow was no more of a mystery than yesterday. Hewey enjoyed reading blood-stirring novels about cowboys and pirates and knights of old. Walter found satisfaction in guiding a plow and keeping a straight row. He would have been happy to spend his life as a farmer somewhere back in the blacklands.

In Hewey's view, East Texas had been cottoned out. It offered no future that interested him, while West Texas promised a fresh beginning. But his shining hopes had gradually diminished along with the supplies he and Walter had brought on the trip. At the moment, he would trade a month of tomorrows for a plate of beans.

Walter said, "Neither one of us would make a meal for a coyote. Even the buzzards don't pay us any mind."

They had come across an occasional scattering of cattle, which usually hoisted their tails and clattered off into the nearest thicket. Hewey grasped at the tattered shreds of his optimism. "Where there's cows there's bound to be a ranch. And where there's a ranch, they're bound to need cowboys."

The animals were of all colors and ran more to horn than to flesh. Hewey said, "Takes a tough breed to make it in this western country."

"You sure *we're* tough enough?"

Hewey set his jaw. "Our name's Calloway, ain't it? Pa carried a Yankee bullet in him for twenty years, right up to the day he died. We've just got to take another hitch in our belts."

He would have to punch a new hole to make his any tighter.

Sundown came with no sign of a dwelling or watering place. But at dusk Hewey saw the flicker of a campfire. Walter said, "Maybe they'll give us somethin' to eat."

Hewey said, "We ain't goin' to ride in there and beg. Us Calloways have never begged for nothin'."

Walter said, "Maybe they'll hear our stomachs growl."

Hewey assumed the lead as he usually did, being a year or so older. He put his horse into an easy lope and did not slow until he was within rock-throwing distance of the fire. He saw nobody.

A stern voice spoke from behind a bush. "You-all lift them hands to where I can see them."

Hewey did not spot the man at first, or the gun, but his gut told him they were there in the dusk. "Friend," he said shakily, "we ain't out for no trouble."

A tall, lanky man walked into the open, holding a pistol. He said, "You must be pilgrims, or you'd know not to charge into a camp like that. You always holler first to find out if you're welcome."

A shiny badge reflected firelight. Law officers made Hewey uneasy. Back where they came from he had had a couple of run-ins with old Sheriff Noonan, a man with a stern commitment to the letter of the law. There was, for instance, the time Hewey had slipped over to Old Man Babcock's farm one night and whacked off all the pigs' tails. A penful of bobtailed pigs looked funny to Hewey, but Babcock and the sheriff had not seen the humor in it. The jail cot was the hardest bed Hewey had ever tried to sleep on.

He said, "Don't shoot, mister. We'll ride on and not bother you no more."

Moving closer, the man gave each brother a moment's study, then slipped the pistol back into a holster on his hip. The frown slowly left his thin face. "I had to be certain of your intentions. Name's Len Tanner."

"Ours is Calloway. I'm Hewey, and he's Walter. Pleased to make your acquaintance." Hewey kept looking at the badge. It was circular with a star in the center. "You a sheriff?"

"Texas Ranger." Tanner touched his forefinger to the badge. "Pretty, ain't it? Had it made out of a Mexican peso."

Hewey judged that Tanner was well into middle age. Firelight exaggerated the facial creases and the roughness of a skin weathered by sun and wind. It crossed Hewey's mind that a ranger must lead an exciting life, maybe better even than a cowboy's. But he did not dwell on the notion long, for he knew he was too poor a marksman to be accepted into such a demanding organization. He could not hit a barn from the inside.

The campfire drew his attention. A small coffeepot sat on the coals. A half-cooked slice of beef lay in a skillet on the ground. Tanner had probably set it off to one side when he heard the horses coming. Hewey said, "I'd trade you a good pocketknife for some of that."

Tanner shook his head. "Already got a knife." Seeing Hewey's disappointment, he added, "But you're welcome to share my supper. Didn't cost me nothin' anyway. It's contraband."

"Contraband?" Hewey thought that was some kind of illegal whiskey.

"I was trailin' a pair of thieves that butchered another man's beef. They ran off and left the meat behind."

"You didn't catch them?"

"I know where they'll light. Most criminals ain't weighted down with brains." He fetched a tin cup out of a canvas bag and tapped it on his knee to dislodge a scorpion or anything else that might be in it. He handed it to Hewey. "Help yourselves to the coffee. I'll heat the skillet again."

Hewey filled the cup. The rim burned his lips. He handed the cup to Walter. "Hot. Needs to be blowed a little."

Hewey had no compunctions about sharing a cup. He

was used to drinking from cisterns and wells that had a community cup for use by anyone who came along. He said, "I remember a story about some yahoo that dragged into town starvin' to death for water. They asked him why he didn't drink at one of the wells he passed along the way, and he said, 'I couldn't. I had no cup.'"

Tanner chuckled at the story and told a couple of his own while he waited for the steaks to get done. He watched bemused as Hewey and Walter wolfed down the meat, which was sizzling hot from the skillet. "Sorry I got no gravy." He fried a second helping, then sat back while the brothers finished that, too.

He asked, "How long since you boys left the cotton patch?"

Hewey said, "Does it show?"

"You've both got lint in your ears. What brings you out so far from water? There ain't a decent farm in a hundred miles."

Hewey said, "That's the way we want it. We're lookin' for cowboy work."

Tanner grunted. "Cowboy life ain't exactly like the storybooks tell it. You're up before daylight and out till dark. You sweat for thirty days to earn a piddlin' wage that you can blow in thirty minutes."

Walter asked, "Does rangerin' pay better?"

"Not always, but a ranger don't have to put up with a bunch of bawlin' cows. Ain't nothin' dumber than a cow unless it's a sheep."

Hewey said, "We know. We've done some cow work ourselves."

Tanner responded, "A horse is a little smarter, but not much. I've been throwed off and stomped on more times than I've ever been shot at, even bein' a ranger."

Hewey nodded. "I notice you've got to look quick if

you want to see these cattle around here. They're up and gone before you can say scat."

"They ain't housebroke. Some'll run you ragged, then try to put a horn through your gizzard. But if you're bound and determined to chase cows, good luck to you. I do better chasin' outlaws."

Hewey's imagination ran free as he pictured the adventures this lawman might have experienced. "How long you been a ranger?"

"I started in the Indian times before the big war. Wasn't much more than a skinny button then."

He was still skinny, Hewey thought, but long past being a button.

The talkative Tanner related stories about chasing and being chased by Comanches, and about long searches for criminals of every stripe. He said, "For a while of late I was down on the Ryo Grandy, chasin' after border jumpers from both sides of the river. Big state, Texas is, and I've crossed every river in it just about. Got the scars to prove it."

He rolled up his sleeve to show a raised mark about five inches long. "That's one of the littlest. A knife blade done that."

Hewey chilled at the thought of cold steel.

Tanner asked, "Ever hear of Rusty Shannon and Andy Pickard?"

Hewey had not.

Tanner said, "Good men, both of them. Me and them rode many a mile together. They're out of the rangers now. Old Rusty's married and got two young'uns. Andy took him a pretty young wife, too."

Hewey asked, "You ever been married?"

"Naw, horses and dogs like me, but I don't shine in the womenfolks' eyes. The Lord didn't choose to make me handsome. He just made me lucky instead."

After breakfast Tanner gave the brothers most of the meat that remained. He ignored their polite objections. He said, "It don't take much for a skinny old hull like me. You two need it to keep your strength up in this big dry country."

Hewey regretted parting company with the ranger, but Tanner was headed southward. Watching him ride away, Walter said, "He's a great talker. You reckon half of what he told us really happened?"

"If it didn't, it ought to have." Hewey touched spurs to his horse and started west. "We ain't findin' work settin' here."

At the middle of the afternoon he saw dust ahead, stirred by a herd of cattle. "Maybe somebody can point us to a job of work." He moved his horse into a lope. He was halfway there before Walter caught up with him.

Two horsemen appeared from within a clump of mesquite brush, brandishing pistols. A scowling rider with two weeks' growth of mottled whiskers demanded, "Who are you, and what's your business here?"

Staring into two formidable-looking muzzles, Hewey felt a chill. He had never been drawn to guns. He stammered, "Nothin'. We don't even rightly know where we're at."

The man's belligerence slowly subsided. "You-all ain't nothin' but a pair of punkin' rollers. We thought you might be cattle rustlers. In this country we got to be careful." He holstered the pistol and gave a silent signal to his younger partner to do the same. The second man had not used a razor in a while either, but his stubble was more like fuzz than whiskers. "Just lookin' over the country, are you?"

Hewey's voice steadied. "What we're really lookin' for is a job."

"Cowboys, are you?"

"We've been up the trail once."

The man considered for a minute. "Me and Chum here could use a little help. How about six bits a day and found?"

"Found?"

"Grub and all the ground you need to roll out your beddin'."

Six bits wasn't much, Hewey thought, but it beat what they had been doing. The thought of regular grub made up for a lot. "Just tell us what you want done."

"Fall in behind them cows and help us keep them movin'. Me and Chum ain't been makin' good time by ourselves."

Hewey said, "We can do that." He started to ride up but paused. "What do we call you, mister?"

"Call me Mr. Smith. You don't have to *mister* my partner. Just call him Chum."

Hewey rough-counted about a hundred cows in this bunch, and most had calves. He could not see that driving them offered much challenge. They appeared to have been driven far and hard already. Heads down, they drooled and dragged their feet. Many calves had fallen to the dusty rear, unable to keep up with their mothers. Cows kept stopping and turning back, bawling for their offspring. The smell of their saliva and fresh, warm manure was strong in Hewey's nostrils.

Smith and Chum left Hewey and Walter in the dust and took positions farther ahead. After a while Smith turned back, agitated. "You're lettin' the drags fall behind. Punch them up."

Hewey said, "These calves ain't got much left in them to punch. How much farther do they have to go?"

The answer was curt. "I'll let you know when we get there. Keep pushin'."

Walter rode over beside Hewey. "He's goin' to walk the hooves plumb off of them."

Hewey shrugged. "They're his, so it's none of our worry as long as we get paid." Nevertheless, he disliked seeing animals punished, especially small calves. "I don't see where it'd make much difference if it took a little longer. Cows don't know what time it is."

He noticed that most of the cows were branded CC and earmarked with a swallow fork. Several bore a J Bar brand and a different mark.

Walter started to speak. "You don't suppose . . ." He broke off in mid-sentence. "No, they wouldn't be."

"Be what?" Hewey asked.

"Nothin'. I don't know why I said anything."

Hewey puzzled over what Walter might have been thinking, but he did not dwell on it long. "We've got what we came for, a payin' job that'll feed us."

Smith did not stop the drive until after sundown. Chum built a small fire to boil coffee and fry just enough bacon to neutralize the hunger pangs. He took the bacon away from the heat while it was a little raw. "We got to put this fire out. They can see it for a long ways in the dark."

Hewey knew it was best not to question the boss, but he asked anyway. "Who is *they?*"

Smith said, "Indians."

"I thought all the Indians were on the reservation."

"Never can tell when some of them bucks may bust out. A herd like this would be easy pickin's."

Hewey thought Smith was overcautious. It had been years since he had heard of any Indian trouble. "All the Indians I ever saw was tame ones."

Smith studied their back trail, his eyes narrowed. "You boys are too young to remember the old days. Once you've heard a war whoop, you never forget it."

Hewey looked in all directions. "I don't see anything."

"It's when you don't see anything that you'd better be extra careful."

Hewey hoped Smith would tell about some of his adventures with Indians, but unlike Tanner he was not a talker. He held his cards close to the vest. As he poured a second cup of coffee he said, "You boys take the first watch. Me and Chum will relieve you after midnight."

The cattle were so leg-weary that they bedded down easily once the cows and calves had paired up. Hewey saw little danger that they would stampede in the night.

The moon was full. He rode a slow circle around the herd and met Walter coming from the other direction.

Walter said, "I ain't heard you singin' to them."

"With my voice, they'd jump and run."

"Yeah, I've heard you in church. You ain't no nightingale."

Pa had taught Hewey how to tell time in a general way by the position of the stars as they made a slow circle in the night sky. He judged it was considerably past midnight when Smith rode up to him and asked, "See or hear anything?"

"Nothin' but a cow with the croup. No Indians."

"There's other things to worry about besides Indians. It'd be a shame if cattle rustlers was to take this herd before we can get it to the ranch."

"Where's that?"

"Other side of the Rio Grande." Smith jerked his head in a southward direction. "Better get a little sleep. We'll be drivin' them hard again tomorrow."

"The pace is tough on the calves."

Smith's voice was sharp. "I'll worry about the stock. You just do what I hired you for."

Hewey shrugged. Though he felt sorry for the cattle, it was none of his business if the boss worked them down to hide and bone. It just didn't seem logical for an owner to mistreat his property. This herd was worth money.

He met Walter before reaching camp. Hewey said, "I could use a cup of coffee."

Walter said, "Chum told me not to start that fire again. He's worried about cow thieves seein' it."

"No self-respectin' cattle thief would be out stirrin' around at this time of the night," Hewey said. But orders were orders, and they hadn't earned but six bits apiece so far.

In the dark Hewey had a hard time finding a place smooth enough to spread his blanket. Something kept poking him in the back. He finally got sleepy enough to ignore it. By the time he came fully awake, the sun was rising. He saw that Walter was sitting up, listening.

Walter said, "I hear horses runnin'."

Hewey flung the blanket aside and stood up. He saw two horsemen moving south in a long lope, leaving the herd behind.

"That's Smith and Chum," he said. "Must be chasin' a runaway cow."

"Looks more like they're *bein'* chased." Walter pointed to horsemen approaching rapidly from the north. Four men split off in pursuit of Smith and Chum; four others came toward the herd.

Hewey felt sudden apprehension. "They may be the cattle thieves Smith was worried about."

Walter's expression was grave. "Or maybe the real thieves are them two we hired on with."

Hewey's eyes widened as the suggestion soaked in. "You think we been drivin' stolen cattle?"

"It crossed my mind."

"Then we're in a mess of trouble." Hewey expelled a long breath. "I wish you'd told me what you was thinkin'."

"You're the oldest. You're supposed to be the smartest."

"I ought to've suspicioned them myself. I was just too anxious about gettin' a job and somethin' to eat."

Walter's voice was shaky. "Those people look pretty mad."

"Just try to appear innocent, like we don't know nothin'. That ought to come natural."

The four riders seemed to bristle with guns. Hewey assumed the oldest was the leader. He was a smallish, skinny man of middle age or perhaps a little past. It was hard to tell through several days' growth of whiskers. He pointed a pistol that appeared from Hewey's angle to be larger than he was. The man wore a dusty, misshapen old felt hat with deep grease stains and a wide brim tattered along its edges. He looked as if he might have crawled out from under a freight car. He gave Hewey and Walter a blistering look and declared, "Thought you got my cows cheap, did you? Two Cs beef comes awful high."

A young man with a round, chubby face grinned with anticipation. "Let's hang them, Mr. Tarpley."

Tarpley's reply was curt. "Use your head. There ain't a tree around here big enough to hang a man on."

"Just thought it'd be a good lesson to them."

"In the old days we could take thieves like these and give their necks a stretchin' without havin' to go to the courthouse. Now it'd stir up a narrow-minded sheriff and a dozen swivel-jawed lawyers."

Hewey struggled for voice. "We ain't thieves."

"We caught you red-handed with my cows. I'd call that thievin'."

"But we didn't know they was stolen. Me and Walter, we just hired out yesterday. The man said they was his."

"What man was that? What was his name?"

"Smith."

"We seen two run off. Who was the other one?"

"The only name we heard was Chum."

Tarpley snorted. "Smith! I reckon you-all are named Jones?"

"No sir, I'm Hewey Calloway, and this is my brother Walter. We just come from over in East Texas."

The chubby boy said, "If we can't hang them, can we shoot them?"

Tarpley snapped, "Shut up, Fat."

Another cowboy put in, "I kind of believe them, C.C. They look too green to be cow thieves. Probably a couple of farm boys fresh off of the plow."

"What would you know about farm boys, Grady Welch?"

"I was one myself, greener than a gourd vine when I came out here. I was a lot like these two."

Tarpley seemed to give at least some consideration to what this cowboy said. "We'll have to let the sheriff sort it all out." He looked back at Hewey. "You boys got any guns?"

Hewey pointed to his saddle lying on the ground. "Walter don't. I got a six-shooter in my saddlebags, but I can't hit anything with it."

"Damned few cowboys can. Fat, go fetch it to me. Then you boys saddle up. You're goin' to help us drive these cows and calves back to where they come from."

Hewey thought about asking him if they would be paid for the work, but Tarpley did not appear in a mood to discuss wages.

The four riders who had pursued Smith and Chum returned empty-handed. "Sorry, C.C.," one said, "but their horses was faster than ours. One of them was that half Thoroughbred you used to match races with."

Tarpley scowled. "Ain't but one thing lower than a cow thief, and that's a man that'd steal your best horse." He jerked his head as a signal. "Let's take them cows home."

TWO

TARPLEY GRUMBLED ABOUT THE CONDITION OF THE cattle. "They're drawed pretty bad. You boys been runnin' them, looks like."

Hewey said, "I told Mr. Smith we was pushin' them too hard. He said he was afraid cattle rustlers might catch up to us."

"Wasn't rustlers he was afraid of, it was me. There was a time when cow thieves shivered at the name of C. C. Tarpley. They ain't forgot my reputation. I'm surprised you didn't recognize my brand."

"Like I told you, me and Walter are strangers here. We just hired out yesterday."

"I got to have more than your word about that."

Hewey watched, puzzled, as Tarpley moved away. The rancher hardly fitted his vision of a big, important cowman. Instead of boots he wore a pair of old lace-up shoes crusted with dirt. His saddle could have been a veteran of the first drive up the Chisholm Trail, and his clothes looked as if they might have been cast off by some passing tramp.

The cowboy named Grady pulled up beside Hewey. He sat in his saddle with the ease of a man who knew his way around a horse. Though he wore a loose shirt with a ripped sleeve clumsily repaired, his broad-brimmed felt hat was carefully shaped. His boots appeared to be custom made. His leather chaps bore silver conchas, which hadn't come cheaply, and inlaid silver hearts decorated his spurs. In contrast to Tarpley, he looked as if he were trying to live up to an image shaped by the penny-dreadful magazines.

Hewey said, "Mr. Tarpley don't look like a cattle baron to me. I'd expect to see him swampin' out a saloon."

Grady smiled. "He may not look like much, but when he shows up at the bank, they call out a brass band." He rolled and lighted a cigarette and offered the sack to Hewey. "What part of East Texas are you boys from?"

Nervous, Hewey spilled more tobacco than went onto the paper. He passed the sack back to Grady without offering it to Walter. He was trying to shield his kid brother from bad habits. "Our pa sharecropped over in the blacklands."

"I'm from the piney woods myself. Came out here four years ago."

"Been a cowboy all that time?"

"That's about all there is to do unless you want to herd sheep. That's left mostly to the Mexicans."

Tarpley hollered, "Grady, I wouldn't get too sociable with them boys. They're liable to contaminate you."

"They've got honest faces."

"So did Billy the Kid."

The cattle were allowed to set their own slow pace, grazing as they went. By late afternoon Hewey guessed they had not traveled more than five or six miles. They came to a large pool where runoff from a recent rain had gathered in a depression. The cows and calves picked up the pace as they smelled the water. They eagerly crowded into it, some standing belly deep while they drank.

Hewey was feeling dry himself. He was not sure he wanted to drink where the mud had been stirred, but he changed his mind when he saw Grady kneel and scoop up water in his cupped hands where no cattle or horses had been. Grady said, "I'm thinkin' about growin' me a mustache. It'd serve as a strainer."

Hewey tried to do as Grady did. After a couple of tries he managed to hold enough water in his hands that he could get a decent mouthful. As he expected, it tasted of mud.

Grady said, "This beats drinkin' out of a cow track. Done that a few times."

Hewey looked back toward C. C. Tarpley. "Ain't you afraid I'll contaminate you?"

Grady smiled. "C.C. barks loud, but he ain't got any teeth, hardly. He's a damned good cowman, even if he has got the soul of an old pirate."

"Pirate?"

"He's big and intends to get bigger no matter what it takes. He's a dried-up, skinny little feller, but he's tied together with rawhide."

Hewey grimaced. That did not bode well for him and Walter.

Tarpley decided to make camp so the cattle could water again when they wanted to. He did not feed much better than Smith had. Pursuit of the cattle thieves had been undertaken too quickly to allow for much preparation. Somebody had thrown a bag of Arbuckle's coffee and a smoked ham into a canvas sack. That had been dinner. Now it was supper, and it would be tomorrow's breakfast if it lasted that long. In the pressure of the moment no one had thought to pick up the little food that had remained in Smith's camp. That had probably become some coyote's supper by now.

Hewey noted that everybody in the outfit was on the lean side except for the one called Fat. It occurred to him that cowboy life might not be the best choice for somebody who loved to eat.

Grady warmed a slice of smoked ham on a stick, holding it over a small fire. He offered it to Hewey, who cut off half and handed the rest back. He said, "I'd think a cow outfit would be eatin' beef."

Grady said, "Only if it's a stray. C.C. thinks too much of his cattle to eat them."

Fat glared at Grady. "It ain't right to feed them cow thieves when the rest of us ain't got enough."

Grady retorted, "A wagonload of groceries wouldn't be enough for you, Fat."

Fat said something under his breath and stalked away. Grady said in a low voice, "Don't pay no attention to Fat Gervin. He was born on the wrong side of the bed and been gettin' up that way ever since."

"At least he's got a job."

"The only place he makes a hand is at the table. I think C.C. keeps him on just so he's got somebody to holler at that's afraid to holler back."

"Right now Mr. Tarpley scares me a little, too."

"Don't let him. He's stubborn as a mule and tight as the bark on a tree, but you never saw anybody gentler when it comes to his livestock. He don't wear spurs because he don't want to hurt a horse. He won't hardly even cuss a cow, not out loud."

A hawk soared overhead and screamed a warning as the riders approached its nest. Hewey envied the bird.

He wished he had its wings and could simply fly away from here. "I don't know what he's liable to do to me and Walter."

"I wouldn't worry too much. They don't hang cow thieves anymore. For a first offense they just send them up for five to ten years."

Grady made a thin smile, but his comment sounded too much like the truth to be funny.

Toward noon the next day Hewey saw a couple of windmills ahead, towering over the scrub mesquite and greasewood. Beyond lay a long, flat-topped desert mountain. Grady said, "We're comin' to the ranch headquarters."

Fat Gervin drew in close, smiling wickedly at Hewey and Walter. "We're short of trees, but we could hang them inside a windmill tower."

Grady said, "Don't bedevil the boys, Fat."

Gervin's face flushed. "You know I don't like anybody to call me that. My name is Frank."

"C.C. calls you Fat."

"Mr. Tarpley ain't just anybody. He's the one that pays me."

"I'll try to remember that, Fat."

Tarpley rode back from the point of the herd. "We'll turn them loose on the water and let them scatter on their own. First, though, there's a few Jessup cows in the bunch. We'll cut them out."

He did the cutting himself. The rancher quietly worked his horse in and out of the herd with an ease that came from long years' experience. Grady had lauded Tarpley's abilities as a cowman. Hewey could see what he meant.

Tarpley removed about a dozen cows from the herd. They bore a J Bar brand. Several had calves not yet branded. He said, "Shorty, you and Baker drive them back onto Eli Jessup's land. *Way* back. Be damned if I'll let that old land hog fatten his cows on my grass."

Hewey said, "Doesn't sound like he's got much use for this feller Jessup."

Grady replied, "He'd ride bareback a hundred miles to attend old Eli's funeral."

A spotted dog came trotting out to meet the horsemen. It barked a welcome, then trotted alongside Tarpley's horse, escorting his owner in.

The headquarters was utilitarian. The only natural trees were a few large "granddaddy" mesquites with thick, gnarly trunks shielded by dry, rough bark. Evidently no one had taken time or trouble to plant domestic varieties. Hewey counted three frame structures, unpainted but not yet old enough to have turned the gray of weathered lumber. One was obviously a barn. He assumed a long, narrow building to be a bunkhouse. A small, square one appeared to be a family residence. A woman and a girl stood on the narrow front porch, watching the riders approach.

Grady said, "That's C.C.'s wife and daughter."

"It don't look like much of a house for an owner."

"C.C. says there'll be time to build a big house when he's got enough land and cows to suit him. With his ambition, that ain't likely to be soon. Jessup's ranch is bigger than his, and it plagues him like a case of hives."

Hewey noticed that Fat kept staring toward the house, probably at Tarpley's daughter. From here he would guess her to be sixteen or so, just ripening. She was no great shakes for looks, however.

The dog separated itself from the riders and moved into the shade of the Tarpley house.

Tarpley's gaze lighted upon Hewey and Walter.

"Over yonder is a dugout that I lived in when I first come here. It ain't got but one door. We'll put you boys in there till we can get the sheriff to come out." He nodded at Grady. "Bar the door from the outside and keep watch on it. Fat'll relieve you after a while."

The pudgy cowboy turned red in the face at the use of his uncomplimentary nickname. Hewey had noticed that no one except Fat called the boss "Mr. Tarpley." Everybody else said "C.C."

Grady jerked his head as a signal for Hewey and Walter to follow him. The dugout had been built into a low, gravelly bank. Its roof was of mesquite branches and bear grass clumps weighted down with dirt. The door was of rough lumber, dry and splitting. Grady opened it and looked inside.

He said, "Ain't exactly the Menger Hotel, but it's probably cooler than the bunkhouse. You might want to look it over to be sure you ain't got company. There's somethin' about dugouts that just naturally draws rattlesnakes."

Dismounting, Hewey untied his blanket from behind the cantle of his saddle and paused at the door. The place smelled musty. "What about our horses?"

"I'll take care of them, and I'll see to it that the cook feeds you after a while. Make yourselves to home."

Walter said, "Right now I wish we *had* a home."

Grady shooed a couple of chickens outside, then pushed the door shut. Hewey flinched at the sound of a wooden bar falling into place. The interior seemed gloomy and dark at first. As his eyes adjusted, he saw light streaming in from wide cracks in the door and holes in the roof where the dirt covering had thinned and either washed or blown away from the dry branches that supported it.

He said, "Kind of like bein' in jail."

Walter said, "I wouldn't know. Never been there."

"I have, by invitation of Sheriff Noonan. The old reprobate always took things too serious." Hewey looked up at the low roof. He could see blue sky in places. "A man could probably dig through there in a little while."

"And then what? We're out in the middle of nowhere."

"Every place is somewhere, and there's always someplace to the west of it. Come dark we could catch our horses and git."

"And get chased all the way to El Paso? I say we keep tellin' them what really happened. Pa always said the truth'll come out if you wait long enough."

"Like after five to ten years in the pen?"

"We ought to be able to get some character references from back home."

Hewey shook his head. "Not from Sheriff Noonan. He's had it in for me ever since the night I took his paint horse from in front of the jailhouse and tied it at Big Bessie's. Everybody in town knew that horse."

"You never was one to think much about consequences."

Despite the gloomy situation, the memory made Hewey smile. "His wife wouldn't even speak to him."

Walter said, "The truth finally came out. The truth'll come out for me and you, too."

"I always knew I might have to pay the fiddler when I pulled that stunt on old Noonan. But gettin' in this mess wasn't my fault."

"I'm not blamin' you for it." Walter spread his blanket on the dirt floor and stretched out. "The fact is, I always wished I had a little of your recklessness. But every time I felt tempted I stopped and thought about it first, and then I didn't do it."

"Thinkin' too much spoils the fun."

"Are you havin' fun now?"

Hewey admitted, "Not much." He looked up again at the roof and thought how easy it might be to dig out. Maybe after dark. . . .

Sometime in the late afternoon he heard the bar slide away and the bottom of the door drag against the hard-packed earth. The bright light hurt his eyes. Grady Welch motioned for him and Walter to come out. "Supper's ready at the kitchen. C.C. says it's all right for you-all to come down."

Hewey asked, "And risk contaminatin' the crew?"

"He's startin' to lean a little in your direction, so don't do anything to abuse his hospitality."

Hewey promised, "We'll even try to be nice to Fat Gervin."

He and Walter followed Grady to the bunkhouse. The kitchen took up one end of it, sharing its space with two plain dining tables and four wooden benches. Grady showed the brothers where to wash. He said, "The cook's kind of contrary. Old Soapy always wants you to wash your hands whether they need it or not. He'll think better of you if you'll comb your hair, too. There's a comb layin' by the washpan."

A cracked mirror was attached to a post. Hewey looked at himself and rubbed his rough chin. He saw that he needed to shave. He tried to do that every week or two.

Grady washed first. Drying his hands on a community towel, he said, "You never want to get the cook mad at you. The worst a boss can do is fire you, but a contrary cook can starve you to death."

The cowboys were already at the tables, their plates filled. A couple slid down the bench to make room for

Hewey, Walter, and Grady. Fat Gervin got up and moved to the other table.

Grady passed Hewey a platter containing several slabs of fried steak. He said, "Here, have some of Old Man Jessup's stray beef. And you'll be wantin' some whistle berries, too." He handed over a bowl of red beans.

Hewey was heartened to see that most of the men evidenced no hostile feelings, though he and Walter remained under suspicion. Fat was an exception. Hewey heard him mutter something about bad company, but it seemed to have no adverse effect upon his appetite.

Tarpley was not there.

Grady said, "C.C. don't often eat with the hands except when we're out with the wagon. It hurts him to watch cowpunchers puttin' away so much high-priced grub. The missus fixes for him up at the big house."

If that was Grady's idea of a big house, Hewey thought, it would be interesting to see what he called a little one.

The cook leaned against the doorjamb, watching with satisfaction as the men devoured the results of his labor. He was a wizened little fellow built on lines similar to Tarpley, except that his stomach stuck out like a pregnant woman's. He wore a flour-dusted sugar sack tied around his belt as an apron. The brand name showed through in reverse.

Hewey ate until his stomach hurt. He could not remember when he had had such a good meal, or as big a meal. He told the cook, "These sure are good fixin's."

Soapy replied dryly, "That's what C.C. pays me such a big salary for."

Walter said, "It's mighty generous of Mr. Tarpley to feed us like this."

Gervin gave the Calloways a narrow look from the other table and said, "It's customary to give condemned men a good last meal."

Hewey tried to think of an appropriate retort. He decided it might be wise to keep his mouth shut, though it was a strain.

Grady spoke for him. "Fat, it ain't etiquette to talk with your mouth plumb full and your head plumb empty."

A few snickers around both tables indicated that the other cowboys agreed with Grady. Face coloring, Fat bowed his head and shoveled a big chunk of steak into his mouth. Gravy trickled from his lower lip and down his broad chin.

Hewey made up his mind that if the opportunity ever came, he would set fire to Fat's shirttail.

The cook walked to the open door and peered out. "We got company comin'. Three men." Flour and dried dough stuck to the hand he raised to shade his eyes. "Looks to me like one of them is that ranger."

Grady got up from the bench and joined Soapy at the door. "Damned if it ain't. I better go tell C.C." He trotted away.

Fat grinned at Hewey, his eyes mocking. "The rangers been known to make short work of cow thieves."

Hewey felt fresh hope. He said, "If it's the same ranger me and Walter met the other evenin', he can vouch for us." He reached with his fork and speared another slice of steak from the platter. "I believe I feel like eatin' a little more." He glanced toward the other table. "If it's all the same to you, Fat."

He heard a commotion out in the yard, a voice raised in sharp command and a sullen response. A tall, lanky man stepped into the open doorway and said, "You-all got any supper left? Me and my prisoners are as lank as gutted snowbirds."

Hewey heard hurried footsteps and Tarpley's voice. "Who you got here, Len?"

Len Tanner turned back to respond. "A couple of boys that taken a likin' to other folks' cattle. Recognize them, C.C.?"

Tarpley said, "Can't say that I do, but they don't look like Sunday schoolteachers." He exploded, "By damn, that's my good Thoroughbred he's ridin'!"

Hewey left the table and went outside. There, handcuffed to their saddles, he saw the pair who had left him and Walter with the stolen cattle. He declared, "That's the ginks I was tellin' you about, the ones that called theirselves Smith and Chum."

Smith looked daggers at him. Chum trembled a little and stared at the ground.

The ranger said, "Smith ain't the name his mother gave him." He took a small notebook from his pocket. "They're both here on the fugitive list." He took a better look at Hewey, then at Walter, who had come out to stand at his brother's side. "Well, I see you boys found yourselves a job."

Hewey nodded toward the prisoners. "We did, with them. We didn't know they was drivin' stolen cattle."

Tarpley jerked his thumb at Hewey and Walter. "Do you know these boys, Len?"

"Yeah, we shared a camp a few nights ago. They was lookin' for work. I'm glad they found your place."

"They didn't. I brought them here as prisoners." Tarpley walked up to the older thief, who sat on the Thoroughbred. "Are these boys tellin' it straight, that you hired them without lettin' them know those cows was stolen?"

Sullenly the thief said, "I don't admit to nothin'."

Hewey told him, "You owe us six bits apiece. We won't charge you for that second day."

Smith growled, "You'll keep your mouth shut if you know what's good for you, farm boy."

Tarpley gave Hewey a look of regret. "I ought to've known you were tellin' the truth. Nobody would make up an excuse as dumb as yours. You'll have to admit, though, you boys looked suspicious."

Walter spoke. "Like I told you, Hewey, the truth always comes out."

Tanner had sized up the situation. "C.C., wasn't you tellin' me you've been shorthanded? These boys are lookin' for a job."

Tarpley gave Hewey and Walter a solemn appraisal. "Most of the cowpunchers that drift through here have got too high an opinion of theirselves. The price of cattle bein' what it is, a man can't afford to pay what they think they're worth."

Hewey said, "We figure a dollar a day wouldn't be too much."

Tarpley raised one eyebrow. "I heard you say you hired on to these thieves for six bits a day. Would you charge an honest man more than you'd charge a thief?"

Hewey considered. "Money ain't the only thing in life. It's just that when you don't have any it can be sort of inconvenient. Six bits will do." He turned to his brother as an afterthought. "Won't it?"

"I reckon."

Tarpley said, "Money is wasted on cowboys anyway. They blow it every time they get to town. Better it stays with a man who knows how to invest it."

Tanner said, "Would you mind, C.C., if I took the Calloway boys to town with me? I'd like them to swear out a deposition against these two renegades."

C.C. nodded. "Sure, take them. I ain't put them on

the payroll yet anyway. Time enough to do that when they get to work."

Tanner said it was too late to escort the prisoners to town and asked if Tarpley had a place where they might be kept overnight. "Otherwise I'll have to handcuff them to a wagon wheel or somethin'. Not that they don't deserve it."

The rancher said, "Use that old dugout over yonder. That's where I put these boys."

Hewey declared, "Maybe it ain't my place to speak up, but that roof ain't too sturdy. I was figurin' on bustin' through it tonight so me and Walter could get away from here. These two could do the same."

Smith gave Hewey a look that could have withered cotton. His lips moved in silent threat.

Tarpley said, "Maybe cuffin' them to a wagon wheel is the best idea after all. That old dugout always did leak."

While Tanner led the rustlers toward a wagon, Walter said in a subdued voice, "You ought to've kept your mouth shut, Hewey. That Smith will hate you from now on."

"That's all right. I don't like him, either."

THREE

WHOEVER NAMED THE TOWN UPTON CITY MUST have been a reckless optimist, Hewey thought. But at least it had the bare essentials of urban civilization. He saw a modest stone courthouse and adjacent jail, a general store, and a blacksmith shop. Tanner pointed to a boarding house where transient drummers, lawyers, and the like could bunk and get a decent meal. "They'll even feed cowboys if they're washed and curried," he said. "It doesn't cost so much that you have to sell your horse to eat there."

Hewey was more interested in a square-fronted frame building that sported a sign reading SPIRITOUS LIQUORS AND BILLIARDS. "That means saloon, don't it?"

Tanner grunted. "I didn't figure you farm boys would have much use for a place like that."

Hewey said, "Walter don't, but he's just barely come of age."

Walter declared, "I'm old enough. I'm just not crazy about the taste of whiskey."

Pa had never held with whiskey except for medicinal purposes. However, he had been sick a lot after Ma was buried.

At the moment the saloon might as well be a hundred miles away. Hewey was too broke to buy a drink. Smith hadn't paid the six bits he owed, and it seemed unlikely he ever would. He had been surly as a chained dog all the way to town.

Chum was mournfully quiet, his eyes downcast. Now he looked at the courthouse and adjacent jail with palpable fear. He murmured, "I hear they got a gallows in there."

Tanner replied, "No such of a thing. See that big mesquite in the courtyard? They use that. It's cheaper." He winked at Hewey. "But if you was to decide to turn state's evidence, I think they might let you bust rocks instead of stretchin' rope."

Smith growled to his accomplice, "You'll keep your mouth shut if you know what's good for you."

Tanner said, "If he knew what's good for him he wouldn't have gone with you in the first place. But I guess he's a slow learner. I remember an old horse I had once...." He launched into a tale about a mount that never could learn to stop eating when he was full. He kept foundering himself until finally one day his stomach exploded and he died. "It was such a mess that they finally decided just to burn the barn down."

Chum looked ill.

Tanner said, "I expect you buzzards have been in better jails than this, but you got to remember that this is ranchin' country, and ranchers hate to pay taxes. If you want a nicer jail you'll need to do your stealin' in a rich county."

Holding the pistol, Tanner started to dismount. Smith suddenly lunged at him. He caught the ranger off balance and pushed him out of the saddle. Tanner landed on his back. Smith whirled his horse around and bumped violently into Hewey's.

The impact jerked Hewey's foot out of the stirrup and twisted it. His spur jabbed into the flank of Smith's mount. The horse squealed and made a high jump. Smith sailed from the saddle and flopped on his stomach. Tanner pushed up onto hands and knees and grabbed him before he could get to his feet. Smith wrestled and cursed but could not break loose from the ranger's determined grip.

A gray-haired man with bent shoulders and a look of dyspepsia had stepped out of the jail to meet the riders. A star shone prominently on his vest. He quietly thrust the muzzle of a pistol against Smith's chin and said, "How do, Tanner. You want me to shoot him?"

"No, it'd cause me too much paperwork." Breathing hard, Tanner roughly pulled Smith back to his feet. He gave Hewey a look of gratitude. "Thanks, cowboy."

Hewey's heart was still thumping from the unexpected action. "I didn't do nothin'. He bumped into my horse."

Smith flashed Hewey a look of hatred.

Probably thinks I got him throwed off on purpose, Hewey thought. *If I'd had time I'd have gotten out of his way.*

The sheriff resembled old Noonan back in East Texas. He said, "Tanner, I ain't got bunks enough for four prisoners. A couple of them got to sleep on the floor."

Tanner dusted himself off. "Just two prisoners, Jed. The other two are witnesses."

The sheriff frowned. "They all look like outlaws to me." He gave Walter a closer study. "Except maybe that youngest one."

Walter grinned at Hewey.

The sheriff asked Tanner, "What's the charges?"

"Cow theft here, and there's paper on them back East for considerable worse."

"Stealin' beef, hunh? Well, they'll see mighty little beef in my jail. They'll get corn bread and beans."

Tanner said, "If the judge is around, I'd like him to take these two cowpunchers' deposition."

"Far as I know, he's in his office."

Tanner said, "I'll help you get these prisoners stoppered up good and tight. Then I'll take these boys over to the courthouse and have them tell the judge all they know."

Smith glowered at Hewey. "I'll remember you. I'll come lookin' for you when I get out."

Tanner said, "Hell, feller, you ain't *gettin'* out."

He saw to it that the pair were placed in separate cells. Smith might intimidate his partner with shouted threats, but he would be unable to get his hands on him. Hewey figured Chum for the type to break down and confess all.

From behind the bars Smith demanded, "When do we get somethin' to eat? That ranger ain't let us have nothin' since breakfast."

The sheriff said sourly, "You'll eat when I get in the mood, and right now I ain't in the mood." He turned to Hewey and Walter. "Have I got to feed these two as well?"

Tanner shook his head. "They've earned a good supper over at Mrs. Pearson's boardin'house."

Hewey pointed out, "Me and Walter are flat broke."

"I expect the judge will authorize the county to pay for it since you're here as witnesses."

The sheriff said, "Just see that it ain't charged up to jail expenses. The commissioner's court has been ridin' me about the high cost of upkeep over here."

As had been the case with the sheriff, the silver-haired judge's first impression was that Hewey and Walter were Tanner's prisoners. His severe countenance softened when the ranger explained why he had brought them. He summoned a clerk to take dictation while Hewey and Walter described their experience with the rustlers.

Tanner read the two men's true names from his fugitive book. "Let the record show that the one who calls hisself Smith is Olin Trumble, wanted in San Saba County for horse theft, armed robbery, and murder." He glanced at Hewey. "He's accused of murderin' the man who testified against him in the horse stealin' case." He flipped several pages. "The other one is Chumley Barringer, wanted in Tarrant County for armed robbery, assault with intent to do bodily injury, and stealin' a hog." He shook his head. "Looks like a man who commits armed robbery and assault ought to have more ambition than to steal a hog."

Hewey barely heard the last part about the hog. His mind was on the part about Smith-Trumble murdering a man who testified against him. It shook him a little. "Sounds like he don't turn loose of a grudge."

The ranger assured him, "You don't need to fret about him comin' to get you. When them people over at San Saba get done, he'll have a permanent rope burn right under his jaw."

"I'm not worried." Hewey swallowed, for he could still see in his mind's eye the look of hatred the thief had shown him. "But if you're goin' to send them somewhere else, what do you need statements from me and Walter for?"

The judge said, "You're cowboys. If the courts back East don't do their duty, we'll bring those two back here for trial on charges of cow theft. We want your words on paper, signed and notarized, because cowhands drift. By the time we needed you, you might be anywhere from Mexico to Montana."

Tanner said, "Let's put our horses away, then go eat."

Hewey was uncertain about his appetite after hearing Smith's threat.

The livery stable was nothing more than a modest wooden barn with several corrals out back. The owner leaned against the doorframe and nodded what passed for a welcome. He was dressed like a cowboy, and a broke one at that. Hewey would not have taken him to be a businessman.

Tanner said, "Sandy, we'd like to put our horses up for the night."

The stableman gave Hewey and Walter a quick looking over. "I seen you come in to town a while ago. Looked like you had some prisoners."

Tanner said, "Couple of fellers got careless with other people's stock. These boys ain't them."

"Just two is all there was?"

"Two is all I caught, but coyotes sometimes run in packs."

Hewey guessed the stableman's nickname came from the color of his shaggy hair. The man opened a corral gate for the horses. "Throw them in there. You can stow the saddles in the barn. You want me to feed them, I guess?"

Tanner said, "Naturally. I'll need you to write me out a receipt so I can turn my expenses in to the state."

"It won't be but a couple of dollars."

"Without a receipt they won't pay me back. They'll complain if I ask for an extra two bits. For a dollar, they'll holler like a stuck pig."

"You'll get your receipt. Just seems like a lot of fuss over a little of nothin'."

Hewey tended to agree with the stableman. Money had never been of primary concern to him. So long as he had enough to put a little jingle in his pocket, he felt rich. At the moment, however, if a dollar would buy a whole saloon, he couldn't afford a bar rag.

Tanner asked the stable owner, "How's cow business, Sandy?"

"Slow. My kids would go hungry if I didn't have this stable. The little man has got an uphill battle, but I ain't goin' to be a little man forever. I'll have a herd as big as Tarpley's and Jessup's someday."

Tanner looked back as they walked away. "You've got to give Sandy credit for ambition. He's tryin' to build a herd of his own, but he's squeezed between C.C. and Eli. Wherever a blade of grass comes up, there's a Two Cs or a J Bar cow waitin' to graze it."

Hewey said, "That's why I'd rather be a cow*boy* than a cow*man*. I don't have to worry about things like that."

Walter said, "I think Sandy has got the right idea. A man ought to try to build somethin' of his own."

They turned toward the boardinghouse. Tanner said, "It'll be good for a change to have a meal cooked by womenfolks. A man gets awful tired of fixin' for himself wherever the night catches him."

He explained that the boardinghouse served the town in lieu of a hotel. "Better watch your manners. Old Lady Pearson don't like the smell of whiskey, and she don't stand for monkeyshines. She's been known to grab a cowpuncher by the scruff of his neck and throw him plumb off of the porch. She's a woman of powerful opinions."

Mrs. Pearson met the three as they ascended the steps. Her greeting was civil but hardly warm. "Mr. Tanner, I do not fancy feeding prisoners at my table."

The ranger had to explain to her as he had explained to the sheriff and the judge. "These ain't prisoners,

ma'am, they're witnesses. They've been of help to me
on a case."

She continued to give the brothers a stern appraisal,
especially Hewey. "Well then, maybe." Barely more
than five feet tall, she was built for strength rather than
speed. Hewey guessed she would tip the scales at close
to two hundred pounds, much of it pure muscle. Tanner
had said she had been married twice, burying one husband and running the other out of town. She was not
looking for a third.

She asked suspiciously, "You-all been at the saloon?"

Tanner assured her, "We've come directly from the
courthouse. These boys are sober as old Judge Stone."

"I've seen Judge Stone when he couldn't make it up
onto the porch. But you-all come on in. We'll be ringin'
the supper bell directly. You know where to wash."

Tanner said, "Thank you kindly, ma'am."

Strong women made Hewey uneasy. He had a feeling
it was their intention to take over the world, if they had
not already done so. Some reckless politicians were
even talking about letting women vote, a radical notion
from Europe or some other foreign country.

Walter made it a point to wipe his boots on an old
piece of rug that lay just outside the door. Mrs. Pearson
noticed and nodded approval. She said, "Sometimes
when I see a cowboy with good manners I get to hopin'
this old world may survive its tribulations after all."

"Yes, ma'am," Walter said, hat in his hands.

Hewey wiped his feet, too.

Several men stood on the back porch, awaiting the
call to supper. Hewey tried to guess at their occupa-
tions. It was difficult to tell which might be a lawyer and
which a whiskey drummer. He decided it didn't matter
much. They were all peddling something.

A young woman stepped out onto the porch and rang

a small bell. Hewey guessed that she was not Mrs. Pearson's daughter, for he saw no resemblance. She was taller but probably weighed little more than half as much. Her face was pleasant enough, even a little shy. He would not regard her as pretty, but she was not really plain, either. She was hard to classify. He might not have given her a second look except that the only women he had seen in a while had been Tarpley's wife and daughter, and then only at some little distance. The daughter was definitely what he would call plain. Being C.C.'s offspring, she could not help it.

Some of the men made a rush toward the long dining table. Hewey started, but Walter caught his arm and said, "Let's show them that cowboys do have manners."

Hewey grunted. "More than lawyers and drummers, anyway." He watched two men grab for the same chair and try to glare one another down.

Hewey noticed that Walter was looking at the young woman. It occurred to him that his brother's show of manners was not altogether for Mrs. Pearson.

The landlady held onto one chair at the head of the table. "Judge Stone is comin'. This seat is his."

The judge walked in, leaving his derby hat on a rack in the parlor. Mrs. Pearson held the chair out for him. She glanced at Hewey, Walter, and Tanner, then nodded toward the far end of the table, away from the judge and away from the meat and potatoes.

If he had had any doubt, Hewey knew now what she thought about cowboys. She seemed to have doubts about rangers, too.

She stood back from the table, watching the men eat. At length she called, "Eve, you'd better fetch another platter of biscuits. I don't suppose any of these gentlemen have noticed the high cost of flour."

The young woman appeared, holding a pan from

which she replenished the biscuit platter. Walter said shyly, "They're mighty tasty, ma'am." He broke a biscuit in two and slathered butter on half of it. Watching the young woman instead of the biscuit, he spread some of the butter on the heel of his hand. She noticed and smiled. Walter blushed and started to lick the butter from his hand, then thought better of it. When the woman looked away, he wiped his hand on the underside of the cotton tablecloth.

Mrs. Pearson brought out a pan of cobbler pie, giving the judge the first helping, then letting the pan work its way down to the cowboy end of the table. By the time it reached Hewey it was empty. He poured molasses into his plate, mixed butter in it with a table knife, then swabbed it up with a biscuit. That was his notion of a sensible cowboy dessert anyway.

The boarders began leaving the table. Hewey grabbed another biscuit to take with him.

Walter said, "That was an awful good supper, Mrs. Pearson." Though he spoke to the older woman, his gaze was on the younger one.

Mrs. Pearson turned away but said over her shoulder, "Even a cowboy deserves a decent meal once in a while. God knows they don't get many in a cow camp." She followed the judge to the door, complimenting him on his dignified appearance. He was a steady customer. Cowboys just dropped in occasionally and could not be depended upon for repeat business.

The young woman smiled at Walter. "Come again."

"I will. What time do you serve breakfast?"

"At seven in the mornin'."

"I'll be here at six, settin' on the porch and waitin'." Walter started to leave, but turned back. "I heard Mrs. Pearson call you Eve. You kin to her?"

She said, "No kin. I just work here."

"I'm Walter Calloway. It's a real pleasure to make your acquaintance." As an afterthought he said, "I guess you know Mr. Tanner. And this other one here, he's my brother Hewey."

"Howdy," Hewey said.

He stooped to retrieve his hat, which he had tossed at the rack on his way in but missed. It lay on the floor. He waited until he was on the porch before he put it on. Mrs. Pearson stood there, watching the judge's departure. She said nothing to the cowboys or Tanner.

Out of earshot, Hewey said, "The old lady wasn't real tickled about us bein' here, but I don't reckon she has any compunctions about takin' the county's money."

Walter said, "Eve was awful sweet, though."

Hewey frowned. "Kind of forward with her, wasn't you?"

Walter looked puzzled. "I'm generally a little uneasy around womenfolks, young ones especially. But there was somethin' about Eve . . ."

"You look like you got gas on your stomach. What you need is a strong shot of whiskey."

Tanner grinned. "I'll set you-all up to a drink."

Hewey took only one. He knew this was coming out of Tanner's pocket, not the county treasury. He doubted that the ranger had much of a bank account.

They slept on a pile of hay in the wagon yard and had breakfast at the boardinghouse on the county's dollar. Eve stood on the porch and watched as Hewey and Walter rode away toward the ranch. Walter kept looking back.

THE COWBOYS HAD A bronc hemmed against the fence in a round corral. Grady Welch took a firm grip on the horse's ears. "Throw the saddle on him, Fat."

Resentful at the use of the nickname, Fat lifted the saddle from the ground. He dropped it and ran for the fence when the bronc jumped in his direction. For a man of his weight, he moved with alacrity. Grady grumbled under his breath. "Help me here, Shorty."

The bronc tried to kick and pitch, but Grady did not lose his hold on the ears as Shorty fought to put the saddle into place. When the cinch was tight, Grady said, "All right, Hewey, he's yours."

Watching the pony's efforts to fight, Hewey had second thoughts about being so quick to volunteer. "Kind of wiggly, ain't he?"

Grady said, "Playful, is all. There ain't nothin' to it. You just plant yourself in the middle and keep one leg on each side. Anybody can do it. Except maybe Fat."

Hewey was well aware that close to a dozen men were watching him, including Tarpley and Walter. He clamped his teeth together in determination and reached for the saddle horn. He swung up and firmly planted both feet in the stirrups. "Turn him aloose."

Grady released his hold on the bronc's ears and stepped quickly out of the way. The horse kicked at him in passing, but missed. Grady shouted, "Show him who's boss."

The bronc made several ineffective crow hops. Hewey's confidence came back in a rush. He turned his head in a search for Walter and saw his brother sitting on the fence. He shouted, "Like Grady said, there ain't nothin' to it."

He was unprepared when the bronc suddenly twisted back and seemed to turn himself wrongside out. Hewey's neck felt as if it had snapped in two. He was aware of two high jumps, both ending with a jarring impact as all four hooves struck the hard ground at one time. For a moment he was suspended in the air with nothing under him. The horse was gone. Hewey's rump struck first. The back of his head thumped solidly against the packed earth. His teeth came together with an audible click and bit his tongue.

He lay stunned, aware that the bronc was still pitching, empty stirrups slapping against its sides.

Grady leaned over and extended his hand to help Hewey to his feet. "You can't just lay there and let him get away with that," he said. "If he thinks he's run his bluff on you, he'll try it every time."

It took Hewey a minute to regain enough breath to answer. He rubbed the back of his aching neck. The bronc had stopped pitching but still circled the pen in a run. "You sure he was bluffin'? I had a notion he meant business."

"A colt like that has always got some play in him. You don't want to let him get the idea that you're afraid of him, do you?"

"No, I wouldn't want him thinkin' that." Hewey waited in vain for someone to volunteer to take over for him. "All right, catch him. As long as I've still got a chip to play, I don't quit a losin' game."

Grady grinned. "All this fun and gettin' paid for it, too. What man wouldn't love this kind of a job?"

Hewey lasted longer the next time. He expected the quick reversal and leaned into it. He managed to survive several jumps before he lost one stirrup and then the other. He struck the ground feetfirst. It was not as painful as before.

Grady said, "You're gettin' the hang of it."

The tiring bronc was dripping sweat as Hewey got on him again. This time the reversal was slower, and the jumps were not so high. Hewey gripped hard with his knees and remained in the saddle until the horse wore itself down and quit, heaving for breath.

Grady walked out to hold the animal while Hewey dismounted, his legs quivering from fatigue. "You done good, Hewey," he said. "You're beginnin' to look like an honest-to-God west-of-the-Pecos cowpuncher."

Beaming, Hewey looked toward his brother. "Told you, Walter. We've about got this cowboy thing whipped."

Tarpley had been watching from the other side of the fence. He said, "Someday you're liable to be worth a whole dollar a day. Maybe in a year or two."

FOUR

BY THE NEXT SPRING'S BRANDING TIME, HEWEY AND
Walter had diminished C. C. Tarpley's fortune by
about two hundred dollars apiece at seventy-five cents a
day. Walter still had most of his earnings stuffed in the
toe of a sock under the cornshuck mattress that covered
his cot. Hewey had barely enough left to buy tobacco.
He contended that money was meant to be spent so the
poor folks could get their share. He did not consider
himself poor folks, not at six bits a day.

He had invested in a new saddle at twenty-seven dollars, boots like Grady Welch's, a wide-brimmed hat,
and a pair of leather chaps to turn away mesquite
thorns. To replace his cheap OK spurs he had bought a
pair with silver-plated shanks shaped like a woman's
leg. He considered that he made a handsome shadow on
horseback.

Walter had inherited Hewey's OK spurs. He said the
horses couldn't tell the difference.

Tarpley had not wasted his assets on unnecessary

equipment or by building a lot of corrals, which would have made the cowboys' work easier. His position was that if they didn't want to work, they shouldn't have hired on. Most of the branding was done in the open. A skeleton crew held the gathered herd in check while the calves were roped and dragged out to a fire where the branding irons were heated. Flankers threw them down and held them while the animals were branded and ear-marked, the bull calves castrated.

It was an honor of sorts to be chosen to do the roping. The job was usually assigned to the most accomplished in use of the loop. Among the Tarpley crew, that meant Grady Welch. Grady had been in the saddle a couple of hours, catching smaller calves around the neck, larger ones around the hind feet, and dragging them out to flankers, including Hewey and Walter.

One mark of an experienced roper was hands scarred by rope burns or missing parts of one or more fingers, pinched off between rope and saddle horn.

Grady bent over in pain, hugging his right arm tightly against his chest. He rode back toward the fire, his face twisted. Hewey saw that his sleeve was torn, his arm an angry red.

"Rope got twisted around my wrist. Like to've burned my arm off."

Tarpley walked over to look. He was conservative with sympathy, as with all else. "Better go to the wagon and get some of Soapy's bacon grease. Rub it in real good."

Walter said, "Maybe he'd better go to a doctor."

Tarpley replied, "It's too far to town. Bacon grease'll fix about anything except a broken leg." He waved away any further discussion and went to what he saw as his larger and more immediate problem. "Just lost my best heeler. Hewey, I've noticed that you're gettin' handy with a rope."

"Been practicin' with Grady."

"Then climb aboard Grady's horse and get at it. Can't have flankers idlin' around here drawin' a wage and not doin' nothin' to earn it."

Hewey's elation at being trusted with such a responsibility was compromised by guilt inasmuch as it had come at Grady's expense. He said, "Find you another flankin' partner, Walter," and mounted Grady's horse.

Under Grady's instruction Hewey had roped at anything that would move and much that would not. The chickens had learned to run at the sight of him. A tomcat that headquartered in the barn was missing some of its fur. A hoe handle had never fit Hewey's hands, but a rope felt just right.

For a while he caught every unbranded calf at which he aimed. He had not missed a loop. He hoped Tarpley was paying attention, but he doubted that he was. Tarpley took it for granted that his men could do any job to which he assigned them. If they couldn't, they didn't belong with the Two Cs. The only exception was Fat Gervin. Hewey often wondered why Tarpley tolerated him. When it came to cowboy work, he was as useless as teats on a boar hog.

Hewey's arm eventually began to tire, and he started missing a loop now and again. Fat, working as a flanker, began offering unwanted advice. "Try ropin' left-handed. You couldn't do no worse." Then, "You goin' blind? I could do better with a sack over my head."

Hewey was tempted to step down and *put* a sack over Fat's head. Following Grady's lead, he had been roping the larger calves by the hind feet because they could put up less of a fight than if caught around the neck. He made his way slowly through the herd and picked the biggest unbranded bull calf he could find. It was probably close to being a yearling. He dropped a small loop around its neck and began drawing the animal toward the branding fire. It kicked and pitched and bawled in anger and fear. Hewey said, "Caught him first loop, Fat. He's all yours."

Fat didn't want him, but pride would not let him back away with everybody watching and hoping to see him make a fool of himself. Tentatively he reached to grab a leg. The calf kicked him in the belly with a lightning-fast hind foot. Fat reeled. The cowboys began shouting advice, most of it bad.

Fat grabbed the agitated animal around the neck and bounced about like a ball on the end of a string. The calf shook him off and stepped on him. Walter and Shorty moved in to bring the animal down. Fat was on his knees, wheezing, trying to suck breath back into his lungs.

Hewey was tempted to taunt him, but seeing a scarlet hue in Fat's round face was enough.

After a time he saw Grady trotting from the chuck wagon toward the branding fire, a distance of two hundred yards. The branding was always done far enough away from the wagon to keep dust from settling on the food. He assumed Grady was ready to resume heeling calves, so he rode partway to meet him. Grady was almost out of breath as he hurried up to Tarpley.

"Trouble comin', C.C." He turned and pointed.

Four horsemen approached from the north. Squinting, Tarpley cursed under his breath. "Eli Jessup. Can't be lookin' for much of a fight, only bringin' three men with him."

Grady argued, "He can do a right smart of damage without help. Folks tell me he charged a Comanche camp once all by himself."

Tarpley grunted. "Wasn't but two Indians in it, and one of them was crippled. If he could fight like he can brag, ain't no tellin' how much mischief he could do."

Hewey had been hearing the Jessup name for months, but he had never seen the man until now. He knew only that bad blood had existed between Jessup and Tarpley for years. Both men wanted to become the biggest rancher in West Texas. It was not a distinction that could be shared.

Jessup was no taller than Tarpley but outweighed him by forty or fifty pounds. On windy days Hewey thought Tarpley needed to carry rocks in his pockets to keep from blowing away. In contrast to Tarpley, Jessup dressed more like a banker than a dust-eating rancher. He wore a vest and a string tie, and his hat looked new. His saddle bore the marks of an expert saddlemaker. It was evident that he had money, and he liked to spend it, at least on himself. His principal facial feature was a bushy but well-combed mustache, mixed gray and black. He had a broad nose, perhaps broken in some long-ago fight, and sharp eyes that tried to burn a hole in whatever they looked upon.

He paid no attention to anyone except Tarpley. He rode up so close that Tarpley could have touched the horse's nose. Though a blind man could see what was going on, he asked, "Are you brandin'?"

Tarpley met the question with contempt. "Of course we're brandin'. Did you think we was throwin' a dance?"

"Thought I ought to come over and be sure you wasn't losin' your eyesight in your old age, maybe puttin' your brand on calves that rightfully ought to carry a J Bar."

"If I was goin' to steal cattle, I'd steal better than that scrub stock you raise."

Hewey looked for a reaction in Jessup's face. The rancher never changed expression as he said, "How would you know? You couldn't tell a cull heifer from a high-grade bull. Mind if we ride through your herd and look for any stray J Bars?"

Tarpley frowned. "Nobody cuts my herd but me. But if it'll ease your mind, the first thing we done was to cut out the J Bar cows and their calves. They wasn't hard to spot. I got two men right now drivin' the sorry specimens back onto your range and off of my grass."

"*Your* grass? Most of this land still belongs to the state of Texas. As a taxpayer, I'm a part owner. I got as much right to use it as you do."

"The same goes for your place. We're both just squatters if you come right down to it. But I don't aim to be a squatter forever. I buy every acre I can as soon as it comes on the market."

"Well, don't you get any notions about buyin' anything out from under me. I moved in when the Comanches moved out, and I got a shotgun claim on every acre of it."

Jessup jerked his head as a signal for his three cowboys to leave with him. But one lanky, lazy-looking rider hung back. He grinned at Grady Welch, a gold tooth shining. "How do, Grady. Why don't you come over and work for a *good* outfit again?"

Grady grinned back. "Howdy, Snort. How long since you threwed a real fumble, stumble, and fall-down drunk?"

"Too long. We'll get together one day and see which of us can soak up the most brave-maker without fallin' over dead."

"You'd have the advantage. You've had a lot more practice than me."

"Like hell. If me and you was to both quit drinkin', the whole state of Kentucky would go bust." Snort saw that his boss was fifty yards on his way. "Got to go before he fires me again. He's already done it twice this month. See you in town, Grady." He rode off with a careless ease, letting his shoulders sag.

Hewey observed that the animosity between the two owners was not shared by their hands. He felt drawn to the Jessup cowboy on first sight. He asked Grady, "Who's your friend?"

"Snort Yarnell. He's a top hand and a good old boy, but he don't give a damn whether school keeps or not. Been fired off of nearly every ranch on the Pecos River. He acts like he's still just twelve years old."

Tarpley growled, "A man with any gumption about him had rather herd sheep than hire out to Eli Jessup. Let's get back to work before the irons go cold."

TARPLEY'S CATTLE WERE SCATTERED over more than three hundred square miles fronting on the Pecos. It was not fenced—fencing cost money—so Tarpley and his crew worked twenty or so square miles at a time, rounding up all the cattle within a rough circle. After the calves were branded, the herd was turned loose, the wagon was moved, and the next circle was worked. Each lapped over the edges of those adjoining it to pick up any unworked cattle that might drift. It took all spring to get the branding done. Not until the wagon was ready to return to headquarters did Tarpley reluctantly pay off the cowboys and allow them time to go to town.

He told them, "Now, don't you-all do anything to cause me shame. Upton City is a nice quiet little place, and folks there have got a lot of respect for C. C. Tarpley. I'm even thinkin' of startin' a bank there one of these days, when I've got a little spare money saved up. It'll be a place where you boys can put your earnin's and see them grow."

Hewey did not say so, but the thought came to him

that Tarpley would probably charge his borrowers a lot more interest than he would pay to his depositors. Besides, if a man put his money in a bank, there was always a risk of it being robbed. If he invested it in a rousing good time, nobody could take that away from him.

Walter said, "I'm leavin' the biggest part of my money here so I don't spend it in town."

Hewey argued, "Mine can't do me any good if it's here and I'm there. What if a bronc was to throw me off and break my neck? I'd rather go to my rest rememberin' the fun I had instead of thinkin' about the money I left layin' here goin' to waste."

"C. C. Tarpley didn't get where he is by spendin' all his money on fun and frolic."

"And where is he? Does he own this ranch, or does it own him? I'll bet he lays awake half the night worryin' about losin' it. I don't own nothin', so I got no worries."

Walter said, "The time'll come when you'll want to get married and settle down. You'll be glad if you saved somethin'."

"Get married and take on all that responsibility? I remember how hard Pa worked to keep Ma and us fed and a roof over our heads. What good did it do him? Ma died, and we set out on the drift. Pa went to his grave a tired old man with nothin' to show for all that work."

"He went knowin' he'd tried his best. He felt justified in the sight of the Lord."

Hewey frowned. "The Lord ought not to've worked him so hard. He ought to've let him have more pleasure along the way."

"Pa had his own idea of pleasure. Even with all his troubles, he never gave up his dreams. He was a happy man."

"I'm a *happier* one, not havin' any troubles."

* * *

GRADY AND HEWEY LED the cowboy procession. Walter and the others were strung out behind for fifty yards. They all spurred up when the town came into view. Fat shouted, "Look out, Upton City, here comes the Two Cs. Bring out the women and the whiskey."

Grady told Hewey, "The women in Upton City are mostly too young, too old, or too married. Anyway, Fat wouldn't know what to do with one even if he could catch her."

Hewey had noticed the lack of women on his previous visit. The only ones he had seen close up were Eve and Mrs. Pearson. "If it wasn't for the saloon, they could call this place Saint's Roost."

Walter pulled up beside Hewey. "I'm hungry enough to eat a side of beef by myself. I'm goin' to the boardin'house and see if supper's ready."

Hewey frowned. He knew supper was not the primary reason Walter was interested in going to the boardinghouse. "It's been months since we was here last. Like as not, she's married some dry-goods drummer by now."

"Then again, maybe she hasn't."

It would not do to let their horses stand all night tied to a hitching post. Grady led the Two Cs men to the stable so their mounts could be freed of the saddles and receive the unaccustomed luxury of being fed oats.

Hewey said, "If we deserve a holiday in town, so do they."

A boy of twelve or so met the horsemen at the stable's front door. Grady said, "Where's Sandy at?"

The boy said, "Dad is out lookin' after his cattle. Left me to watch things."

"Pretty big responsibility for a boy your size."

"I can handle it. He always lets me do it when he's gone from town. And he's gone a lot."

Grady accepted that. "Give them a good bait of oats, but watch that none of them kick the others out of the way and founder theirselves. When it comes to feed, these Two Cs horses ain't got good manners."

The boardinghouse would not have been Hewey's next choice of a place to go, but his stomach was talking to him. So was Walter.

Hewey gave in to his brother's argument. "All right. I doubt that the boys can soak it all up before we get there. Ain't good to drink on an empty stomach anyway. You get drunk too fast, and then you're through."

Grady warned, "Remember now, you've got to sidle up to Mrs. Pearson on her good side, or she won't let you in the house."

Hewey said, "If she has a good side, she kept it turned away from me."

The landlady met the three on the porch. Grady removed his hat and made a wide sweep with it as he bowed. "Mrs. Pearson, there's three lank and hungry cowpokes here who can't wait to be blessed by your wonderful cookin'. My old mother back in the piney woods couldn't match the fixin's that you lay on your table."

A tiny smile managed to escape before she covered it with a frown. "Save your sweet talk for them too young to know better. I can recognize blarney when I hear it." She gave Hewey and Walter a second examination. "Seems I remember you two. Wasn't you here once with that ranger Tanner?"

Hewey said, "Yes, ma'am, we was."

"Too bad what happened to Tanner afterwards."

Hewey blinked. "I didn't know anything had. Out at the ranch, we don't hear much."

"He was deliverin' two prisoners from here to somewhere back East. One of them managed to hit him over the head, then shoot him with his own pistol."

Hewey sucked in a sharp breath. "Kill him?"

"No, just bunged him up some from what I heard. He might've bled to death, but the other prisoner stayed and took him where he could get help."

Walter asked, "Do you know who the prisoners were?"

She shook her head. "All I know is that they were in jail here for cattle rustlin'. They were wanted somewhere else for worse."

Hewey said, "Smith and Chum. It'd be Smith that done the shootin'." Remembering Smith's threat, he felt cold. "So now he's on the loose. No tellin' where at."

Walter said, "I wouldn't think he's mad enough to come back here lookin' for you. Too much risk. He probably rode for Mexico as fast as his horse could carry him."

"I guess." Hewey tried to dismiss the thought, but it would not leave him. He felt that he needed a drink more than he needed supper.

Walter followed Mrs. Pearson through the door and said, "Are you comin'?"

"Go ahead on. I'll be along." Hewey stood on the porch a minute, staring into the distance. He knew the notion was foolish, but he could not help feeling that Smith-Trumble might be out there somewhere right now, drawing a bead on him.

Grady clapped him on the shoulder. "Don't worry, nobody's goin' to hurt a Two Cs cowhand. C. C. Tarpley wouldn't stand for it."

Hewey's reply held a touch of sarcasm. "That sure makes me feel better."

Several men waited in the parlor. For all Hewey could tell, they might have been the same ones he saw the last time, though they probably were not. He just did not pay a lot of attention to drummers and lawyers.

Judge Stone came in and placed his derby hat carefully on the rack. He recognized Hewey and moved toward him. "You've heard what happened to your friend Len Tanner?"

"Just now, from Mrs. Pearson."

"He should have retired from the Rangers a long time ago. Instead, he's back on the job, chasing outlaws again."

"Maybe that's all he knows to do."

"Age must be making him careless, or he wouldn't have let a criminal seize the advantage."

"I hear the other prisoner helped Len."

"That helped lighten his sentence when he went to trial," the judge said. "Meanwhile, Trumble is back in every Ranger's fugitive book."

"I just hope he's not out here somewhere lookin' for me."

"I am sure he has more pressing matters on his mind than going after revenge on some dollar-a-day cowboy."

"Six bits," Hewey said.

Eve came out of the kitchen, carrying a platter of sliced roast to the table. She glanced toward the men in the parlor, her gaze lighting upon Walter. He gave her a quick bow. "How do, Miss Eve. It is still *Miss,* I hope."

"Certainly," she said, staring at him, evidently trying to remember who he was. "Oh yes, you were in here a few months ago with your brother. I remember you sittin' on the porch the next mornin', waitin' for breakfast."

"Yes'm, that was me. And a good breakfast it was."

"We do our best to please." She went back to the kitchen.

Walter turned to Hewey, beaming. "Told you she wouldn't be married."

"I don't see where that makes any difference. You're too young to think about marryin'. You couldn't afford it in the first place."

"I won't always be workin' for six bits a day."

"No, the time may come when you're makin' a dollar. That still won't be enough."

THE SALOON WAS AS plain as every other commercial building in town, constructed of rough-sawed lumber that had never been blessed by a coat of paint. A dozen or so horses were tied to hitch racks and posts up and down the street. Approaching the open doors, Hewey could hear several voices raised in what was meant to be song. He would classify it as noise.

He said, "The boys have got a head start on us."

Grady responded, "We'll catch up."

Fat Gervin sat at a table alone, his head bent forward. He was singing something completely different from the rest of the men. The words were so slurred and the tune so off-key that Hewey had no idea what song it was supposed to be.

Grady said, "It don't take much for Fat. He can get drunk just sniffin' the cork." He led the Calloways to the bar. The bartender did not bother to ask what they wanted. He poured whiskey into three glasses and shoved them forward. His only greeting was, "Two bits apiece."

Hewey dug into his pocket for the bankroll that had been resurrected from near death when Tarpley had paid his hands. Two bits for a larruping good supper and two bits for a shot of whiskey. A sound investment, he thought.

Grady remarked to the bartender, "The boys couldn't carry a tune in a washtub. You ought to get a piano in here."

The man wiped up a few drops of whiskey with a dirty rag. "There ain't two people in town could play it.

Anyway, the music I like best is the sound of coins ringin' on this bar."

A loud, whiskey-tinged voice shouted from a back corner, "Hey, Grady, about time you got yourself in here." Snort Yarnell lifted a bottle for him to see, then tipped it over when he set it back on the round table in front of him. "Bring us a fresh bottle. This soldier is dead."

Grady asked the bartender, "How long has Snort been here?"

"Long enough to drink up more money than he could earn in a month. I can't seem to get him full."

"I'll try." Grady reached across the bar and grasped a bottle, then nodded for Hewey and Walter to follow him. Snort arose to extend his hand and almost overturned the table. "You boys light and squat. I want you to meet some of my J Bar compadres." He called the names of three punchers who shared the table with him. They all shook hands. Hewey knew he would not remember the names for five minutes.

Grady uncorked his bottle and poured seven drinks. "How come you in town, Snort? Did Jessup finish his brandin'?"

"Nope, still at it. Brandin' camp is just a little ways out of town. But my nose got sore from all that burnin' hair, and my ears were ringin' from all them bawlin' cattle. Decided it was time me and my compadres took ourselves a little vacation."

"You left before the brandin' was done? You're liable to get fired again."

"Already been, but it don't matter. I got to countin' and found I had more than fifty dollars in my pocket. Why should I keep workin' when I'm damned near rich?" Snort drained his glass without stopping for breath.

Grady said, "You won't be rich long, not at this rate."

"Then I'll go back to work. There's always more work out there than a man can get done, but there ain't that many good times. I figure I better enjoy myself before I get stomped to death by some outlawed bronc." He winked. "Or shot by some jealous husband."

Dryly, Grady said, "Yeah, a handsome feller like you is always a big threat around the womenfolks."

Hewey thought Snort was about as homely a cowboy as he had seen yet. His nose was large and his ears stuck out. The gold tooth called attention to the fact that the rest were crooked. When the Lord had passed out looks, Snort was probably asleep behind the barn. Drunk, maybe.

Snort said, "Drink up, boys. Next bottle is on me and Old Man Jessup. I'm squanderin' his wealth one drink at a time."

The seven had just about polished off Grady's bottle when Hewey heard spurs jingling and footsteps thumping on the wooden sidewalk outside. Four men strode in. One he recognized as rancher Eli Jessup. The others' clothing and boots proclaimed them to be cowpunchers. He thought he remembered seeing one with Jessup the day the neighboring rancher had shown up at Tarpley's branding. He stood better than six feet tall and ax-handle broad in the shoulders.

In a voice that rattled glassware, Jessup declared, "Yonder they are," and led the others toward the corner where Snort sat.

Snort raised his glass. "The J Bars have arrived. You boys set yourselves down and have a drink."

Jessup's eyes crackled. "Drink hell! You-all are goin' back to work right now." He jerked his head toward the door. Three J Bar men quickly stood up and weaved their way outside. He did not have to tell them twice.

Snort just sat there. Jessup demanded, "What about you?"

Snort showed no reaction. "You fired me."

"Well, you're unfired. Damn you, you gutted my brandin' crew. Now get up from there and find your horse."

Snort grinned and poured another drink.

Jessup turned to the big cowboy. "Bring him, Mitch. Get him back to the wagon. Alive if you can." He strode across the room and out the door, shouting orders at the men who had already retreated outside.

Mitch seemed to tower over Snort. "You look like you've had enough. Mr. Jessup said fetch you."

Snort's jovial grin soured. "I ain't ready to be fetched. The night's still young, and so am I."

"It ain't polite to ride off before the work's done. Mr. Jessup got his feelin's hurt. When his feelin's are hurt, he sees to it that the rest of us hurt too." The cowboy extended a muscled arm that would do credit to a blacksmith. "I'll help you up."

Snort gripped the edge of the table with both hands. "I ain't goin'. Old Eli fired me."

"You heard him say he's unfired you. Now come on."

"I'm a free-born citizen of the sovereign state of Texas. Go tell him I'll stay fired as long as I want to."

Mitch grabbed Snort's arm and tried to pull him away from the table. Two of the newly arrived Jessup cowhands moved to help.

Grady pushed quickly to his feet. "Snort ain't goin' anyplace he don't want to. Turn him aloose."

Mitch struck Grady in the face. Hewey jumped up and grabbed Mitch, shoving him against the wall. "Ain't nobody hits a friend of mine." He punched the cowboy in the stomach. It felt as hard as a cedar stump. Hewey knew he had hurt himself more than he hurt Mitch.

Somebody grabbed Hewey's shoulder and jerked him backward. Hewey tripped over a chair and fell. He came up swinging, only to meet Mitch's fist. It jarred him like the kick of a mule. Two men immediately piled on him, knocking him flat on the floor. Mitch and one other became heavily involved with Grady.

Snort Yarnell continued to sit in the corner, happily watching the fight as if he had bought a ticket. He grabbed the bottle when one of the combatants fell against the table. The glasses all rolled to the floor. "Sure has got noisy in here," he said.

Hewey was in a bad way, the two men holding him down and punching him about the head. Walter joined the fray, pulling one of the men off and driving a fist into his face. The other Two Cs punchers gathered around, shouting encouragement but not joining in. Like Snort, they remained enthusiastic spectators.

Hewey half hoped the sheriff would show up and stop the fight, for he was getting the worst of it. Instead it was Snort who brought the fracas to an end. He tugged at Grady's shoulder, then reached down and got hold of Hewey's shirt. "Grady, Hewey, you've had fun enough. Now stop whuppin' up on friends of mine. Hell, you're *all* friends of mine. Ain't no use in friends fightin' friends."

Grady felt of a bruised jaw and mumbled, "We done it to help you, Snort."

Hewey rubbed bleeding knuckles against a trousers leg.

Snort told Mitch, "I'll go back to camp with you in the mornin'. I'll be broke by then anyhow. Now all you boys have a drink. Ain't no use in anybody carryin' a grudge. We're all friends here."

The J Bar hands and the Two Cs men eyed each other warily. Snort put one arm around Mitch and the other around Hewey. "You-all shake and let's uncork another bottle."

Hesitantly Hewey extended his hand. Pain shot through him when Mitch gripped it. He managed a half-hearted smile, though his lower lip was split.

Snort said, "Let's drink to Eli Jessup. And to C. C. Tarpley—the two biggest skinflints on the Pecos River. May they live long, and die of the piles."

The cowboys took kindly to the toast.

Hewey heard a thump. Fat had slumped forward, his head striking the table where he sat alone. His bottle rolled off onto the floor, but Fat made no effort to retrieve it. He did not know it was gone.

Jessup reentered the saloon and did not appear pleased to see that the combatants had made peace. He placed his knotted fists on his hips and shouted, "Any man of mine not back at the wagon by mornin' don't need to come back at all." He stomped out.

There was a man, Hewey thought, who ought to be an officer in the army. Or at least a fancy-house bouncer in Hell's Half Acre.

Snort said, "Don't worry, boys. He needs us to get the brandin' done. Come mornin' he'll be his natural self. Still mad as hell."

In a little while a stranger walking in would not have been able to tell the J Bars from the Two Cs. They were mixed up together, all trying to sing at the same time but in three or four different keys.

The proprietor smiled, counting the change spread across his bar.

FIVE

AWAKENING, HEWEY FOUND HIMSELF LYING ON A pool table in the back of the saloon. He did not remember how he got there. Rising up on one elbow, he thought every muscle in his body had declared war on him.

Walter lay on the floor, half covered by his blanket. His eyes were open. Hewey could not see a mark on him. His part in the fight had been minimal.

Walter said, "You all in one piece, Hewey?"

"I don't know. Feels like I'm scattered a little."

Grady was sitting up, leaning against a back wall. Snort lay under a table, snoring. The rest of the Two Cs and J Bar hands were lying here, there, and yonder.

The front door opened. The bartender walked in, stopping to survey his domain. He said, "Looks like the walls are still standin'. You boys get up. I need to swamp out in here."

Hewey vaguely remembered the bartender leaving about midnight, admonishing the cowboys to keep track of their drinks so everybody could settle in the morning. It would have been easy for the men to have left early without squaring up what they owed, but few would have considered doing that. It was accepted as holy writ that they paid for what they drank and settled for what they broke.

Hewey looked around for some notion of the damage. Beyond a few smashed glasses, the only casualty he saw of last night's little wrestling match was a broken chair.

The bartender built a fire in a fat-bellied, flat-topped stove and set a large coffeepot on to boil. "If you boys want the hair of the dog, come over to the bar. If you'd rather have coffee, it'll be ready directly."

Most of the punchers elected to wait for the coffee, though Snort and Grady stumbled to the bar and leaned on it for support.

Walter said, "I'm for havin' breakfast over at the boardin'house. What about you, Hewey?"

Hewey started to shake his head, but it hurt too much. "How do I look?"

"If you feel as bad as you look, you've got one foot in the grave."

"Then go by yourself. That old lady'd probably take a broom and sweep me out into the street."

After Walter left, Hewey made his way by stages to the stove to listen to the coffee boil. The bartender brought a glass of water and poured it in to settle the grounds. "Help yourselves, boys."

Hewey's joints hurt, and his cheek and nose were sore to the touch. His knuckles were skinned and bruised. He poured a cup of coffee and sat down to hold it between his hands, hoping its warmth might draw out some of the ache. It struck him strange that the J Bar men he had fought with last night sat at the table with him, as friendly as if nothing had happened. They looked to be in about as bad a shape as he was. There was probably a lesson in this somewhere, he thought. He would study on it when he felt better.

Grady asked him, "Where's Walter?"

"Said he was goin' to the boardin'house for breakfast. I think mainly he wanted another look at that young woman."

"Eve? I ain't surprised. She's a nice girl, and pleasant to the eyes."

"Sort of skinny, I thought."

"She comes from good folks, but poor as church mice. They've had a hard time keepin' groceries on the table. That's why she works for Mrs. Pearson."

Hewey thought about Pa. The problem in East Texas hadn't been dryness so much as used-up soil and ravenous insects, poor markets and high interest. A farmer's life was seldom peaches and cream. It was more often skim milk and clabber. "Walter's too young to be thinkin' about women. Ain't nothin' but a kid."

"You're not payin' attention. He's twenty-one at least. If he wasn't thinkin' about women there'd be somethin' wrong with him." Grady arched an eyebrow. "Anything wrong with *you,* Hewey?"

"Nothin' except bein' dumb enough to get into somebody else's fight." Hewey gave Snort a critical glance. "I don't see no bruises on you."

"They're friends of mine."

"I wish you'd told us that before."

"I started to, but then it turned into a dandy scrap. Broke up the monotony."

"And like to've broke my jaw."

After partaking of the bartender's coffee, the J Bar cowboys started riding off in the direction of their branding camp. Mitch said, "I wish I could invite you fellers out to the wagon for breakfast, but Old Eli would paw and beller about feedin' C. C. Tarpley's hands. Even if the beef is C.C.'s."

Snort grunted. "Bellerin' don't hurt him. A little aggravation helps keep his blood from clottin' up."

Grady demurred. "Thanks anyway, but if we was to go to your wagon, C.C. might think we was swappin' sides."

Mitch said, "There ought not to be any sides, but I guess that's the way it is when you get two old mossy-horns buttin' heads. Let's just try to see that none of us hands gets caught up in their feud."

Grady looked regretful. "Old men start the wars and send young men off to fight them."

Mitch put his horse into an easy lope to catch up to the other J Bar cowboys. Snort held back a minute. He said, "I thank you, Grady, for takin' my part last night." His big hand was heavy on Hewey's shoulder. "And Hewey Calloway, you're a good old boy. Hell, we're *all* good old boys."

Slouching in the saddle, he rode after his friends.

The Two Cs hands made their way to the general store. They breakfasted on crackers, sardines, and canned tomatoes. None wanted to visit Mrs. Pearson's boardinghouse. She probably would not let them in, and even if she did, they would not want to hear her lecture on abstinence and clean living. After last night, they were already convinced anyway.

Walter wandered back after a while, picking his teeth and looking much too contented. Hewey said, "I can tell you've been talkin' to that girl."

Walter smiled. "Eve told me about her folks, and I told her about ours. She said there's a dance tonight in Shelby's barn. Since we don't have to be back at the ranch yet, I thought I'd go."

"You don't know how to dance."

"I've watched it done. Ain't nothin' to it. You just walk in a circle and drag your feet."

"You want to get your arms around that girl, is all. That's dangerous. Women are always out to hook you for whatever they can get."

"What would you know? The only women you've ever spent time with were at Big Bessie's, and places like hers."

Hewey's cheeks stung. "That ain't so." He knew it was.

"You weren't near as sneaky as you thought you were. I always knew where you went."

Hewey could not think of a good response. "Anyway, what do you want with a skinny farm girl? First thing you know, she'll be sweet-talkin' you about gettin' married. You'll end up workin' in a store or pushin' a plow because there ain't no cowboy can support a wife."

"Who's talkin' about gettin' married? I don't hardly know her yet."

"Be careful, or you may get to know her a lot more than you intended to. She'll have one ring on her finger and another one in your nose."

Hewey knew he had to nip this thing in the bud. He just didn't know how.

SHELBY WAS A HORSE trader who had built a barn at the edge of town. Part of it had a wooden floor fit for dancing. It bore the strong smell of horses and horse liniment, hay, and old leather. That was little hindrance to the citizens of Upton City. It was a ranch town, and they were used to such things.

Hewey was hesitant about going to the dance. He would rather spend the evening in the saloon, quietly contemplating life's deeper meaning, but he felt that

Walter needed a chaperone. He might be past twenty-one, as Grady had pointed out, but to Hewey he was still a kid whose inexperience made him vulnerable. He could be manipulated by people who might have their own interests in mind rather than his.

He still felt sore in most of his joints, and he knew without looking in a mirror that his face was swollen. He asked Walter, "Reckon anybody'll notice?"

Walter studied him critically. "Not if you stay in the dark end of the barn. If you're worried about what people might think, you don't need to go over there. I'm old enough to take care of myself."

"I wish I was as sure as you are." Hewey ran a comb through his hair and found another tender spot he had not known about. "I promised Pa I'd look out for you."

"What could happen to me here? Bein' in this town is like bein' in church, almost."

"I've been to funerals in church." Hewey paused. "And a weddin' or two."

Word had gone out that Shelby did not want any drinking in his barn, which had indicated to Hewey that this dance would be about as much fun as a memorial service. But as he and Walter walked toward the sound of fiddle music he saw that though the letter of the law might be observed, its spirit was being broken like a barroom mirror. He observed men stashing bottles in wagons and buggies and in a couple of bushes just outside the door.

He said, "Maybe the night ain't lost after all."

Walter frowned. "You ain't goin' to get drunk, I hope."

"Me? You know I wouldn't do such as that and embarrass you in front of your girl." The idea suddenly seemed to have a lot of merit.

Walter said, "She's not my girl. Yet."

A goodly crowd was already in the lantern-lit barn when Hewey and Walter arrived. Besides town folk, many had come from ranches for miles around. Hewey found himself looking at the faces, searching for the cattle thief named Smith-Trumble. He realized how foolish that was. In this town where he was known, and in a crowd like this, was surely the last place Smith would want to be.

He recognized a couple of the J Bar cowboys he had seen the previous evening. They evidently had sneaked in from Eli Jessup's branding camp. A few of the Two Cs cowboys were there, too. One was Fat Gervin. His belly stretched a clean new shirt that was still wrinkled from being folded in a stack at the general store.

Hewey found a dark corner where his bruises and contusions would not be so obvious. He watched the dancers stepping with enthusiasm to an Irish jig played loudly, if not quite in tune, on a fiddle and a banjo. He picked up the rhythm and tapped his foot. This was his kind of music.

He hoped Eve would arrive with some man, which might discourage Walter from pursuing her. He was disappointed, for she and Mrs. Pearson came through the door together. Fat Gervin immediately hurried toward her, but Walter got there first. She curtsied, and he shook her hand as he would shake with any cowboy he met.

Mrs. Pearson gave Walter a critical study. He looked well-brushed and combed, but it was obvious that her suspicions were not allayed. The music and the sound of dancers' feet sliding across rough pine prevented Hewey from hearing what she said. Walter took Eve in his arms and moved awkwardly onto the floor with her. Mrs. Pearson watched like a mother hen concerned about a wayward chick.

Hewey had been right about Walter not knowing

how to dance, but he made a creditable effort. Eve offered him guidance. After a few tunes he had improved considerably.

Walter danced Eve over to where Hewey stood. He said, "Look at her, Hewey. She's the prettiest girl here."

Hewey could not argue with that, but the competition was not substantial.

Eve scrutinized Hewey's bruised face. "What happened to you?"

"Horse," he said, hoping that was enough.

Her smile broadened. "I heard that the horse had a J Bar brand on him." She danced away with Walter.

A gruff voice demanded, "Ain't you dancin', Hewey Calloway?" Snort Yarnell had walked up behind him.

Hewey asked, "You been fired again?"

"Naw, me and Old Man Jessup have come to an understandin'. He goes where he wants to, and I go where I want to. A lot less aggravation that way. Looks like your little brother's havin' hisself a time."

"Too good a time. Look at that grin on his face. Like a possum lickin' cream."

"Yeah." Snort nodded gravely. "If he ain't careful, his cowboy days are numbered. That'd be a waste of good talent. What you goin' to do about it, Hewey?"

"Damned if I know. Somethin'."

"I know what *I'm* goin' to do. There's several bottles of good drinkin' whiskey out yonder in a bush, not doin' nobody any good. Join me?"

"Don't mind if I do." Hewey looked back. Fat Gervin was watching Walter and Eve with envy in his eyes. Hewey said, "Wait a minute, Snort. I believe I just gave birth to an idea." He walked to where Fat stood, his gaze wistfully following the pair. "Howdy, Fat."

Fat flashed him a resentful look. "Frank's the name."

"I was wonderin' if you'd do me a favor, Fat. That

girl has been dancin' with my brother ever since she came. Won't let him dance with anybody else. Him and me would both take it as a favor if you'd go out there and cut in."

Fat instantly shed his resentment. "It'd be a pleasure. Thanks, Hewey."

"It's you that deserves the thanks." Hewey watched with satisfaction as Fat worked his way through the dancers and tapped Walter on the shoulder. Hewey could not hear the words, but he saw the look of surprise on Eve's face and dismay on Walter's. Fat danced away with Eve, leaving Walter standing in the midst of the dancers. He weaved through the crowd to where Hewey waited.

He looked puzzled. "I don't understand. What's this cuttin'-in business?"

"You ain't been to many dances. Generally the girl lets somebody know she'd like to change partners. Like as not, she gave Fat a signal."

"She wouldn't do that. We were havin' a good time."

"*You* were, anyway. She probably got tired of you steppin' on her feet. Come on. Me and Snort were fixin' to have a drink."

Outside, Snort was talking to a lanky rancher whose shirttail was halfway out and whose string tie was undone, dangling beneath a prominent Adam's apple. Snort hailed Hewey. "Come over here and meet somebody."

The rancher extended a bottle toward the brothers. "You fellers look like you could stand a little drop of kindness."

Walter hung back, turning so he could watch the open barn door. Hewey accepted the offer and took a long drink. He was no connoisseur, but he knew this was not ordinary over-the-bar whiskey. "Prime stuff."

The rancher nodded, pleased. "Kentucky's finest.

You can taste the bluegrass. You-all friends of Snort Yarnell?"

Hewey said, "Like we'd known him all our lives."

Snort grinned. "This here is Alvin Lawdermilk. Got him a ranch out yonder way." He waved his hand vaguely. "Yonder way" could have been in any direction.

Lawdermilk said, "It ain't near as big as C.C.'s or Old Man Jessup's, but it's mine."

A woman came out of the barn and stood in the doorway, peering into the darkness. Lawdermilk quickly moved behind a wagon. "My wife Cora," he said. "She don't hold with strong drink." He watched until the woman went back inside. "I've got to take a chaw of tobacco to cover up my breath."

Hewey said, "You sure she'd rather smell chewin' tobacco than whiskey?"

"She don't like either one, but she can't holler much about the tobacco. Her old mother dips snuff. Boys, that woman's breath would knock a skunk into the ditch."

Walter declined Lawdermilk's offer of the bottle. "I still can't believe it," he lamented. "I didn't take Eve to be the fickle type."

Hewey said, "Just shows that a cowboy ought to stick to horses. With a horse, he's either gentle or he throws you off. He don't leave you wonderin' where you stand."

Lawdermilk nodded. "I love my Cora dearly, but there's days when I wonder if we're both speakin' the same language. There's times when I almost wish I'd never got married. Of course I always get over that notion when I set myself down to the table."

Walter looked inside the barn again. Fat was waltzing with Eve, clumsily bumping against other dancers. He said, "It beats me what she can see in him."

Hewey shrugged. "Some women like them chunky. There's more to get ahold of. I know this has got your goat, but you'll be a better man for knowin' the truth. Now, let's go over to the saloon. They've got the right medicine to treat what ails you."

Lawdermilk said, "That's a dandy idea. I believe I'll go with you. The first round is on me."

Hewey asked, "What about your wife?"

"She's already mad anyway. She'll be over it in two or three days."

Snort laid a big hand on Lawdermilk's shoulder. "Alvin, you're a good old boy."

Walter was still nursing his first drink at the bar when Hewey, Snort, and Lawdermilk were working on their third. Grady Welch had joined them, breathing heavily after dancing with most of the younger women. He seemed unaware of Walter's distress. He said, "You ought to be out at Shelby's barn, Walter. Fat Gervin is beatin' your time."

That was spark enough to light Walter's fuse. He turned toward the door. "I'm fixin' to go see about that."

Hewey grabbed at him but missed. He apologized to the other men. "I'd better try to keep my little brother from gettin' himself in trouble." He followed Walter out into the night and down toward the barn, where the fiddle and banjo continued to play in lively rhythm. He shouted, "Hey, Walter, hold up!"

Walter slowed but did not stop. Hewey trotted to catch up to him and said, "You oughtn't to do anything that'll make you look foolish. Accept it, you ain't no ladies' man."

Walter kept walking, not attempting a reply. As they neared the barn they saw two men escorting Fat out the door, holding firmly to his arms. They gave him a shove and ordered, "Don't you be comin' back."

Fat seemed bewildered. Hewey asked, "What's the trouble, Fat?"

Fat looked back. "All she had to do was to say no. Her bein' just a waitress, I thought . . ." He fixed a baleful gaze on Hewey. "Next time you want somebody to take over a gal, don't pick on me." He trudged off in the direction of the saloon.

Walter turned on Hewey. "What did he mean, take over a gal?"

Hewey feigned innocence. "Damned if I know. Fat don't always make sense."

Mrs. Pearson came out, Eve at her side. She spotted Walter and made straight for him, her face severe. "It's your fault. You left me with that awful Fat Gervin."

Walter sputtered, "What happened?"

Mrs. Pearson answered, "He made an indecent proposal to Eve, that's what, and she slapped him. It was his good luck that a couple of gentlemen hustled him out of the barn quick. Some of the young men were gettin' ready to stomp on him."

Eve demanded, "Why didn't you cut back in?"

Walter said, "I thought you wanted to dance with him. I thought . . ."

Eve said, "I don't know where you got such a fool idea."

Walter stammered. "But Hewey said . . ."

Now both Walter and Eve turned their anger on Hewey. Defensively he raised his hands and backed up a step. "I must've made a mistake. I never was good at readin' women's minds."

Eve declared, "I'll bet you can read my mind now."

He thought for a few seconds that she was going to strike him. He would not know how to handle that.

Walter said, "Eve, I did enjoy dancin' with you. I'd be pleasured to dance with you again if you'll go back in there with me."

She shook her head. "I'm too mad to face that crowd

anymore tonight. And I'm too mad to stand here talkin' to you. Next time you think about askin' me to dance, don't."

Walter looked as if he had been knocked down by a runaway wagon he had not seen coming. "Eve . . ."

Eve turned away toward the boardinghouse. Mrs. Pearson gave both brothers a withering glance. "Good night, *gentlemen*."

As the women moved away, Walter called after them. "I'll be over for breakfast. Maybe we can talk."

Mrs. Pearson said, "There won't be any empty chairs."

Hewey tried to measure his words. "Someday you'll look back on this and be glad it turned out like it did. You could've got yourself trapped, and she'd pretty soon have you hooked up to a plow. You're too good a cowboy to waste your life like that."

Walter snapped, "The next time you feel like buttin' into my business, don't." He strode away, making it clear that he did not want Hewey to walk with him.

Hewey thought, *I'm just tryin' to keep him out of trouble. It's a good thing Pa ain't here to see this.*

Lying on the pool table, he slept fitfully. He was assaulted by dreams of Eve and Mrs. Pearson beating him with broom handles, of Eve driving away in a wagon with Walter. When that nightmare faded, he was certain he saw the rustler Smith-Trumble coming after him with a pistol. As he awakened for the tenth time, fighting his blanket, he gave up any attempt at sleep. Walter was lying on the floor, awake. He turned away when he saw that Hewey was looking at him.

Hewey said, "I'm thinkin' about goin' over to the boardin'house and apologizin' to that girl."

Walter's voice was crisp. "You've caused trouble enough already. Stay away from her."

Hewey fished for the right words. "I never had no thought of hurtin' you. I've always looked out for you the best I could, like a big brother is supposed to."

"I'm not as little a brother as you think I am. I'm a grown man, and I can handle myself pretty good, thank you."

"I reckon you're right. It ain't my place to do the thinkin' for you anymore."

He lay back down on his blanket and began trying to figure out the best way to keep Walter and Eve apart.

SIX

C. C. TARPLEY POKED HIS HEAD IN THE BUNKHOUSE door after the crew returned to the ranch from their holiday in town. "Anybody here sober?"

Grady feigned innocence. "C.C., you know nobody in this outfit ever drinks."

"Only when they get the chance." Tarpley beckoned Hewey, Walter, and Grady outside. "You-all come and go with me. I've got somethin' to talk to you about." Looking around to be sure no one else could hear, he led them to a corral fence and leaned his bony shoulder against it. "Boys," he said, "I hope you-all will do somethin' for me."

That sounded as if they had a choice. They didn't if they wanted to keep working for the Two Cs.

Tarpley said, "I been tallyin' the figures. Our brandin' came up a mite short. The way it looks to me, somebody's been skimmin' off part of the crop. I see the fine hand of Eli Jessup in this."

Grady suggested, "It was dry last year. Maybe the cows didn't breed up like they ought to."

"Ain't nothin' wrong with our cows, or our bulls, either. They know their job." Tarpley's eyes narrowed. "Old Eli's still brandin'. Now, I ain't exactly sayin' he's a thief, but on the other hand there's no bounds to his ambition."

Hewey doubted that Tarpley's ambition knew any bounds, either, but the boss wouldn't want to hear that.

Tarpley lowered his voice as if he were divulging a military secret. "I'd like for you boys to sneak out of here and scout around over Eli's country. I've got a hunch you might find some J Bar–branded calves suckin' on Two Cs cows. If you do, I'll put the sheriff onto that old reprobate like I'd sic a dog onto a coyote."

Grady frowned. "I know most of the boys that work for Eli, and they're good folks. They'd quit before they'd be a party to such as that."

Tarpley looked annoyed at having his judgment questioned. "Maybe you don't know them as well as you think. There's many a man will forget about his conscience if there's enough profit to be had."

Grady argued, "But every once in a while Eli gathers up Two Cs strays and sends them back here where they belong. He could just as easy keep them."

Tarpley sniffed. "Maybe he does that just so I don't suspicion him."

Hewey said, "If he catches us pokin' around over there, he'll be the one that calls for the sheriff."

"See to it that you don't get caught. Stay away from where he's still gatherin' and brandin'. Scout around where he's already moved on."

Grady reluctantly nodded acceptance. "Eli's got a lot of country. How long do you want us to keep lookin'?"

"Till you're plumb satisfied one way or the other."

Hewey glanced at Walter. One good thing about this assignment: it would keep him away from town and that girl. He said, "This might take a right smart while. We'll need to pack plenty of grub."

Tarpley's face pinched at the thought. "Go easy on the expenses. Money don't come easy around here."

Hewey already knew that.

Tarpley added, "Don't tell anybody where you're goin'. I wouldn't want the word getting' to Eli. I'd wager ten dollars—well, maybe five—that he's got a spy or two on this place. On my payroll!" The idea that some of his money might be going to an enemy spy appeared to cause him considerable pain.

Hewey immediately thought of Fat Gervin but rejected the idea. Not that Fat was above such a thing, but he didn't seem to have that much ambition.

Tarpley added another bit of advice. "Don't you boys flash any firearms. That'd just give Eli's crew an excuse to shoot you. If you do happen to get caught, just say you were drunk and got lost. That'll sound logical."

Grady looked as if he had bitten into a sour apple. When Tarpley was gone, he said, "Me, get lost? I know every cow trail and rabbit track from here to Pontoon Crossin'. We won't find any Two Cs calves over there. Old Eli ain't no cow thief, even if he is as ornery as a sore-footed badger."

Walter shrugged. "The boss may not always be right, but he's the one that pays us."

Grady started for the kitchen. "Let's go jaw with Soapy."

They tried to get supplies without letting Soapy in on the secret, but the cook was a step ahead of them. He said, "C.C. has always suspicioned that Eli is stealin' from him, but I think you boys are off on a snipe hunt. When it's over you'll be holdin' an empty sack."

Hewey said, "It's C.C.'s sack. We'll be drawin' our six bits a day, regardless."

"Six bits? I'm gettin' a dollar and a quarter and don't even have to climb on a horse."

Grady impatiently turned toward the door. "Throw the stuff in a couple of sacks, Soapy. We'll saddle up and come back for it."

Hewey objected, "Just a couple of sacks? That'll be lean pickin's if we're out for very long."

Soapy asked, "Ain't you ever et jackrabbit?"

"Never did."

"No matter. With you-all doin' your own cookin', most of it won't be fit to eat noway."

HEWEY WAS INCLINED TO agree with Grady and Soapy about the futility of the mission Tarpley had assigned. They seemed confident that however numerous his faults might be, Eli Jessup was not one to steal cattle from his neighbors beyond the common practice of slaughtering strays for beef. On the other hand, the saving grace might be that the trip would keep Walter occupied. Hewey's brother had spoken to him but little since the incident at the dance. Perhaps a change of scenery would have healing powers.

Hewey had envied Len Tanner as he listened to stories about adventures the ranger had known. Crossing over onto Jessup's range provided a tingling sense of adventure and risk. Maybe he had not been born too late after all.

"Eli has got a good bunch of boys workin' for him," Grady said, "but it's best we don't stumble into any of them. They might feel duty bound to tell him they saw us. Eli's got the same suspicious mind as C.C. He'd figure we're out to steal from him."

Hewey asked, "How do we know where to go, and where not to?"

"I worked for Eli my first year out here. I know his country and the way he works. Wherever we find the calves already branded, we can be satisfied that he's finished workin' that part of the place."

It did not take long to find the first J Bar cattle. Hewey's limited experience told him Jessup's range was stocked more heavily than Tarpley's. Jessup probably figured Tarpley received more rain—just another reason to resent him—but the fact was that he had more cattle searching after a limited amount of grass. No wonder Jessup was always looking for more land and allowing his stock to push over Tarpley's outer perimeter.

It was not easy to see the J Bar cattle close up. Worked recently, they were leery of horseback riders. Hewey, Walter, and Grady had to circle around and hold them up for a good look at the brands.

The first group set the pattern. Grady checked them over and said, "Not a Two Cs amongst them."

Near nightfall Grady pointed to a distant windmill. "Pretty good water there. It'll be a place to camp for the night and rest the horses."

Hewey said, "We could rest them for a week, no more good than we're doin'."

Walter said, "We're followin' orders and earnin' our time."

Soapy had wrapped some beef and put it in one of the sacks. Grady said, "We'd just as well eat hearty. It won't keep long anyway. After this it'll be sowbelly and whatever we can find. We might manage to kill us a javelina hog."

Hewey frowned. "They don't look fit to eat, with those long teeth and all that bristly hair."

"You don't eat the hair. Javelinas are fair to middlin' if they ain't too scrawny."

Hewey had seen several of the wild pigs. Scared up by the horses, they would go clattering away into the nearest brush, snorting and grunting in alarm. They were a far cry from the domestic hogs Hewey remembered on the farm. It had not occurred to him that they might make a decent supper.

Frying steak in a small skillet over a cow-chip fire, Grady said, "Ain't far from here to the old Butterfield Trail. There was thousands of immigrants passed over it, goin' and comin'. You could tell which ones was headin' west, full of faith and hope. They left ham bones and tin cans behind them. Comin' back east, they was usually wore out and draggin' their feet. All you found in their camps was rabbit fur and quail bones."

Hewey said, "I expect when they got to this part of the country it looked like the jumpin' off place to hell."

"Charles Goodnight called the Pecos River the grave of a cowman's hopes. But it's not as poor as it sometimes looks. A man has just got to know how to manage it. C.C. does pretty good. Eli tries to wring more out of it than it can give."

His stomach full, Hewey stretched out on his blanket and watched the evening star brighten in the darkening sky. The night birds tuned up for their evening concert, and somewhere in the distance a cow bawled for her strayed calf. He felt contented with the world.

"Grady," he said, "is there anything you'd rather do than be a cowpuncher?"

"I've studied on it some. Never came up with anything better."

"Me neither." Hewey looked at Walter, but Walter had nothing to say.

AFTER FOUR DAYS OF hunting they still had not found any Two Cs calves except a few following Two Cs mothers. These had simply strayed onto Jessup's land after branding. Even a cow ought to have more judgment, Hewey thought. The grass was better on the Tarpley range.

Riding away from the last bunch they had inspected, Grady declared, "I told C.C. this was a wild goose chase. If Jessup was goin' to steal, he's too big a man to mess around with penny-ante stuff like this. He'd do it in a big way. I've got a good mind to give up this foolishness and go home. If C.C. doesn't like it, he can fire me. There's always other jobs."

That might be so for a top hand of Grady's caliber, Hewey thought, but he and Walter did not yet qualify.

He had enjoyed this little adventure for its own sake, whether anything came of it or not.

Grady said, "We've still got grub. If nothin' else, we could go over to the river and fish for a few days. C.C. doesn't expect us back so soon."

Walter had not talked much during the trip, especially to Hewey. He rode most of the time in brooding silence. Now he protested, "That wouldn't be playin' the game square with C.C."

"The game we're playin' ain't exactly square either," Hewey replied, "trespassin' on another man's land, stirrin' up his stock."

Grady said, "I was just lettin' off a little steam. No, I wouldn't shortchange C.C. We'll keep lookin'."

The next day they found about twenty cattle shaded up in a mesquite thicket where a shallow depression held water after a rain. They started pushing them out into the open for yet another perfunctory look at brands. The cattle balked at first, reluctant to give up the shade.

Grady made a pass around the bunched cows and calves, giving the brands little more than a glance. Then he pulled up short and took a second look at a heifer calf. He turned back to examine more closely another calf that had recently been rendered a steer. A remnant of dried blood still clung to its hind legs. He dropped a small loop over the calf's neck to hold it.

"Hewey, Walter, come look at this."

Hewey and Walter drew in closer. Hewey saw nothing remarkable. "It's a J Bar, and the cows are J Bars. Just like all the others we've seen."

"Look again. That brand don't go all the way to the hide. It's just a hair brand."

Hewey did not grasp the significance. "Somebody didn't take the time to do a good job."

"Somebody knew damned well what he was doin'. The hair'll grow out after a while, and then there won't be any brand. Soon as its mammy's milk dries up and this calf weans off, it'll be a maverick. Anybody can burn his own brand on it. Chances are Eli would never know."

Walter looked puzzled. "How did they manage to do this under Jessup's nose?"

Grady explained, "Whoever done it worked out ahead of Eli's brandin' crew. He was smart enough not to be greedy about it. Just sleepered a few here, there, and yonder. Eli's boys would be too busy for a close look. They'd see the fresh brands and figure these calves just drifted over from an earlier gather."

Hewey got the picture. "Next fall or winter somebody'll gather up the mavericks and brand them for their own."

Grady said, "He put Eli's earmarks on them, but a sharp knife can alter those."

Walter mused, "Who would think of such a thing?"

"It's an old trick. Probably started with the vaqueros in Mexico, like most everything else we do."

Hewey said, "Kind of odd. We came over here tryin' to prove that Eli is a thief, and instead we find out he's the victim."

Grady frowned. "Maybe not the only one. Our brandin' count came up short. I'll bet somebody's been doin' the same thing to us."

Walter said, "We'd better go by town and tell the sheriff."

Hewey suspected Walter had another motive for a trip to Upton City. He said, "No, the sheriff would ask why we were on Jessup's land in the first place. He might even figure it was us that did the hair brands. And if he didn't, Jessup would."

Grady agreed. "We'd best not say anything to the sheriff, and we sure don't want to tell Eli. But if I get the chance I'll whisper in Mitch's ear, or Snort's."

They had not ridden more than a mile when Hewey saw the chance coming. He looked back and saw two riders. He said, "Somebody's catchin' up to us from behind."

"Hell," Grady wheezed. "We better think of somethin' quick."

As the horsemen neared, Hewey recognized Snort Yarnell and the foreman Mitch. Snort gave a loud yell from fifty yards away.

Mitch seemed to suppress a grin as he reined up. "Howdy, Grady. Ain't you a long ways from where you belong? I thought Eli fired you off of this place three or four years ago."

Grady said, "Eli never got the chance to fire me. I quit."

"He'll want to know what you-all are up to, sashayin' around over his country."

Grady struggled for a reply. Hewey spoke up, saying the first thing that popped into his head. "We're trailin' after some horses that strayed or got stolen."

Mitch shifted his attention to Hewey. "Name's Calloway, ain't it? Seems like me and you had a slight disagreement in town."

"It didn't amount to much. We had a drink together afterwards. Several of them, the best I recall."

Mitch asked, "What kind of horses was they?"

"Horses?"

"The ones you're trailin'."

Hewey said, "Oh, them. One was a roan, kind of between a gray and a blue, thirteen hands high, stockin' on his right forefoot. And there was a black with a blaze face, carries some kind of a Mexican brand on the left hip. Walks a little paddle-footed." He amazed himself at the ease with which he picked the descriptions out of thin air. He could only hope that Mitch did not ask him to repeat them.

Mitch studied the ground. "You say you've been trailin' them. I don't see no tracks here."

Hewey said, "We lost the trail back yonder a ways. We're tryin' to pick it up again."

Mitch sniffed. "Except maybe for Grady, I never saw a Two Cs hand who could track a steer herd through a cornfield. You boys had better give it up and go back home before Eli puts the law on you for trespass."

Hewey tried to sound plaintive. "What about those horses?"

"We'll scout around. If we find them we'll send them

home. If we don't, C.C. can afford a little loss. He's got more cows than old Abraham."

Hewey nodded regretfully. "He'll be awful disappointed."

Snort moved up beside Hewey. He grinned, his gold tooth shining. "What color did you say them horses was, Hewey?"

Hewey realized Snort hadn't believed a word of it. He said, "Don't you remember?"

Snort shook his head. "I thought I wore the crown as the best liar in this part of the country, but after listenin' to you I'm afraid that crown don't set easy on my head anymore."

Grady shrugged. "Hell, Mitch, there ain't no horses. Hewey just made that up."

Mitch nodded. "I figured that."

Grady said, "C.C. sent us over here to hunt for Two Cs calves carryin' the J Bar brand. We didn't find any, but we found somethin' else you ought to know about." He described the hair-branded calves. "Don't let Eli know we told you. He'd lay it onto us."

Mitch frowned. "He'd blame you, anyway. He's got a suspicious mind when it comes to Tarpley and the Two Cs." He was deep in thought while he rolled a cigarette, then offered the sack to the others. "Best thing to do is for us to hunt down those sleepered calves and brand them on the sly. The less Eli knows about it, the better." Another thought came to him. "Whoever done this to us has probably done the same thing to the Two Cs."

Grady said, "If they have, C.C. would probably blame it on Eli. We'd best find them and brand them without makin' any noise about it."

Mitch agreed. "I wish the two knotheads would get together. They could fix this problem. But they'd probably go at one another like two old bulls and get somebody hurt. Somebody like us."

Grady said, "Kind of makes me homesick for the piney woods. But we had a lot of knotheads there, too. The whole world's infested with them. Come on, we'll show you them calves we found."

The calves were with their mothers, back in the shade of a thicket. Mitch dropped a loop over the neck of one and dragged it into the open. "Would you-all build a fire? I've got a cinch ring."

The two cows pawed dirt and threatened while Mitch used the heated ring to burn a proper J Bar on their bawling calves' hides. As soon as their offspring were released they led them back into the thicket in a long trot.

Snort had been staring off into the distance as if he had little interest in the proceedings. He said, "Eli would want us to escort you three off of his property. It wouldn't be much out of the way for us to go by town."

It would be considerably out of the way. Mitch said, "Not me. Every time Eli fires you, he hires you back. With me he might make it permanent."

Hewey saw a hopeful gleam in Walter's eyes. He quickly headed it off. "Great idea, Snort, but we'd better get back to the Two Cs and start lookin' for hair-branded calves of our own."

Without thinking about it, Hewey had adopted a typical cowboy's sense of commitment to the outfit for which he worked. So long as he drew its pay, it would be *our* ranch, *our* cattle.

Snort said, "You can do what you want to, Mitch. I'm goin' to town. If Eli asks about me, just tell him the last time you seen me I was headed straight up and anglin' a little to the west."

Watching Snort move away, Mitch shook his head.

"There goes the best-natured old boy I ever knew, only he hasn't got a lick of judgment."

Hewey said, "I like a man who goes his own way, sunshine or rain. I wish I could be like that."

Walter said, "You're closer to it than you know."

They rode half a mile before Mitch reined to a stop, worry in his eyes. "You boys don't need me to guide you back to the Two Cs. I'd better trail after Snort and try to keep him out of trouble. If I can get him to the ranch before daylight, Eli won't ever have to know."

Walter offered, "If you need any help with him, I'll go along."

To Hewey's relief, Mitch said, "I can usually handle Snort, but thanks anyway."

Walter looked disappointed. Hewey knew he was thinking about that girl in town.

He said, "You're a cowboy. You can't afford a woman anyway."

"I may not always be a cowboy."

Hewey was not prepared for that. "A man couldn't want a better life than what we've got right here."

"Yes he could," Walter said.

No fence divided the two ranches. There was only a reluctant and unspoken understanding between Tarpley and Jessup regarding the boundary. In truth, neither actually owned all the land he claimed. Much still belonged to the state of Texas but was too far from Austin for authorities to come and measure each man's use and collect for it. The two ranchers simply paid lease on enough acreage to make a show of legality. They did not acknowledge that they had cattle on the rest.

Anyone else would have had a legal right to turn cattle loose on the unleased land, but few dared. Tarpley and Jessup had reputations that intimidated all but the most determined. Both men had a nagging fear that some interloper would come along and buy the state land out from under them. For that reason, each had bought selected tracts that offered water. Neither was yet willing to make the investment that would give him full title to all the land his cattle grazed.

After reaching the Two Cs, Hewey, Walter, and Grady rode through several bunches of cattle, carefully looking over the calves. Hewey saw the first of the hair brands and pointed. "There's one." It was not obvious. He would easily have overlooked the fraud had he not specifically been looking for it. The ranch's branding crew had innocently passed over these calves because they appeared to have been branded already.

Walter said, "And here's another."

The rest of the calves bore normal brands.

Grady said, "Let's brand them here and now."

They built a small fire and heated a cinch ring. Hewey and Walter held the calves down while Grady laboriously burned the brands.

Hewey said, "There's apt to be more."

Grady nodded. "C.C. ain't expectin' us back yet. We've got enough grub to keep us for several more days. What say we three stay out and hunt for hair brands? C.C. don't need to know."

Hewey said, "Whatever you say. I wonder who done this?"

"Some small owner, tryin' to get bigger."

Hewey tried to remember the small owners he had met. "What about that feller Lawdermilk? Alvin Lawdermilk."

Grady said, "I don't want to believe it could be Alvin. He seems like a good old boy. But you never can be sure about people."

Hewey said, "We ought to let the rest of the crew know what's happened so they can be on the lookout, too."

Grady agreed. "All except Fat Gervin. He'd run to

C.C. like a schoolboy tattlin' to the teacher. Then C.C. might go gunnin' for Eli. There's a good chance we'd have to bury two stubborn old men, and maybe some of ourselves."

SEVEN

THE SHERIFF WAS WAITING WITH TARPLEY WHEN
Hewey rode up to the corrals on a young horse he
was training. *Oh, hell!* Hewey thought. *C.C. has found
out about those hair brands.* The Two Cs crew had
found and quietly rebranded more than a hundred
calves in the weeks since the discovery was made.
Hewey gripped the hackamore rein tightly and stepped
down as far from the saddle as his legs would reach.
The bronc had a worrisome habit of pawing at a dismounting rider.

Trouble showed in Tarpley's face. "The sheriff's got
somethin' to talk to you about, Hewey."

Hewey felt an anxious moment, though he could not
remember that he had committed any serious breach of
the peace. He had not even been to town lately. *Those
damned calves. They're going to cause a war between
C.C. and Eli Jessup yet,* he thought.

The sheriff's expression was as dark as Tarpley's.

"Calloway, you remember the two fellers you testified against?"

The subject was not what Hewey expected. "Seems to me like I do." He tried not to be infected by the older men's mood, but it made him feel cold.

"You probably heard that Trumble—you called him Smith—got away from Ranger Tanner some time back. He swore he would come back someday and get you."

"Seems to me like I remember that, too." Hewey had thought about it every day.

"There's a rumor that he's been seen. I don't know that I believe it. If I was him I'd be in California by now, or maybe sailin' to China. It don't make sense that he'd risk his neck just to get even with an ordinary cowpuncher like you. But criminals don't think like normal folks. Their brains are set in their heads sideways."

Walter had ridden up behind Hewey. He had heard most of it. Worriedly he said, "Maybe you'd better get away from here for a while."

Hewey appreciated his concern, especially because Walter had not been talking to him much.

"Where? I hate to just ride off and leave a good job. C.C. has been talkin' about givin' us a raise."

Tarpley spoke quickly, "I ain't said when that'll be."

The sheriff asked, "How good a shot are you, Calloway?"

Hewey twisted the hackamore rein. "I couldn't hit a bull in the butt with a shotgun."

"Too bad. You've got to figure that Trumble is right peart with a firearm. That's one of the few things most criminals are good at."

Hewey tried to rationalize. "If he was hell-bent on it, he could've found me easy before now."

The sheriff agreed. "It's probably a false rumor, but we'd better not forget that he cussed you every day he spent in my jail. He blamed you as much as he blamed Tanner. And you heard what he done to Tanner."

Hewey said, "I testified because I was sore about him leavin' me and Walter to take the punishment for him. Besides, Tanner told me it was my bounden duty."

Tarpley said, "It happens I've got a job that'll take you away from here for a while. And you'll still draw your wages. By the time you get back, maybe Trumble will be on cornbread and beans again. Or smellin' flowers from the underside."

Hewey said, "I'm listenin' with both ears."

"I had figured on sendin' Grady, but you'll have to do. An old cowboy named Jerome Padgett wrote that he's located a herd of cows for me. They're somewhere south of San Antonio. He wouldn't tell me just where. I guess he was afraid I'd go around him and do him out of a commission."

Hewey said, "Surely you wouldn't do that."

"I thought about it, but I might need him again sometime. Anyway, I'm buyin' out the brand and eight hundred head that go with it. I'd like you to receive them for me, then help Jerome drive them out here."

Hewey grinned at Walter. This was the kind of work he liked. Despite bad weather, indifferent food, and several wild and wet river crossings, he had enjoyed the trip he and Walter made up the trail to Kansas with a herd out of central Texas. He told Tarpley, "If I get started, I can travel a good ways before sundown."

"Tomorrow mornin' will be soon enough. I doubt that Trumble will get to you before dark."

"I'm not afraid of Trumble. Well, not a lot."

"Come over to the house after supper. I'll give you directions and write a letter for you to carry."

Hewey recognized that if he left here alone, Walter would be without his supervision and counsel. There was no telling what mess his brother might get himself into. He asked, "Can I take Walter with me? I may need his help."

Walter made a quick objection, but Tarpley seemed not to hear it. He said, "I figured on Jerome Padgett hirin' whatever extra men he thinks he'll need. Down there they're mostly Mexicans, and they work cheap. But go ahead and take Walter if you want to. He's not costin' me much more than a Mexican would."

"I'm much obliged."

Walter was not, but he said nothing. His sour expression indicated that he would have much to say later.

Tarpley appeared ready to turn away, then paused. "One more thing. I'd like you to take Fat Gervin with you."

Hewey's jaw dropped. Fat would be about as much help as a broken leg. "What do we need with Fat?"

"I'd like to be shed of him for a while."

"Why don't you just fire him?"

"Can't. For some reason my wife and daughter have got attached to him. There's enough things botherin' my life without two naggin' women addin' to the load."

The last thing Hewey needed was Fat Gervin like a two-hundred-pound weight on his shoulders. But it was Tarpley's ranch, and his call. "Whatever you say. I just wish you'd tell him that I'm the boss till Jerome Padgett takes over."

"If he gives you any trouble, go off and leave him. You'd be doin' me a favor, and the womenfolks would blame you instead of me."

Hewey found little consolation in that. He said, "Maybe Padgett will run him off, and neither one of us will get blamed. What kind of feller is this Padgett?"

"He's had as many birthdays as I have. There ain't much cow country that he hasn't left tracks in. As a young'un he drove herds all the way to New Orleans before the Yankee war. But don't worry about his age. He's forgotten more than you'll ever know about punchin' cattle."

That satisfied Hewey. "Maybe me and Walter can learn some things from him."

"Just watch and listen. Sober, he's a better hand than even Grady Welch. But he's got the same weakness as Snort Yarnell. It'll be up to you to keep him away from whiskey."

"How can we tell him what to do if he's bossin' the drive?"

"Figure it out as you go along. It's part of what I'm payin' you for."

Tarpley and the sheriff retreated toward Tarpley's house. Walter turned on Hewey, his voice sharp. "You had no call to volunteer me. You're just tryin' to keep me away from Eve."

"The last I saw, she was doin' that for herself."

"Only because you put me in a bad light with her. I've got a good notion to tell C.C. that I ain't goin'."

"Bosses don't like bein' told what a man won't do. The trip'll be good for you. I'll bet by the time we get back you'll forget all about that farm girl."

"I'll take you up on that bet. Twenty dollars. No, better make it ten."

Fat Gervin was unsaddling his horse. Walter asked, "Are you fixin' to tell Fat that he's goin' with us?"

"Not me. He'll take orders better if they come from C.C."

After putting away a healthy feed of red beans and Jessup beef, Hewey told Walter, "Let's go over to the big house and get our instructions." He used the term *big house* with a touch of irony.

Walter said curtly, "You go. You dragged me into this."

"Pa would be disappointed if he could see the way you're actin'. Our ma wouldn't be proud, either."

"If Pa had had you for a brother, he never would've got to marry Ma in the first place. Then where would me and you be?"

Fat Gervin sat on the edge of the narrow porch, talking to C.C.'s daughter. She seemed to be hanging on every word. Poor girl, Hewey thought. Even if she *was* plain as a board fence, she could do better than Fat if she lived in a town where she had a chance to meet more young men. As it was, she seldom saw anyone other than the Two Cs cowboys. Even among those, he thought, any would be a better catch than Fat.

He tipped his hat. "Evenin', Doreen. Is your daddy in the house?"

Tarpley hollered from inside. "The door's open."

Hewey hoped for Doreen's sake that Tarpley was keeping one eye on her and Fat, but the rancher was hunched at a battered rolltop desk. It appeared old enough and battered enough to have fallen out of an immigrant wagon on the Butterfield Trail. Tarpley looked up over a pair of black-rimmed reading glasses and nodded toward a rawhide-bottomed chair. "Set yourself down. I'm finishin' a letter for you to give to the seller, along with a draft on a San Antonio bank. You'll have to write in the figure after you and Jerome have done countin' the cattle. He could count a herd of jackrabbits, but he don't read and write very good." His eyebrows raised. "You *can* read and write, can't you?"

"Sure. I went plumb through the fourth grade. Our pa was real particular about us gettin' an education."

"Fourth grade is plenty for a cowboy. All he needs is to know more than the cows. Now looky here." He spread a map across the desk and traced with his forefinger. "Best thing is for you to go east and strike the head of the Middle Concho. Follow it to San Angelo. From there an old military road will take you down through the hills to Friedrichsburg and on to San Antone. That's where you'll find Jerome Padgett. He'll take you to where the cattle are at. I gather that they're a ways south of San Antone."

"How come he lives in San Antone but the cattle are someplace else?"

"He doesn't *live* anywhere. Home is wherever he happens to drop his bedroll of an evenin'. When you get to San Antone, hunt up a feller name of Patrick Appleby. Lives a couple blocks east of the Alamo. He can help you find Jerome."

"Do we follow the same route comin' back?"

"That'll be up to Jerome. He knows how to travel through the settled country without a bunch of mad farmers gettin' the whole outfit throwed in jail. He'll likely go around the towns. He wouldn't want a bunch of town dogs stampedin' the cattle through somebody's front parlor."

Tarpley told Hewey he could draw on the San Antonio bank for necessary supplies. "Go easy, though. I ain't fattenin' up a bunch of lean and hungry cowhands."

Mrs. Tarpley came out from the kitchen and offered Hewey a cup of coffee. She was a dainty little woman with a subdued voice she probably didn't get to use much when her husband was around. Tarpley told her sternly, "He's just et." She retreated back into the kitchen before Hewey could accept the offer. Tarpley said, "Too much coffee can addle the brain near as bad as whiskey."

Hewey arose. Tarpley held up a finger. "Now listen good. I don't want everybody to know about this till we get the cattle home and situated. I got my eye on some land for sale on the other side of the river. If Eli gets wind of what I'm doin', that greedy old devil will bust a gut tryin' to buy it out from under me."

"He won't find out from me and Walter."

"If you run into any J Bar hands and they ask, tell them you're goin' back East to visit your folks."

"Ma died years ago. Pa just lasted a few years longer. Me and Walter ain't got any folks."

"Well then, just lie to them. Those J Bar hands will believe anything."

"Have you told Fat that he's goin' with us?"

Tarpley looked toward the front door. Fat still sat on the porch with Tarpley's daughter. "Nope. As you leave, tell him to come in here. I'll spoil his evenin' for him."

Hewey was pleased to comply.

HEWEY AND WALTER SADDLED their horses soon after sunrise. Fat lingered at the breakfast table, throwing them late in getting started. He was puffed up like a toad when he finally appeared at the barn. He avoided speaking, but it was clear that he did not relish the prospect of a long ride to South Texas and an even slower cattle drive back. He mumbled to himself as he dragged his rigging out of the saddle shed.

Hewey was not eager for his company. He said, "We're startin'. You can catch up when you're ready." He led a packhorse carrying enough supplies to last through the trip. Tarpley did not trust merchants along the way because they tended to take advantage of travelers who had no other recourse. He owned half interest in the Upton City mercantile and got his goods at wholesale.

Walter did not speak half a dozen words the first couple of miles. Hewey tried several times to get him to break his silence, but to no avail. Then Walter veered off to the west.

Hewey pointed eastward. "San Angelo's thataway."

"Upton City is this way. I ain't goin' anyplace till I get things straight with Eve. Go by yourself if you don't like it."

Hewey did not like it, but he saw that Walter was going to be stubborn. He never had been able to understand stubborn people. "You don't know if she'll even talk to you."

"I'll do the talkin' if she won't."

"C.C. will count the days we're gone."

"I don't figure on marryin' C.C., but one of these days I'm goin' to marry Eve."

Walter's jaw was set like Ma's used to be when she made up her mind to something. Once she went that far, Hewey had never seen her back off. He saw nothing more to be said or done for now. Maybe while they were gone Eve would attach herself to some other poor cowpuncher or some Fort Worth drummer and let Walter go on being free like a man was supposed to be, the way Hewey was.

Fat had been trailing behind, his mood morose. He brightened as he realized they were headed for town. He caught up and stayed up.

They reached the boardinghouse before midday. The noon dinner crowd had not begun to gather. Walter dismounted and boldly walked up the steps and onto the porch. He rapped his knuckles on the doorframe.

Mrs. Pearson appeared, carrying a dish towel. She placed both hands on her broad hips. "Well?"

Walter declared, "I've come to see Eve."

"We're busy fixin' dinner. Anyway, she's already said about all there was to say to you."

"Maybe so, but I've got something to say even if she

ain't." He pushed past a flustered Mrs. Pearson and entered the house.

Hewey had never seen Walter be so assertive. It seemed a pity to waste all that newfound boldness on some farm girl so thin she hardly threw a decent shadow. He tied the horses and followed. He hoped Eve might throw a pan of dishwater at Walter and prove that Hewey had been right all along. Such a show would be worth seeing.

Eve was sliding a tray of biscuits into the oven when Walter spoke her name. Startled, she burned her hand and lifted it to her lips.

Walter blurted, "I've got somethin' to say to you."

She stared at him with wide eyes, the hand still against her mouth.

"Eve, I tried to tell you before, but you wouldn't listen. I thought you wanted to dance with Fat Gervin. I ought to've known it was all Hewey's doin'. I wouldn't hurt you for the world. I'm willin' to hurt Hewey, though, if it'll make you feel better. I'll beat him to a pulp."

Hewey backed up a step.

Eve shook off her surprise and offered Walter the slightest hint of a smile. "You'd whip your own brother? For me?"

"If you say so. He's not much of a fighter."

The look she gave Hewey indicated that she was thinking about it. He backed up a little more.

She asked, "Why? You don't know me, hardly."

"But I'm goin' to know you a lot better. One of these days I'm goin' to marry you."

She blinked a couple of times. "How do you know I'll marry *you?*"

"You will when you get to know me. And I'm goin' to see that you get to know me a lot better."

She seemed too stunned to reply.

Walter said, "Me and Hewey are goin' off on a trip for C. C. Tarpley. When we get back, I'll come callin'."

Eve recovered her voice. "I'm still provoked at you. I'm not promisin' you anything."

"I wouldn't expect you to, yet. I just want you to know I'm serious, and I've got honorable intentions."

She cast a disapproving glance at Hewey. "What about *him?*"

Walter said, "He don't count. It's just me and you."

Mrs. Pearson had been taken aback. Now she intervened. "If you men want dinner, you'll have to get out and let us finish cookin'."

Walter said, "Yes, ma'am. We'll be on the porch." He jerked his head at Hewey.

Hewey spoke to Mrs. Pearson. "Fat Gervin's outside. Would you feed him, too?"

Mrs. Pearson looked at Eve, posing a silent question. Eve said, "If he'll act the gentleman, I'll try to overlook his past behavior."

Outside, Hewey told Walter, "You've split your britches now."

"You already split them for me. I'm just tryin' to get them mended."

After dinner, Fat complained loudly about leaving town without a drink. Hewey gave in. "Just one, and then we're leavin'."

Walter hung back to talk to Eve some more. Hewey entered the saloon with Fat. He saw a face he remembered from the night of the dance. Rancher Alvin Lawdermilk leaned on the bar. "Howdy, cowboys. You-all come over and have one with me."

It was evident that he had already had one, or perhaps three.

Hewey was hesitant, for he suspected Lawdermilk

might be the man hair-branding Two Cs and J Bar calves. But Lawdermilk was insistent, declaring, "I don't get to come to town every day, but my mother-in-law has run us plumb out of flour and sugar and stuff. I never seen a woman who could eat so much. Keeps one man busy all day choppin' enough firewood for the stove."

The bartender placed two glasses on the bar, and Lawdermilk filled them. "Belly up, cowboys. Ain't no use puttin' off till tomorrow what you can drink today."

Hewey asked, "How's your calf crop this year?"

"Best I ever saw. Even some of my bulls are havin' twins."

It may not be as good as he expects, Hewey thought. *We found most of those hair-branded calves.*

THEY RODE AT A leisurely pace that would not tax the horses, though Fat griped as if it taxed him considerably. Toward sundown Hewey saw a windmill against the skyline, its cypress-vaned fan turning lazily in a light wind. Though not yet plentiful, mills like this were beginning to spread across dry West Texas to bring water from underground in places where nature had not placed it on the surface. They allowed livestock to graze neglected areas formerly too far from water for animals to walk. They, along with barbed wire, were making it possible for settlement to survive in a desert-like environment.

Hewey said, "That'll be a good place to make camp. The horses need water."

They had left Upton City miles behind, but Walter's mind was still there. Hewey tried to pry some conversation out of him. "I'm not sure where the Middle Concho commences. If we follow this wagon trail east, we ought to find it in fifty or sixty miles. What do you think?"

Walter just grunted.

Fat had been trailing again, hunched in the saddle. Hewey had ignored his frequent requests that they stop and rest.

The windmill pumped water into a man-made shallow depression gouged into the ground. Elsewhere it would be called a pond. Out here it was called a tank. Though the facility was not yet old, small mesquites had already taken root around the edge of the water. Hewey had been told that cattle scattered the seed in their droppings. Several J Bar cows and calves loafed around the surface tank. They retreated fifty yards and turned to watch uneasily as the three men dismounted to let their horses drink.

Fat warned, "This is a J Bar windmill. Old Eli might get us throwed in the calaboose for trespassin'."

Hewey said, "It's a public road, and the Lord furnished the water."

"The Lord didn't put up the mill."

The site was devoid of firewood. Hewey told Walter, "If you'll unpack the chuck, me and Fat will gather some cow chips and get a little fire started."

Walter went about his task in silence. Fat was more vocal. Hewey pulled several handfuls of old grass and stuffed them beneath a small stack of dry chips. He struck a match and set the grass to smoldering, blowing on the blaze to help it take hold. In a little while the chips were glowing and throwing off heat enough to boil coffee and fry bacon. That and a couple of Soapy's cold biscuits made up what passed for a meal.

Hewey leaned back and savored a second cup of coffee. "This is the life we was born for," he said.

"Breathin' the clean outdoor air, eatin' from the fat of the land. We've got good horses to ride and nobody around to boss us. Paradise couldn't be no better."

Fat whimpered, "Sand blew into my plate. The bacon was burned, and the water has got gyp in it."

Hewey said, "You'd complain if they hung you with a new rope."

Walter said, "Fat was born complainin'."

That was as many words as he had spoken since they had left Upton City. Hewey began to hope his brother was finally coming around.

He said, "The way I figure it, the pace we're settin' ought to have us in San Angelo the day after tomorrow. I don't reckon C.C. would begrudge us spendin' a night there and seein' the sights."

Fat braced up. Hopefully he said, "I hear San Angelo is a wide-open town."

Walter frowned. "C.C. wouldn't want us spendin' his money on such as that."

Hewey said, "It wouldn't be his money. I brought some of my own."

"I swear, Hewey, when you die you won't have enough money left to bury you. They'll just drag you off away from the house and throw a little brush on top of you."

"That's how I'd like to go. Spend my last dollar just before I take my last breath, and die with a smile on my face. That way I won't have a bunch of kinfolks fightin' over what I leave behind."

"You don't have any kinfolks except me."

"That's enough. As long as me and you stick together, ain't nothin' can throw us."

He heard hooves and the rattle of a vehicle on the rutted trail. A buggy approached, drawn by two horses. Another horse with a rider trotted alongside. "Somebody's travelin' kind of late."

Fat declared, "Oh Lord, that's Eli Jessup comin' yonder. Told you we might wind up in the calaboose."

Hewey said, "Don't worry. If he says anything, I'll give him back his water."

Jessup drew on the reins and stared at the three cowboys. Hewey recognized the rider as Jessup's foreman, Mitch. He said, "Light and hitch, Mr. Jessup, Mitch. Have some coffee."

Jessup climbed down, his legs stiff, his face weary. His heavy mustache seemed to droop. "Seems to me I know you boys. Work for C. C. Tarpley, don't you?"

Hewey said, "Yes, sir, that's a fact."

"I guess you realize you're on my land."

"Just this little bit of it. We couldn't hardly camp in the middle of the county road."

Jessup shrugged his broad shoulders. "I don't reckon you're hurtin' anything if you don't stay long. What you doin' here, anyway?"

Fat started to answer. "We're goin' . . ." Hewey poked him with his elbow and shut him up.

C.C. had told Hewey to lie if pressed. Hewey said, "We're on our way to San Angelo to see if it's all the town that we heard it is." That was not a lie, just something less than the whole truth.

Jessup seemed to find something mildly humorous. He winked at his foreman. "It's enough of a place to give you all the trouble you can handle if you don't keep one hand on your gun and the other on your purse. Ain't I right, Mitch?"

The big cowboy smiled. "It's Snort Yarnell's favorite town. That tells you somethin'."

Jessup looked toward the little campfire. "I believe you mentioned coffee?"

Hewey said, "We'll fix you a fresh pot. It'll just take a jiffy."

While the coffee boiled, Hewey watched the sun sink below the western horizon behind a thin curtain of red and purple clouds. "You-all are welcome to camp the night with us if you'd like to."

Jessup said dryly, "That's kind of you, seein' as it's my land. But me and Mitch have got to get back to headquarters. Got some cows comin' in tomorrow from over on the Concho." He frowned. "I'd as soon C.C. didn't hear about it till we get them settled."

Hewey said, "We won't be seein' C.C. for a while."

"Good. He used to be a reasonable feller before he got old and cranky. Bet you didn't know we was partners once."

Hewey had not known that.

Jessup said, "It came to a point that we was arguin' all the time, so we decided to split everything before one of us got killed. Things rocked along all right till we got to one old roan horse we both wanted. He wasn't worth fightin' over, but C.C. got so belligerent that I had to stand up for my rights. Mighty opinionated, C.C. is. He'd fight a dog over a bone. It's hard to understand a man who'd let a friendship die over one old horse."

Hewey nodded as if he agreed, though it seemed to him there had been two mighty opinionated men in the dispute.

Jessup said, "C.C. ain't spoke a civil word to me since, nor me to him. I've got no use for a man that damned contrary."

Hewey asked, "What ever became of the horse?"

Jessup scowled. "Some horse thief run off with him. I mortally hate a thief."

Jessup drank his coffee and motioned to Mitch. "We'd better be movin' on if we want to get home before the rooster wakes up." He climbed into the buggy and called, "You boys watch out for yourselves. They got sharpers in San Angelo that can steal your underwear without takin' your pants off."

Fat asked innocently, "How can they do that?"

As the buggy departed, Hewey said, "He ain't got horns and a tail after all. At least, I didn't see them."

Walter nodded. "But if C.C. and him ever lock horns, we don't want to be standin' in the way."

EIGHT

THE ROUTE TO SAN ANGELO WAS MARKED BY TWO small round mountains side by side on an undulating plain.

Fat asked, "You know what those make me think of?"

Hewey said, "I can imagine. Don't you ever think about anything except women?"

"Women, whiskey, and good eats. What else is there?"

Walter said curtly, "You do all right with the whiskey and the eats, Fat, but you don't know how to treat a decent woman."

Hewey felt encouraged. Walter was finally beginning to open up.

As the town came into sight, Fat said, "I vote that we spend a little of C.C.'s money and get us a hotel room. He can afford it."

Hewey and Walter had never slept in a hotel room. Hewey could only imagine how it would be to bask in such luxury. "I'll bet even C.C. never stays in a hotel.

Sleep in a wagonyard, maybe, but not a hotel. That's for rich businessmen and whiskey drummers." He looked at Walter. "What do you think? Should we camp on the river and stake the horses out to grass, or put them in a livery barn and get them some oats?"

Walter frowned. "Why ask for my opinion? You'll do what you want to anyway."

"I always like to know what you're thinkin', even when you're wrong."

"C.C. would never pay us back for the stable bill. Whatever we spend, it'll be our own money."

Hewey shrugged. "Then we'll stake them out and spend our money for whiskey."

He had never been to San Angelo. He knew from conversation that it owed its birth to the confluence of the three Concho rivers and to a frontier army post established some twenty years earlier to protect west-bound freighters, immigrants, and a stagecoach line from Comanches and Kiowas. Now Indian troubles were over in this part of the country. Gossips were saying the army's days here were numbered. The military had the same outlook as C. C. Tarpley: never spend a dollar until it has been squeezed like a lemon.

Following the river, Hewey saw a large tent. He said, "Reckon there's a circus in town? I'd sure admire to see an elephant."

Walter said, "It appears to be a camp meetin'. I believe I'll go tonight. I'd like to hear a little preachin' from somebody besides you."

"I wonder what kind of church it is, one that sprinkles you or one that tries to drown you?"

"I was baptized a long time ago. So were you, only you've probably forgotten about it."

"I remember. I must've swallowed a gallon of muddy water. I've shied away from preachers ever since."

They found a place along the river where the grass had not been grazed off. Hewey asked a passing rider if there would be any objection to their camping there.

"Not from me," the passerby said, "but it ain't mine. It's part of the town site, so I reckon it's open to whoever comes."

The three unsaddled and took the load from the packhorse. The rider, appearing to be in no hurry, watched them stake the animals on long ropes that allowed plenty of grazing room.

Hewey asked, "Where can we buy a decent supper?"

The horseman pointed. "Cheapest is a little hole in the wall over on Concho Avenue. The Dutchman'll sell you a big bowl of chili for ten cents. Then there's a Greek place a ways up the street. It'll cost you more, but it's easier on the stomach."

Hewey said, "Greek sounds foreign to me. I reckon we'll take the Dutchman's chili."

Fat had grown fidgety like a horse wanting to be on the go. "You-all suit yourselves. I been told there's a fancy house here where all the women are good-lookin' and ready to play."

Hewey said, "You better not forget where this camp is at. We'll be travelin' about daylight. If you're not here, we'll leave without you."

Fat hurried away at a pace Hewey had seldom seen him achieve unless a cow was chasing him.

The chili joint was easily found, but not before Hewey had located three saloons and mentally filed away their locations for future reference. By the time he and Walter finished the chili and two cups of coffee, they had spent fifteen cents apiece.

To the southeast, across the river, Hewey could see the stone buildings of the sprawling fort. A bugle's notes drifted softly on a light southern breeze as the flag was lowered for the day. He had thought once about joining the army but decided it imposed too many rules for a free spirit. He saw several soldiers and realized they were black. This was a buffalo soldier post.

A large man walked up beside Hewey and pointed with a glowing cigar. "I wisht you'd look at them burrheads tryin' to act like soldiers. Put a uniform on them and they think they're as good as white folks. It's high time the army pulled them out of here. We don't need them anymore."

Walter always sided with the underdog, for he had been one much of his life. He said, "I'll bet when you *did* need them you were glad they were here."

"It was different then. But we ain't seen an Indian in years. We need them darkies to be gathered up and gone."

Hewey said, "What would become of this town if the army was to close the post? It must put a pretty penny in people's pockets."

"We hear the railroad is comin' in. Give us the railroad and we won't need Grierson's brunettes."

Hewey recalled hearing that Grierson was the post commandant's name. He shrugged. What happened to San Angelo or to the military was somebody else's worry. He was just passing through.

He and Walter returned to camp to check on the horses and found them contentedly cropping grass at the ends of their tethers. Hewey said, "Walter, I'm ready for a drink. You comin'?"

Walter shook his head. "I'm goin' to the meetin'. I don't want to have whiskey on my breath."

"Suit yourself. I guarantee I'll have more fun than you will." He walked back down Chadbourne Street and stood on the corner at Concho Avenue, trying to decide which saloon to try. The first proved to be a little fancy for his taste, but he went in anyway. It offered a shiny mahogany bar and a large mirror with a hand-carved frame. On one end of the bar was a free lunch of bread, sausages, and boiled eggs. It struck him that he could have eaten here and saved fifteen cents for a better use.

He ordered a whiskey and stood at the bar alone. He counted a dozen customers, but none paid any attention to him. They looked like bankers and lawyers and drummers, for the most part, not the kind of people eager to strike up a conversation with a dusty cowpuncher just in from the trail. Not even the bartender spoke to him beyond asking his pleasure and telling him the price. The whiskey was first-rate, but the company was cold. As darkness came and the stars began to show, he walked outside to hunt for a friendlier place.

He found it farther down on Concho. It was a plain-looking joint with a simple bar of pine lumber. Instead of a mirror it featured a painting of a woman lounging on a bed with nothing to hide her several charms except a strategically placed wisp of cloth. It was the kind of art he could appreciate. He gave it a careful scrutiny while he sipped at his drink, thinking that Fat would probably appreciate it, too, if he were not entangled with the real thing. The whiskey was not as good as at the other place, but he liked the atmosphere.

Two black soldiers came in and stood a little way down the bar. The bartender poured drinks and said, "Payday at the fort, ain't it?"

"Sure is," one replied. "Our pockets are jinglin'."

The bartender said, "Apt to be a busy night, then."

Hewey heard a low growl. A customer sitting alone at a table glowered at the soldiers through a spiral of cigar smoke. Hewey realized this was the man who had spoken to him at the river.

The soldiers caught the hostile look and did not

linger long. Uncomfortable, they left without ordering another drink.

The bartender complained, "Arlow, payday don't come but once a month. I wish you wouldn't spoil it for me by chasing off my customers."

"Time was when niggers wasn't allowed where white men were drinkin'."

"You've got to understand that I'm in business. I need every dollar I can put together."

"I never could see a man sellin' out his principles for a handful of silver."

An old man at another table impatiently tapped his cane against the floor. "I remember a time when the Comanches had me surrounded. I was mighty glad to see them black boys come ridin' over the hill. I'd've been pleasured to stand and drink with them, and I'd've paid for the whiskey."

Arlow glared. "You old fart, ain't it time you was home in bed?" He went back to his drink.

Another black walked in. He was not wearing a uniform. The bartender looked him over, then nodded in recognition. "I didn't hardly know you in them town clothes, boy. What went with the soldier outfit?"

"Finished my enlistment. I ain't leavin' nothin' here but my tracks. First, though, I'll have some of the best whiskey you got."

"The best? You sure?"

"I can afford it. I got my musterin'-out money."

The barman reached down and fetched a bottle with a label brighter than the one from which Hewey's drink had come.

Hewey felt the change in his pocket and said, "I believe I'll have a little of the same." The bartender poured it. Hewey raised it in salute. "Here's to the United States Army."

Arlow pushed up from his table, face reddening. "What kind of a white man are you, drinkin' with a darky?"

Hewey's face warmed. "I'm a free-born citizen of the sovereign state of Texas, and I'll drink with whoever I want to."

Arlow declared, "Maybe you've got a little tar in your blood, too." He turned, jabbing his cigar in the soldier's direction. "You've had your drink. Now get your black butt out of here."

The soldier straightened as if standing at attention on the parade ground. "I was born in bondage, but now I'm as free as any man. I'll leave when it suits me."

Arlow grabbed the cane from the old man's hand and struck the soldier across the side of the head. "I don't take sass from no uppity nigger."

The sudden move took Hewey by surprise. He saw the soldier hunch down, then bring his fist up like a hammer. Arlow's head jerked under the blow. He grabbed at the bar but landed heavily on his shoulder. He came roaring to his feet and drew a pistol from his boot. As he charged past, Hewey stuck out his foot. Arlow tripped and fell forward, striking his head against the brass rail at the foot of the bar. He lay too stunned to move. Blood trickled from a gash on his forehead.

The soldier held his hand against the place where the cane had struck him. His ear was bleeding. The bartender said, "There's hell to pay now, boy. You'd better git before Arlow gets up. He's got a streak of mean in him a yard wide. He's apt to kill you."

"He hit me first."

"But he's white, and you ain't."

The soldier replied, "I said I'd leave when I'm ready. Well, I reckon I'm ready." He nodded a silent *thank you* to Hewey and disappeared out the door.

The old man picked up his cane. It had a little blood

on it. He wiped it off on Arlow's trousers leg, then swung it and gave Arlow a smart lick across the rump. He dropped the big man's fallen pistol into a tobacco-stained spittoon. "Old fart, am I?"

The bartender turned a baleful gaze in Hewey's direction. "You tripped Arlow, didn't you?"

"He just ran into my foot, is all. Some big men are clumsy."

"He ain't much on forgiveness. If I was you, I'd be as smart as that darky and make myself scarce, too. I'd get plumb out of town."

Hewey saw that Arlow was beginning to stir. He said, "Sometimes you got to choose between bein' brave and bein' smart." He gulped the rest of his drink, took a lingering look at the painting, and walked out into the street. He tried to look nonchalant, but he glanced back toward the saloon for any sign of pursuit.

He considered going to one of the other whiskey joints but decided that Arlow might come looking for him. He thought of the camp meeting. Arlow would not expect to find him there. For that matter, Hewey surprised himself a little. He wondered how the camp-meeting idea had come to him.

He heard the crowd singing an old gospel song. He remembered the melody but not the words. Something about salvation.

The tent was lit by lanterns. Its sides were rolled up to let fresh air circulate. Hewey walked slowly around it until he saw his brother sitting on a bench, sharing a hymn book with an elderly woman. *At least,* Hewey thought, *he doesn't have his mind on romance.* He edged into the tent and made his way to Walter's side.

Walter's eyes widened as if he had seen the dead come to life. He whispered, "How come you suddenly got religion?"

Hewey wondered if Walter could smell his breath. "Don't you think it's about time?"

"It's considerable overdue."

The woman looked over her glasses at them and frowned her disapproval of their talking during the service. Walter went back to singing. Hewey could not see the hymnbook from where he stood, but he figured it was just as well. His voice might break up the proceedings.

Men came down the aisle with a collection plate. *I would get here just in time for that,* Hewey thought. He dug two bits from his pocket, changed his mind, and increased his contribution to four bits. He would have spent that on drink anyway had it not been for Arlow. Walter smiled at Hewey's show of generosity.

It's worth it if he finally gets over being mad at me, Hewey thought.

As the preacher wound down a strong sermon against sin and extolled the virtues of tithing, movement outside the tent caught Hewey's eye. Arlow and two friends were studying the crowd. Hewey turned his head away, hoping Arlow would not see him.

The service broke up after a closing hymn. Hewey motioned for Walter to lead the exit on the opposite side of the tent from where Arlow had been. But Arlow had moved. He accosted Hewey in the edge of the lantern light and tapped him with his forefinger. His head was bandaged.

"Ain't you the punkin' roller that tripped me in the saloon?"

Hewey put on his most innocent face. "A saloon? I'm a church-goin' man." He feared his breath would betray him, but Arlow's was so strong that he could not have smelled anyone else's.

Arlow shoved his face close to Hewey's. "I'd swear you're the same bird. Maybe if the light was better . . ."

He seemed inclined after a moment to give Hewey the benefit of the doubt. "We're lookin' for a nigger that attacked me. I don't reckon you've seen him?"

"How would I know him, seein' as I was here at the meetin'?" Hewey had noticed a number of black people standing just outside the tent, listening to the service but remaining apart from the whites. He doubted the one Arlow sought was among them. For his own safety the soldier had probably put some distance behind him by now.

Arlow said, "If we find him, me and my friends are goin' to skin him out and hang his hide on the saloon door. And if I find the son of a bitch that tripped me, I'll cut off a strip of his hide and make me a quirt."

He gave Hewey another suspicious looking-over before he and his friends melted away into the darkness.

Walter faced Hewey with his mouth hanging open. "What kind of trouble have you got yourself into now?"

Hewey shrugged. "He must've mistaken me for some other handsome feller."

"If you wasn't in trouble you wouldn't have joined back up with me so soon. I wouldn't have seen you till you came draggin' in about daylight."

As they walked toward camp Hewey decided to tell Walter what had led to Arlow's fall. "Wasn't my fault he didn't see my foot. He ought not to drink so much."

"I never would've thought you'd get yourself in Dutch over a darky."

"It wasn't all that much. You'd have done the same if you'd been there."

"I guess you did right. But we might be smart to break camp early in case he comes huntin' for you in the mornin'."

"Yeah, he's cost San Angelo our business."

NINE

H EWEY AND WALTER BROKE CAMP AT THE FIRST good light. As they had anticipated, Fat had not shown up.

Hewey said, "We warned him he'd better be here."

Walter finished tying their load on the packhorse. "He knows we're takin' the San Antonio road. He can catch up to us if he wants to. Otherwise . . ."

Hewey completed the sentence. "To hell with him."

The military road from Fort Concho to Fort Mc-Kavett led southeastward through rolling grassland and broad flats dotted with dense mottes and scattered big live-oak trees whose heavy branches reached out far enough to shade a goodly number of cattle. Hewey judged it to be good cow country, for those he saw looked fleshier than those out on the Pecos.

They had traveled about two miles when he heard a horse loping up behind them. His first thought was of Arlow. He turned in the saddle to look back. He was unsure whether to feel relieved or not. "I hoped Fat would stay in San Angelo."

Fat Gervin's face was flushed, and he was almost out of breath as he reined up beside the brothers. "How come you-all didn't wait on me? I ain't even had any breakfast."

Hewey said, "Ain't that a shame. You're liable to waste away."

Walter said, "We told you this trip is strictly business. Where were you all night? No, don't tell me. I don't think I want to hear about it."

Fat broke into a broad grin. "There was this girl. Red hair and the bluest eyes you ever seen. It was all I could do to get up this mornin' and leave her."

Hewey asked, "Have you got any money left?"

"Just a little. But I'm tellin' you, boys, she was worth it."

Walter frowned. "What would C.C.'s daughter think?"

Fat's grin slipped away. "You ain't goin' to say anything about it, are you?"

"Not if you hold up your end on the rest of this trip."

They passed a band of sheep scattered over an open prairie. A Mexican herder watched them but showed no reaction until Hewey waved. The herder made a small and tentative gesture in response. Hewey supposed that Mexicans hereabouts, badly outnumbered, adhered to a cautious policy of speaking only if spoken to when dealing with Anglos. The Alamo was not yet forgotten.

Fat's face twisted in distaste. "Sheep! Ain't nothin' stinks worse."

Walter said, "They ain't that bad. A bunch of cows don't smell like flowers either, especially if they been on green feed and their bowels are loose. Folks say sheep are good money makers. When I get a place of my own someday, I'll have me a little flock."

Hewey asked, "How do you think you'll ever get a place of your own at six bits a day?"

"By savin' six bits a day. It'll add up after a while."

"You can have my share of sheep, and the land, too. Any time I take a notion to get up and go, I don't want nothin' holdin' me back."

"What'll you do when you get old?"

"I don't expect I'll live that long."

Hewey caught a glimpse of someone partially hidden in the dark protection of a motte. He thought again of Arlow, but it seemed unreasonable that the man carried a heavy enough grudge to set up an ambush miles from town.

As the horsemen neared the motte, the man warily stepped out into the open.

Fat exclaimed, "A nigger. Probably goin' to try to bum some money off of us."

Hewey recognized the retired soldier whose retort to Arlow had set off a brief tempest in the saloon. He told Walter, "That's the darky Arlow was lookin' for. If he ain't got a horse, he must've walked all night."

The black man approached with his hat in his hand. "I don't reckon you gentlemen would have some water I could borry?"

Hewey lifted a canteen from the horn of his saddle. The soldier clutched it eagerly and took several long swallows without pausing for breath. "I'm much obliged. There's a good spring farther on a ways, but I ain't sure I could've made it there." He looked closer at Hewey. "You're the gentlemen that helped me last night."

Hewey was unaccustomed to being called a gentleman. "It wasn't much. I just stuck my foot out, and be danged if that clumsy Arlow didn't fall over it."

"I thank you kindly. He was cocked and primed to shoot me." The soldier looked back apprehensively. "You don't reckon he might be trailin' me?"

"I wouldn't think so. Most likely he's got his head under his wing this mornin'. Probably can't even remember what you look like. Where are you headed afoot?"

The soldier shrugged. "Someplace where there ain't no trouble. You reckon there *is* such a place?"

"I never found one."

The soldier handed the canteen back to Hewey. "You-all mind if I travel along with you a ways? I know this trail. Been up and down it a good many times."

"Think you can keep up, walkin'?"

"I was infantry."

Hewey said, "Sure, come along." He had neglected to ask Walter, and he looked to him now for belated approval. Fat's opinion did not matter.

Walter said, "Why not? He knows the trail. Me and you might come to a fork and not know which way to go."

The soldier said, "There's a stagecoach stand up ahead. Feller calls it Toenail Station. Says he ain't got nothin' but a toenail hold."

Hewey said, "That's all me and Walter have had most of our lives. By the way, what'll we call you?"

"My old mama named me Gabriel. She said when I was born I squalled louder than old Gabriel's horn. Friends just call me Gabe. That don't sound so high-falutin, and it's easier to write."

Hewey was a little surprised. "You can read and write?" It was his impression that most black folks couldn't.

"Army chaplain taught me. Said just because I chanced to be born a slave wasn't no reason for me to stay ignorant."

"I'm Hewey, and this is my brother Walter." Almost as an afterthought, he added, "That there is Fat Gervin."

Sullenly Fat said, "The name is Frank."

Gabe nodded. "Mr. Hewey. Mr. Walter. Mr. Fat."

Walter shook his head. "*Mister* is what they used to call our daddy, but he was old. You don't have to use it for us."

Hewey suspected he would anyway. The racial divide was still formidable. Blacks and Mexicans were expected to feign deference whether they felt it or not.

Gabe fetched a blanket roll he had dropped at the edge of the motte. It was tied with a rope and had a loop so he could hang it over his shoulder.

Hewey said, "You travel light."

"A foot soldier can't afford to own more than he can tote. Every mile you walk, it gets heavier. How far you-all goin'?"

Hewey said, "San Antonio, then south a ways."

"We been marched all the way down to San Antonio and back several times. They got a big army post there named for Mr. Sam Houston. He must've been a mighty man to get his name put on so much stuff. I don't reckon there'll ever be anything marked with my name on it unless it's a tombstone."

Fat edged up close to Hewey. "I don't see why we're lettin' him come along. Ain't nothin' good'll come of it, travelin' with a nigger. Like as not he'll steal what he can get his hands on and slip away when we're not watchin'."

Hewey winked at Walter. "Then maybe you'd better keep an eye on him for us."

Fat said, "I'll do that. I'll damn sure do that."

They might have reached Fort McKavett in a day if they had pushed, but Hewey saw no reason to do so. Tarpley had given them no specific date by which they must be back at the ranch. There were the horses to consider, and Gabe. Hewey was a little surprised that the soldier kept up as well as he did. A couple of miles would have finished Hewey, for it was the cowboy way to ride horseback if the distance was as much as a hundred yards. Used to walking, Gabe often moved out in front of the horses.

They did not find a convenient spring or creek late in the afternoon, so they made a dry camp. They had water enough in canteens for making coffee, and the horses had drunk their fill a little earlier as they came upon a small natural basin holding water from a recent rain. Supper was three squirrels Gabe had shot with Hewey's pistol. Hewey had tried but had managed only to splinter bark from the trees and send the squirrels scurrying for cover.

He considered giving the weapon to Gabe but decided he might need it in a pinch someday. It could serve as collateral for a small loan if his pockets were empty.

In answer to a question from Walter, Gabe said he had been born in Mississippi to a mother who was a house slave. After emancipation she had continued to work in the same house but drew a small wage that gave her a tentative sense of independence.

He said, "She couldn't read the scriptures, but she would walk ten miles to hear a preacher talk about them. She named all us children after them old fellers in the Bible. She wouldn't name none of us Judas, though. That's where she drawed the line."

Walter said, "Give a dog a bad name and you hang him."

"I never was keen on workin' in the cotton fields, but there wasn't much else I knowed how to do," Gabe said. "Soon as I got my growth I lit out. Went down to New Orleans because folks said you could pick up money right off of the street. I found out folks lied. Wasn't no easy money anyplace."

Walter said, "A man is supposed to sweat for what he gets. Otherwise he can't take pride in it."

"Pride is for them that can afford it. One day a man come along talkin' about the army, and how we could make twelve dollars a month and never set foot in a cotton patch. All we had to do was march a little and shoot a gun." He frowned, remembering. "Oh, how that man lied! He'll get a scorchin' when Gabriel blows that horn."

Hewey did a quick mental calculation. What Tarpley paid him wasn't much, but it beat army wages. Seemed like the meaner the job, the less it paid.

Gabe said, "If all the walkin' I done in the army had been in a straight line, I'd've fell right off the edge of the earth. At least we et regular most of the time."

Hewey said, "Havin' enough to eat and a place to sleep is worth more than money. Ain't that so, Walter?"

Walter replied, "If you have money, them things just naturally come to you. I don't aim to be poor all my life."

Hewey said, "A man ain't poor for not havin' money. He's poor from wantin' too much."

THEY WASHED THEIR FACES and watered their horses in the San Saba River before riding into Fort McKavett.

Gabe said, "We'd all better drink up. It's a ways to the next water."

Hewey replied, "I'm ready for somethin' stronger than water."

Fat said, "Me too."

Fort McKavett was a ragtag town smaller than San Angelo. Citizens had taken advantage of the abandoned fort, using some of the rock buildings for dwellings, barns, and storage, dismantling others for the roofing lumber and window and doorframes. Though limited in size, the place did not lack for enterprises catering to the drinking man.

Walter said, "Ain't much to it, but I guess it's big enough for somebody to get in trouble if he really tried."

Gabe showed a disliking for the place. "If it's all the same, I'd like to stick close by you-all. They've got a reputation here for siccin' the dogs on black folks. The only time us soldiers felt safe was when we stayed in bunches."

Walter said, "I don't see that we need to stop. We've got all the supplies we need."

Hewey said, "We left Angelo quicker than we figured on. Wouldn't hurt to clear the dust out of our throats. There's still aplenty of miles ahead of us."

Fat added, "Thirsty miles."

Hewey picked a small frame structure that might have been thrown together by a drunken carpenter. Some of the nails were bent over, and dents in the wood indicated many false hammer strikes. Uneven red letters painted on a board declared that it served the finest liquors south of St. Louis.

"That takes in a lot of territory," Hewey observed. "Sounds like my kind of place."

Walter looked dubious, but he tied his horse alongside Hewey's. Only a handful of people were on the streets. They seemed to be staring at the newcomers, or perhaps only at Gabe. Nervously Gabe said, "I ain't stayin' out here by myself. I'm comin' in with you."

Hewey's eyes were slow in adjusting to the poor light. There were no customers. He saw a huge man get up from a table and move ponderously behind the crude plank bar. His voice sounded as if it came from the bottom of a barrel. "What'll it be, gents?"

Hewey laid a few coins on the bar, and the barman picked them up with a hand that was as big as a satchel. He seemed to notice Gabe for the first time. He demanded, "Did that boy come in here with you-all?"

Hewey felt his pulse picking up. "He did. We're all in need of a drink."

The barman frowned. "He'll have to get his from the cistern. And he'd better have his own cup, because he ain't drinkin' from the one out there."

Walter said, "We don't none of us really need a drink, Hewey. Let's get out of here." He took a couple of steps. Gabe was two paces ahead of him.

Hewey wanted to make for the door, but he was too provoked to move. He could hardly believe he heard himself say, "He already took our money. We got drinks comin'. Four of them."

Gabe said, "I ain't much given to drink. A sip of water from the cistern would suit me fine."

The proprietor slid several coins across the bar. "Here's your money back. I could whip you in a minute, cowboy, but if we was to fight, we'd bust up this place. I'd as soon not have to do the fixin' afterwards."

Hewey saw that the man was giving him a chance to back away with minimum compromise to dignity. As a boy he had avoided schoolyard fights when he could. Even on the few occasions when he had won, he still hurt. Boyhood bruises and contusions had convinced him it was better to be embarrassed for retreating in haste than to be embarrassed for getting the whey knocked out of him.

He said, "I'd hate to see this joint wrecked any worse than it already is." The saloon looked as if someone had turned a bull loose inside. He counted the money to be sure the bartender was not cheating him.

The barman looked relieved. It would not require much violence to bring the flimsy walls crashing down. "You three are welcome, but next time, leave that darky outside."

Hewey said, "There ain't goin' to be a next time." Fort McKavett would have to get along without their financial support.

Outside, Hewey was torn between anger over the barman's attitude and relief that he had been given a way out of a fight that could have had but one outcome.

Fat was frustrated. "I told you this nigger was liable to be trouble. Now we didn't get nothin' to drink."

Gabe said, "I'm afraid I been a trial to you gentlemen. On account of me, you're leavin' thirsty."

Walter said, "We're lucky we're not leavin' bloody. I swear, Hewey, sometimes your mouth runs a mile ahead of your brain. That barkeep could've cracked us like eggshells. All of us."

"He backed down."

"No, he gave *you* a chance to back down. I was scared you wasn't goin' to take it."

Hewey said, "I wasn't all that thirsty anyhow."

Fat protested, "Well, I was." His eyes were red, his sweaty face flushed from the effects of a long night and little sleep. His shirt was wet under the armpits and along his back.

Several people on the streets stopped what they were doing to watch with curiosity as the four trailed out, a black man walking ahead of three white cowboys on horseback. Hewey looked back in regret. He had not drunk from the river, anticipating something better in town. Now he was thirsty. Walter would probably chide him if he mentioned it, so he did not.

He even felt a brief resentment against Gabe. Had the ex-soldier not been there, they would probably still be in the saloon, enjoying a respite from travel. He realized the feeling was not justified. The problem had not been Gabe himself; it had been the bartender's unjustified reaction to him.

The wagon road became rougher, snaking its stony way between limestone hills and around heavy live-oak mottes. Though Gabe had been strong early in the trip, the uneven ground was wearing him down. Instead of walking ahead of the horses much of the time, he began falling behind. More than once the riders stopped to let their horses "blow" while Gabe caught up.

Walter said, "I'm kind of saddle-weary. Let's get down and set a spell."

Hewey knew that was more for Gabe's sake than Walter's own. "Been hopin' you'd say that."

Fat said, "It's about time. I'm gettin' tired of all this scenery." Sweat trickled from beneath his hat and into his eyes. He wiped a sleeve across his flushed face.

Gabe seated himself on a rock and removed one shoe. He rubbed his foot. "Looks like this sole is goin' to wear plumb through before we get to San Antonio."

Hewey considered letting Gabe ride the packhorse, but they could not afford to jettison any supplies. He said, "We got to see about gettin' you somethin' to ride. You *can* ride a horse, can't you?"

"Fair to middlin', but I ain't no bronc rider. Any old skate would do for me as long as it's got four legs and can walk."

"Maybe we'll come upon somethin' along the way."

They rested a while, then resumed the journey. After a time they came upon a moving set of goats whose long hair shone white in the sun. Hewey said, "What you reckon those are? I never seen the like of them before."

Walter could only shrug.

Fat said, "A goat is a goat."

The animals were driven by a young black woman riding bareback on a dun horse. Gabe exclaimed, "Lordy, would you look at that." He stared, his mouth sagging open. As she approached, he exclaimed, "Young missy, are you real?"

She looked back at him as if she did not believe *he* was real. Crisply she said, "What do you think I am, a ghost? You see me, don't you?"

"But what're you doin' out here in the middle of nowhere?"

"This ain't nowhere. It's somewhere, and I live here. What I'm doin' is, I'm drivin' these goats to the pen so Mr. Hickson can look them over for wormies."

"Them's funny-lookin' critters."

She said, "They're Angoras. Folks say they come from far off, some place called Turkey."

Gabe said, "Never heared of it. Must be back East, in Yankee country."

Fat mused, "Why would anybody want to turn goats loose on good cow range? I'd as soon keep hogs."

The girl said, "These ain't no ordinary goats. Mr. Hickson cuts their hair off, and people weave it into rugs and such. Mohair, they call it."

Fat said, "They're still goats."

Gabe stood as if paralyzed, staring at the girl. She said impatiently, "Would you move yourself out of the way? I'm tryin' to drive these goats."

The riders had already given her room. Gabe quickly

stepped aside. As she rode past him she said, "What're you doin' without a horse anyway? A man afoot out here is as helpless as a newborn baby, and you look to me like you done been weaned."

She went on, following the bleating goats. Gabe stared after her. "Who'd've thought I'd see somethin' like her in a place like this?"

Fat commented, "She's a little dark-complected for me."

Ahead, Hewey saw a ranch house built of chiseled limestone blocks. It lay just off the road a hundred yards or so. Beyond it sprawled several corrals formed of upright cedar stakes set tightly against one another and tied with rawhide. Most of the bark had been stripped off. A gate swung open, and the girl drove the goats through it.

Hewey licked his dry lips. "Maybe we can get a drink of water from that windmill yonder."

A gray-bearded man about as skinny as C. C. Tarpley walked among the long-haired Angoras the girl had just brought in. She slipped the bridle from her horse and started toward the house after giving Gabe a long look. The rancher grabbed a goat by its leg. It let out a plaintive cry as if it were being butchered. It had blood on its forehead. The rancher smeared a black liquid over the wound and turned the goat loose. It bounded across the pen, ramming its way into a mass of animals in a corner.

The three riders went to a nearby windmill and drank their fill of water from an open pipe that drained into a surface tank. Gabe waited until they were done, then cupped his hands beneath the pipe and sipped. The goat man walked over to the picket fence and waited, wiping his face with a red bandanna. "Got to keep watch on these crazy billies," he explained. "They get to buttin' heads and don't know when to stop. If they draw blood, first thing you know they've got a case of screwworms."

Hewey knew about screwworms. Hatched from blowfly eggs in animal wounds, they were a summertime scourge that could cripple or kill livestock and wildlife.

The rancher wore a shapeless hat that should be black but was gray with imbedded dirt and spotted with dried animal blood. His clothes were dusty, stained, and patched in several places. Streaks in his beard revealed him to be a tobacco chewer. Squinting one heavily browed eye, he said, "Hickson's my name. You fellers look like cowpunchers to me, except for that dark-complected boy. What's the matter, he lose his horse?"

Hewey said, "He never had one. I don't suppose you might have one for sale?"

The rancher gave Gabe a speculative study. "Belinda told me about you, boy. Said you looked her over like she was a filly you was thinkin' of buyin'."

"I didn't mean no harm."

"She's my cook's daughter. Just because she's colored, don't get the notion she's somebody you can play around with. She don't have any truck with drifters that come ramblin' through here."

Gabe said, "I had no such notion. Didn't have a notion of no kind."

"Good. Now, about a horse. Might be I have one for sale if you ain't lookin' for a show animal." The rancher jerked his head as a signal for the travelers to follow him to the barn. He opened a gate into another pen and pointed at one of the droopiest-looking animals Hewey had ever seen. It was a bay with rough hair badly in need of a curry comb. A few burrs clung to its long black tail.

The rancher said, "I kind of hate to sell Old Belcher. My wife and kids was all partial to him, but the kids've grown up and left the nest, and my wife died. I don't get much use out of him anymore."

Hewey said, "He looks kind of old."

"Experienced," the man responded. "There ain't much he don't know about handlin' stock." The rancher whistled. The old horse showed no response. "He's been well broke. You don't have to worry about him throwin' you off."

Or running away with you, Hewey thought. He said, "He ain't much for pretty."

"Like I said, he don't look very good. But he'll get you there and bring you back."

If you don't go very far, Hewey thought. But anything beat walking. At any rate the choice was not his to make. He turned to Gabe. "What do you think?"

Gabe appeared less than impressed. "He's got four legs, though I ain't seen any of them move."

The rancher walked up to the horse and slapped it on the rump, raising a little dust and making it take a few steps. "See there? Sound of wind and limb."

Fat said, "I'd hate for any of my friends to see me ridin' an old wreck like that."

Hewey fought down a temptation to ask him how many friends he had.

Gabe said, "I ain't exactly flush with money. What'll you take for him?"

"Like I told you, I kind of hate to part with Old Belcher. He's been like part of the family. But seein' as you need him pretty bad and I don't, I think a fair price would be . . ." He paused to consider. "Say, fifty dollars."

Fifty dollars ought to buy a racehorse, Hewey thought.

Gabe said, "Say, ten dollars."

"Say, forty."

"Say, fifteen."

The rancher made a deep frown. "Boy, you must like walkin'. Say twenty."

"Only if you got a saddle you can throw in. His backbone looks sharp enough to cut a man where it would hurt the worst."

"Done. I got a saddle in the barn. Feller worked here a while and left owin' me money. Consider that you got the horse for twenty dollars and the saddle throwed in free. *Pilón,* the Mexicans call it. You can have his bridle and blanket, too."

The saddle appeared to predate the war. Hewey told Gabe, "I wouldn't trust that cinch too far. If that horse was to jump, it'd likely snap in two."

Gabe shook his head. "I doubt this old horse has got a jump left in him."

Gabe counted twenty dollars from his mustering-out pay. The rancher smiled as he counted again for himself. Satisfied, he asked, "Any of you-all interested in a job?"

Nobody answered.

The rancher said, "I'm in bad need of help. I don't normally send a girl out to do a man's work, but my last hired hand decided to go to San Antone. I pay a fair wage, and I've got a good cook."

Hewey said, "Thank you kindly, but we're workin' for Mr. C. C. Tarpley. I reckon we'll be goin' on."

Hickson looked at Gabe. Gabe said, "I'm with these fellers."

He saddled the horse and mounted him. The stirrups were set short for his long legs, but they could be adjusted if the leather strings weren't too rotten to unlace. Starting through the gate, the horse bumped its head against a post. Gabe dismounted and made a close examination.

He declared, "I do believe this horse is blind."

"Not altogether," Hickson said. "He's still got some sight in his right eye. I told you he don't *look* good."

Hewey's face warmed with indignation, but Gabe seemed to accept the deceit without much surprise. Perhaps he was used to white men taking advantage of him. He said only, "I reckon I'll have to do the seein' for him."

Hewey told the rancher, "You ought to be ashamed, foistin' a blind horse off on somebody."

"I am. Nearly as ashamed as I was when I let a horse trader palm that skate off on me a while back." The rancher shoved the money deep into his pocket. "At least now I'm even again."

"Then you lied about this bein' an old family pet."

"Son, nobody ever lies when they're swappin' or sellin' horses. They just don't let facts get in the way of a trade. I expect when that boy gets to where he's goin' he can sell the horse and get most of his money back. In the meantime he's got transportation cheaper than the stagecoach, even if they'd let him on, him bein' black."

The girl stood on the porch watching as they left. She was grinning.

Gabe said, "She laughed at me for walkin'. Now she's laughin' at me for ridin'. But at least I ain't walkin' no more."

Hewey said, "Yet. You may be walkin' again when that old plug wears out. You may wind up carryin' *him*."

"I feel kind of sorry for the poor thing."

Hewey grumbled, "It'd serve that old scoundrel right if one of them goats butted him plumb over the fence."

Walter said, "You didn't do anything to stop him."

"It was Gabe's trade. Come to think of it, he got the horse and the whole outfit for less than half of what the old man first asked."

Walter said, "So maybe it wasn't such a bad deal after all."

"Still, I wouldn't be surprised to see the old liar's mother crawl out from under the porch and bite him on the leg."

TEN

OLD BELCHER HAD MORE STAMINA THAN HEWEY would have guessed. The bay horse plodded along and kept up with the younger animals, showing little evident strain. It even exhibited an unexpected burst of speed when a startled deer bounded out of a thicket almost under its nose. Caught off guard, Gabe wound up sitting on the ground. Hewey had to chase the frightened horse more than two hundred yards. He caught it only when it ran into a grove of trees and stopped, confused because it could not see where to go.

He led it back and handed the reins to Gabe. "I'm surprised he had it in him," he said.

Gabe rubbed his backside. "You ain't near as surprised as I am. Like to've busted my tailbone."

Fat was the only one who laughed.

Gabe felt better when he saw a town ahead. "That's Friedrichsburg," he said. "Mostly Germans there. They don't mind black folks the way lots of others do."

Hewey suggested, "Might be a good place to pick up a few supplies."

Walter disagreed. "I can't think of anything we need."

"Maybe we'll think of somethin' when we get there."

Fat said, "I can think of somethin'."

Walter gave him a hard look. "You had enough in San Angelo."

Many of the signs were not in English, and Hewey couldn't say *scat* in German. He saw one, however, that contained the word *Bier*. He was pretty sure he knew what that meant. "Might be a good place to stop and think about what we need."

Walter said, "You know what this trip is for. We're supposed to take care of business."

"I can't take care of business unless I take care of *me*."

"Just one beer, then." Walter turned to Fat. "One, do you hear?"

"Who the hell put you in charge?"

They walked into the stone structure, which seemed oppressively dark until Hewey's eyes adjusted. Nobody paid much attention, even to Gabe. Hewey took that for a good omen. Several men stood at the bar or sat at tables, some sipping beer, some drinking stronger stuff. By their dress many appeared to be cowboys, yet they were talking in a language Hewey could not understand. That struck him as strange. He had never run across a cowboy he could not talk to, outside of a few Mexicans.

"I'd better have a second one," he said. "Maybe then I'll savvy what they're talkin' about."

Walter objected. "We agreed on just havin' one."

"You agreed. I didn't. What do you think, Gabe?"

Gabe shrugged. "One is enough. Else I might go to thinkin' I'm white. That could get me killed."

Hewey gave in. "Just one, then." He did not ask Fat's opinion. He knew what it would be, and he did not want to hear it.

Outside, he saw two men walking along speaking English. He hailed them. "How long will it take us to get to San Antonio?"

One of the men looked toward the four tied horses. "Does that old bay belong to one of you?"

Hewey pointed his thumb at Gabe. "Him."

"Most people can make it from here in two days without pushin'. With that old nag, you better figure four."

Gabe watched the men enter the saloon. He asked, "How come everybody makes sport of my horse? He can't help it that he don't look good."

Hewey said, "Maybe they're jealous. They're afoot and you're not."

They had not ridden far when they had to turn aside to make way for two racers thundering along a flat stretch of the road toward them. A couple of dozen men were lined up along the edge of the impromptu track, cheering. A clod of dirt struck Hewey on the cheek as the horses pounded past him. A long-legged brown won the race by a length.

Fat said, "Too bad we didn't get here in time to place a bet. That's the one I would've put my money on."

Walter said, "It's easy to pick the winner after the race is over."

Hewey wiped the dirt from his face. "We ain't in so big a hurry we can't stop to watch a little. Let's wait and see if they match another one."

He pulled in close so he could hear the bystanders' animated conversation. Much was in German and therefore gibberish to him, but some was in English. The gist was that the crowd wanted another run for their money.

A tall man in farmer overalls spotted the four newcomers and ambled up. He asked, "Did you-all come out for the races?"

Hewey said, "We just happened to be passin' by."

The man said, "We're lookin' for another race. That horse you're ridin' looks like it could run."

"No, he's long on looks but short on doin'." But the question made Hewey remember how fast Old Belcher had run when the deer startled him. "We might match this bay if you've got somethin' about his caliber. Maybe somethin' a little lame."

Several men looked over Gabe's mount. Some could not keep from grinning. The man in overalls said, "We've got a little black snide that's been beat by everything in town. But even at that he might peel the hide off of that broken-down nag of yours. To make things fair we could put a heavy rider on him, somebody like Anse there."

The man called Anse was walking proof of beer's fattening qualities. He appeared to weigh well over two hundred pounds. Looking around, Hewey saw a sleepy-eyed little black horse whose forelegs both appeared to grow out of the same place. One hock was slightly swollen.

Emboldened, he said, "That ain't necessary. We wouldn't want to take advantage."

Walter said, speaking with alarm in his voice, "Hewey, what do you think you're doin'? In the first place, Belcher ain't yours to run. He belongs to Gabe. In the second place, what're you figurin' to bet with?"

"We got the expense money C.C. gave us."

"That's meant to get us through the rest of the trip, not to blow on a horse race."

Hewey pulled Walter and Gabe off to one side so no one else could hear. Fat joined without invitation.

Hewey argued, "You saw how Old Belcher ran when that deer spooked him. I'll bet my life's savin's that he'll leave that sorry-lookin' little black standin' still."

Walter retorted, "Your life savin's wouldn't fill a tobacco sack. You're talkin' about C.C.'s money."

"C.C. won't mind, not if we double it."

"I swear, Hewey, that reckless streak of yours scares the hell out of me."

"Ain't nothin' reckless about it when you've got a cinch bet." Hewey looked at Gabe. "What do you say?"

Gabe rubbed his chin, pondering. "Old Belcher's liable to die of heart failure halfway down the track. But my life's been a gamble ever since my old mammy birthed me in a cotton patch. I might even put up a little of my musterin'-out pay."

Satisfied, Hewey returned to the cluster of men. From his saddlebag he fetched up the money Tarpley had advanced and turned it over to the stakes holder. "Bring out that black horse you were talkin' about."

Gabe contributed ten dollars. Fat examined the little he had left after San Angelo and stuck it back into his pocket. "Druther buy whiskey," he said.

Walter stood to one side, offering only silent rebuke.

Hewey immediately had second thoughts when one of the men led the animal forward. This was not the little black he had assumed it would be. This horse was taller. Its trim legs and the proud arch of its neck showed a healthy amount of Thoroughbred blood.

He protested, "You boys have run a ringer on me."

The man in overalls smiled wickedly. "We never done no such of a thing. We just said it was a black horse. We didn't say which one."

Walter stood with his hands on his hips, a stance Pa had often taken when he was about to give Hewey a good chewing-out. "Hewey, you've done it again."

The spokesman asked, "Who's your jockey?"

Hewey looked at Gabe. Dubiously Gabe said, "Belcher left me on the ground the last time."

To call on Fat was out of the question. Hewey said, "You're the lightest of us. You got to do it."

Gabe reluctantly agreed. He dropped the blanket and small pack that had been tied behind the saddle.

Hewey said, "Too bad there ain't any deer to booger him."

Gabe blinked. "I just thought of somethin' that might do just as much good." He lowered his voice. "Give me the borry of that pistol you got."

Hewey hesitated. "I hope you ain't figurin' on shootin' the other horse."

"No, nor mine neither." Gabe held out his hand.

Puzzled, Hewey dug the pistol from his saddlebag, turning away to hide what he was doing. He checked to be sure a cartridge was in the chamber, then handed the weapon over.

Gabe shoved it into a trousers pocket and said, "Me and Old Belcher are as ready as we're goin' to get."

Most of the observers remained at the finish line, a simple mark scratched across the road with a broken live-oak limb. Hewey accompanied the starter, Gabe, and the rider of the black horse down the road to the starting place.

The starter scraped a fresh mark across the road and saw that the two horses stood with their forefeet against it. He raised his arm as a get-ready signal, looked expectantly at the riders, then dropped his arm. Gabe spurred vigorously. Belcher barely moved into a trot. The black horse galloped off ahead of him.

Hewey started thinking about writing Tarpley a letter saying he had been called to South America.

He was startled by a pistol shot. The old bay horse

bolted in fright. The sudden surge forward almost drove Gabe back over its rump.

The shot that so frightened the old bay had a different effect on the black. Spooked, it crow-hopped several jumps before it broke into a run at a tangent, leaving the road. Belcher moved well ahead. Gabe leaned forward, shouting in the bay's ear.

Hewey hollered, "Run, you buzzard bait, run."

Maybe he wouldn't have to write C.C. a letter after all.

Gabe lost his hat but did not look back. The black's rider managed to pull his mount into the road and begin catching up. Hewey spurred into a lope, following the racers. He tried to gauge the distance to the finish line, but the wind made his eyes water.

He began to hear the crowd cheering at the finish line. He could see that the black horse was pushing up close behind the bay. Gabe leaned farther forward, drumming his heels against Belcher's ribs.

Something prodded Belcher to greater speed. Hewey reasoned that the bay had glimpsed the other horse crowding him on the right side. Given his limited sight, Belcher probably saw the black as a potential booger coming after him. The frightened old bay moved back in front by a length.

The cheering died as the horses neared the finish line, for the crowd's money had been on the black one. Hewey heard Gabe shouting encouragement.

Even Walter gave a holler as Belcher crossed the mark. Fat looked solemn, probably regretting that he had not bet. Gabe let Belcher run on another hundred yards, gradually slowing him down. He turned around and let him trot back to where the crowd waited. As Gabe dismounted, breathing heavily, Hewey stepped forward and grabbed the bridle just above the bits. He patted the horse on its sweaty neck. "You done good, old feller. You may be ugly as a mud fence, but you sure looked pretty crossin' that line."

The old bay danced nervously and rolled its eyes, for it was still a little frightened.

Walter said, "You got away with it again, Hewey. I never saw anybody with so much pure dumb luck."

"Wasn't no luck to it. Belcher's a better horse than he looks to be." He turned his attention to Gabe. "Had him a good rider, too."

The stakes holder came forward, his hands full of money, his face creased in a deep frown. "What was that shot we heard just as the race started?"

Admitting what Hewey knew might cause an unpleasant commotion. "Must've been some hunter shootin' at a deer." The other rider might tell about it later, but by then the money would have changed hands, and Hewey intended to be farther down the road.

The man in overalls looked Belcher over from the tips of his ears to his fetlocks. "You boys been doin' this a long time?"

"Doin' what?" Hewey asked.

"Suckerin' people into bettin' against this old skate. He don't look like much, but his daddy must have been part antelope."

"This is the first time we've raced him."

The farmer grunted in disbelief. "Sure, and my name is Ulysses S. Grant. What'll you take for him?"

"He's not mine to sell. He belongs to Gabe."

The man turned to Gabe. "I think me and my friends could clean up, takin' this old horse around to tracks where nobody's seen him. I'll give you fifty dollars for him."

Gabe swallowed. "Fifty dollars? I just give . . ."

Hewey cut him off with a frown.

Gabe caught his breath. "No, sir, him and me have got kind of attached. He ain't for sellin'."

"I'll make it sixty, boy. That's my best offer."

"Thank you kindly, sir, but I reckon I'll keep him." Gabe looked at the black horse that Belcher had just beaten. "But tell you what, I might be in a buyin' mood. That black of yours can't run much, but he'd do for plain ridin'. What'll you take for him?"

"I'd make you an even swap." Seeing no reaction, the farmer said, "And twenty dollars to boot."

Gabe counted on his fingers. "I don't want to trade, but I'd pay you twenty dollars for him, cash money."

"Twenty?" The farmer looked insulted and turned away. Then he turned again. "He's given me about all the disappointment I can stand. He's lost every race I put him in, but I was sure he could win this one. You couldn't give thirty?"

"No, sir, just twenty."

"Take him. Get him out of my sight."

Gabe had bet ten and won ten. Hewey counted out twenty dollars and handed the bills to him. Gabe in turn gave them to the seller. Gleefully he said, "I got me a horse for free."

Hewey started to remind him that ten dollars had been his in the first place, but he did not want to throw cold water on Gabe's moment of triumph. Later he would give Gabe part of the winnings gained on Tarpley's money. It might upset some of these sports to see a black man with so much money in his hands, especially *their* money. He would wait until they were down the road.

Leaving, Gabe rode the black horse and led the tired bay. When they had traveled a while he returned the pistol to Hewey. He said, "Belcher would never make a war horse. He's gun-shy."

Fat demanded, "What's the matter with you, boy? The man offered you sixty. You just paid twenty for Belcher. You throwed away forty dollars clear profit."

Hewey argued, "Money ain't any account by itself. You can't eat it or drink it. All it's good for is to spend on somethin' you want. A horse, for instance."

Gabe said, "I was afeered they might mistreat him, draggin' him around to races, runnin' him till his poor old legs went out from under him. I figured he had more comin' to him than that."

Walter smiled. "You've got a good heart, Gabe."

Gabe shrugged. "I been wooled around a lot in my life. I couldn't let it happen to that horse just so I could make a few dollars. The money'd leak out of my pockets anyway, the first town I come to. He can't help it that he's old."

Fat grumbled, "Forty dollars passed up is forty dollars lost."

They rode through what Hewey considered some of the prettiest country he had ever seen, green rolling hills with narrow, fertile valleys and small creeks fed by bubbling seeps and springs. The four riders stopped beside one of the springs to make camp. The grass was taller than Hewey's boot tops.

Gabe stood in awed silence, surveying the valley. He said, "If we was horses, this here is the kind of place we'd be lookin' for. Water, shade, and all the grazin' we could ever want."

Hewey said, "But we ain't horses."

Gabe rubbed Belcher's neck. "When I see a sight like this, I almost wisht we was." He slipped the lead rope from around the bay's neck and gave the horse a gentle slap on the rump. "Get along, old man. From now on, this is your home."

The horse walked off a few steps, then turned its head to look back. Gabe motioned with his hand. "I got me another horse now. Go on. I done emancipated you." The horse walked a short way, then moved into an easy trot.

Fat said reprovingly, "That's sixty dollars goin' to waste."

Gabe said, "Abraham Lincoln freed the slaves. All I done was free one tired old horse."

SAN ANTONIO WAS THE largest town Hewey had seen, and he felt a tingle of apprehension. Nothing he had encountered on the trail to Kansas or the long trip out to the Pecos River had quite prepared him. It appeared to him that a man could get lost in its narrow, winding streets and never be found. All he knew was that he needed to locate a man named Patrick Appleby who lived somewhere east of the Alamo.

He was not sure he could even find the Alamo.

Ahead he saw a man driving a heavily laden freight wagon. He said, "He acts like he knows where he's goin'. Let's follow him."

As they approached the city's center they were caught up in considerable horse, wagon, and even some oxcart traffic.

"Sure a lot of busy people in this place," Hewey said. "Makes me tired just watchin' them stir around." He began watching for a saloon.

Walter said, "Business first. Drink afterwards."

"I never said nothin' about wantin' a drink."

"But it's on your mind. I can tell by lookin' at you."

Hewey had moments when he regretted bringing

Walter along. Without his brother he could have had a lot more fun on this trip, though he would probably still be a few days short of San Antonio.

Gabe said, "The streets are laid out like a wagon wheel and all lead to the middle. They say it started with the Spaniards' oxcarts comin' in from all directions. If we follow this here street, it'll take us to the Alamo."

Walter asked, "What you goin' to do now, Gabe? You got somewhere to go?"

"No, sir, got no folks anyplace that I know of. I just figured to stick with you fellers if you'll let me. Never have punched cows, but I reckon I could learn."

Hewey said, "Hirin' and firin' for the drive will be up to Jerome Padgett, but you're welcome to stay with us till he says yes or no."

"Thank you kindly. My musterin' out pay ain't apt to last me long."

Fat said, "Not when you throw away sixty dollars at a time."

Hewey was filled with curiosity about the old mission where so many had died fighting for Texas freedom from Mexico, or in the case of Santa Anna's troops, against it. He said, "Been a heap of blood soaked into these streets."

Gabe agreed. "Spanish first, then Mexican and American. Some black folks, too. Comanches killed and scalped people right here between these houses. If I was afeered of ghosts, I wouldn't come to this town at all."

Walter said, "I hope nobody's goin' to cause you trouble on account of you bein' . . . different."

Gabe pointed to a black couple walking along a narrow alley. "There's a good many folks of color here. You never seen the like of mixed-up people: Mexicans, Germans, Polanders, Frenchmen, Chinamen, and some

I got no idea what breed they are. Half the time you can't tell what they're sayin'. I wonder if *they* do."

They came into a plaza. Hewey saw a low stone building whose scars and weathered front made it look as if it could have been there for ages.

Gabe said, "That's the Alamo. That's where they fit so hard against old Santy Anna."

Hewey felt let down. "Kind of small. I figured it'd be a lot bigger."

"You're just lookin' at what used to be the church. There was more to it, but most of it got torn down. They're usin' the old church for a warehouse now."

Walter voiced his indignation. "A warehouse? It ought to be a monument."

Fat said, "You can't blame folks for wantin' to make a dollar."

Hewey pointed. "Accordin' to C.C., that feller Appletree ought to live somewhere yonderway."

Walter corrected him. "Appleby."

"That's what I said."

They turned east after passing the Alamo. Hewey hailed an elderly Mexican. He used the few Spanish words he knew. "Amigo, you know where an hombre named Applegate lives?"

"No entiendo."

Hewey grimaced. "I think he said he don't intend to tell us."

Gabe said, "No, he's sayin' he don't understand you."

Hewey had not expected Gabe to know Spanish. "You speak their lingo?"

"Just enough to get myself in trouble. But maybe I can help a little." He spoke to the Mexican. The only word Hewey got out of it was *Appleby.*

The Mexican launched into a long answer, punctuated with lively hand gestures.

Gabe shook his head. "The best I can figure, he don't know anybody by that name. But if we want to buy some apples, his brother has got a store down the street yonder."

They came across a middle-aged woman carrying fresh produce in a canvas sack. Hewey guessed she had come from an open-air market they had passed. She was Anglo, so maybe he could talk to her. He asked, "Do you know a man around here by the name of Applewhite?"

Anger flashed in the woman's face. "I think you mean Appleby. Are you tryin' to say, young man, that I am a loose woman?"

Flustered, Hewey tried to decide how to rephrase the question. "No, ma'am, we've got business with him. Just thought you might know where he lives."

"Sir, I am a respectable married woman. I cross the street to avoid sharing a sidewalk with Mr. Appleby, or anyone else of his ilk. And I will not stand here and bandy words with anyone who does business with him. Good day."

"Good night," Hewey said as she walked away, her back rigid and her head high. "Mr. Applegate must be a ring-tailed rounder. Kind of like you, Fat."

A thin, brown-faced boy of perhaps ten came skipping down the street, kicking a tin can ahead of him and singing a song in Spanish. Hewey raised a hand to get his attention. "Young'un, do you speak English?"

"Damn betcha," the boy replied. "Soldiers come to see my sister. Teach me many English."

Gabe grinned. "Sounds like the kind of soldiers I know."

Hewey said, "We're lookin' for a man named Apple. Can you tell us where he lives?"

"*Señor* Appleby? Damn betcha. For two bits I show you."

Hewey dug the money from his pocket. "Deal."

The boy kicked the can up against an adobe wall and motioned for the riders to follow him. He cut between two houses and down an alley, then into another narrow dirt street. He pointed to a flat-topped stone house. *"Aquí,"* he said. "Mama and Papa get mad if I go closer. He got no wife, but he got plenty women. Better you knock."

Hewey handed him the two bits. "What you goin' to spend it on?"

"Tortillas and beans." The boy skipped away.

Walter said, "At least it's goin' for a good cause. The kid doesn't look like he gets enough to eat."

Fat said, "I don't either."

Gabe said, "There's a wolf hangin' around just about every door in this part of town."

Walter glanced at Hewey. "Like you say, money's not everything. But it looks like everything when you're hungry."

The doorstep was covered with dirt blown up from the street. Hewey suspected that the only sweeping it ever got was by the wind. He rapped his knuckles against the wooden door and listened. He heard nothing until he rapped a second time. From inside came a rough voice. "What the hell do you want?"

"We come to see you. C. C. Tarpley sent us."

"Come back later. I'm busy."

"We've traveled a long ways. We'll wait."

It was a long wait, at least half an hour, though Hewey had no watch by which to time it. Finally the door opened. A short, fat, balding man scowled at Hewey. Beyond him Hewey saw a woman slipping out a back door. Though he could not see her face, he noticed she had long, black hair that fell to a slender, youthful waist.

The man's scowl deepened. "Who the hell are you,

and what've you come botherin' me for? I got better things to do."

Hewey had seen her. He said, "We need to talk to you, Mr. Applewhite."

"You said C. C. Tarpley sent you. Is that old warthog still alive?"

"And kickin'. He said you can help us find Jerome Padgett."

"I don't help nobody for nothin', and I sure ain't travelin' anywhere to help you find Jerome Padgett. He's done wore out his welcome with me."

Hewey jingled his pocket without drawing out any money. "It'd be worth somethin' if we could locate him."

The sound of loose coin caught Appleby's attention. "I do hate to turn down somebody who's in real need. You-all come on in." He seemed to notice Gabe for the first time and have reservations. But he said, "You can come in, too, I reckon."

Gabe said, "Much obliged," and removed his hat before he stepped through the door. Hewey had kept his hat on until he was inside.

Appleby motioned for everybody to sit down. There were not enough seats, so Gabe sat on the floor, against the wall. A woman's black shawl lay across the back of the chair that Hewey took. She had left in a hurry and evidently forgot it.

Appleby said, "Now, about Jerome. If he owes you money, there ain't a damned thing I can do about it."

Hewey said, "No, sir, nothin' like that. He located some cattle for Mr. Tarpley. We need him to show us where they're at and to help us drive them out west."

That seemed to please Appleby. "West? How far?"

"To the Pecos River."

"That'd keep him gone from here for a long while, wouldn't it?"

"A few weeks at least. He might even decide to stay on with Mr. Tarpley. He ain't bad to work for, only a little cheap."

Appleby traded his frown for a broad smile. "So I wouldn't be pestered with Jerome for a time. That calls for a drink. I suppose you boys do drink?"

Hewey nodded. "We've been known to."

Fat could not contain his eagerness. "We don't understand when they talk Mexican around this town, but we understand that."

Appleby poured a glass for Gabe, but he and Hewey and Fat drank from the bottle. Walter declined. The chubby Appleby became more expansive after a second drink. "Well, sir, I can tell you where Jerome was the last time I heard, and I doubt they've turned him loose. He's in jail."

Hewey was only mildly surprised. Tarpley had told him that Padgett was not given to living by the rules.

Appleby turned the bottle in his hands, studying the label. "You've got to take Jerome the way he is. He ain't goin' to change for me or you or anybody. He's sober most of the time, and he's all business. But when he gets too much of that old kill-me-dead under his belt, you never know what he's liable to do. He may try to hug your neck, or he may try to break it. He can change moods quicker than I can change shirts."

Hewey realized Tarpley had not told him everything.

Appleby said, "He knows the inside of the San Antonio jail like it was his home. The local laws make allowances for him, but he's got himself in Dutch with a sheriff south of here who wouldn't make allowances for his own mother. You may have to wait till he's served out whatever sentence they laid on him."

He finished giving directions, then opened the front

door. "You boys will have to excuse me now. I'm lookin' for a lady to drop in."

Hewey shook his hand. "Much obliged, Mr. Applewhite."

"Take Jerome away for a while and I'll be obliged to *you*."

Walter stopped in the dirt street. "Looks like we may have to get along without Mr. Padgett."

"We got to have him, no matter what it takes." Hewey turned to get his bearings. "Whichaway is south?"

ELEVEN

THE STONE COURTHOUSE WAS BOXY AND PLAIN, WITH-out the ornate cupolas and clocks and gargoyles popular in so many towns given to boasting about their prospects. The conservative structure bespoke a county where tax-hating citizens voted down civic projects that might cost them money. The jail, hunkered beside it on the square, was a small fortress with thick stone walls and heavy bars. It appeared that the county expected its prisoners to be bent on breaking out and was deter-mined to thwart them.

Hewey said, "It'd be tough to bust him out of there."

Walter said, "It'd be stupid to try. We'd end up in there with him. Or dead."

Hewey eyed the courthouse with apprehension. He always dreaded meeting a sheriff. He stopped a passerby and asked, "What kind of sheriff you got in this town?"

The farmer hooked his thumbs in the straps of his overalls and looked Hewey over before he answered.

"Depends. If you're a quiet, honest, law-abidin' citizen, and you like a quiet, honest, law-abidin' town, then Old Quincy is your man. But if you ain't, you'll hate to see him comin'."

Must be kin to Sheriff Noonan back home, Hewey thought.

Walter asked, "You want me to talk to him?"

Hewey was tempted, but he said, "Naw, C.C. put me in charge. It's up to me to do it. I just ain't got the least notion what to say to him."

He turned to Gabe, but Gabe was no help. "I always go way around any white man with a badge on. They'd rap me up 'side the head for just lookin' at them. I'll stay out here and watch the horses."

Fat said, "Me too. I ain't paid enough to butt heads with no officer of the law."

Maybe the sheriff won't be there, Hewey thought hopefully. If he wasn't, they could put this off for a time. But he had found that the longer he stood back and looked at a bad horse, the tougher the ride when it finally came. He said, "Walter, at least *you* can come along and back me up."

Walter trailed a couple of steps behind Hewey as they entered the courthouse. The various offices were identified by small signs standing out at right angles to the doorframes. At the end of a short hall a sign read SHERIFF.

A middle-aged man with sleeves partially rolled up and glasses perched halfway down his nose was hunched over a desk, laboriously writing a letter. The steel-tipped pen scratched audibly against the paper. He raised his graying head to peer at Hewey over the rims of the glasses. His dark eyes seemed to bore through Hewey and fasten on Walter behind him. He had heavy eyebrows and a salt-and-pepper mustache almost as large as Eli Jessup's. He declared, "You two look like you've been whipped about the shoulders with a wet rope. You come to report a murder or somethin'?"

Hewey asked, "Are you the sheriff?"

The man laid down the pen and tapped thick fingers against a star-shaped badge on his shirt. "That's what it says on here. Name's Quincy Ames."

Hewey couldn't read the lettering that far, but he recognized the attitude. It was just like Sheriff Noonan's. "We come to see you about a man named Jerome Padgett. We're told you've got him locked up."

The answer was firm. "Just as tight as I can. You got a grievance against him?"

"No, sir, nothin' like that. We got business. Can we see him?"

"When I let him out of jail."

"How soon'll that be?"

The sheriff stood up and moved to a calendar on the wall. "This shows he's been in here for ten days. He'll be out in another fifty, if I don't find some reason to keep him longer. Come back then, and we'll see."

"We can't wait that long."

The sheriff's brow took on several deep wrinkles. "If you're fixin' to make trouble, I've got some empty cells left. Then you can talk to him all you want."

"No, sir, we didn't come to make trouble. We were sent to see him about some cattle business. If we don't, we'll be in trouble with our boss."

"Who is your boss?"

"Name's C. C. Tarpley, out at Upton City."

The sheriff grunted. "I remember him. Little dried-up wart. Carries a dollar around till he's rubbed the writin' off before he'll spend it."

"That's him."

"If you boys are workin' for him, you've got my sym-

pathy. Maybe you ought to just write him a letter sayin'
you quit, then see if you can find a job around here. It'd
probably pay better anyway."

Hewey and Walter looked at one another. Hewey had
a feeling the sheriff was offering him good advice, but
he said, "Our pa always preached that a man doesn't
quit till he gets the job done."

Quincy gave Hewey a long stare that made him start
to sweat. Finally he said, "Sounds like your pa had a
good handle on things. Tell you what: out of the good-
ness of my heart I'll let you go and talk to him, but
that's all. See how quick you can wrap up your business." He looked down at Hewey's waist. "Either of you
packin' iron?"

"No, sir. Somethin' else Pa said was that the only
thing a pistol is good for is to shoot yourself in the foot.
I keep mine in my saddlebags."

"That's good. The only thing better would be to sell it
or give it away." Quincy took his hat from a rack. It had
a high, uncreased crown, a broad brim, and sweat stains
around a band of rattlesnake skin. "Come on over to the
jail with me."

Walking out of the courthouse, Quincy noticed Gabe
and Fat sitting at some distance apart on the square's
perimeter fence, near the tied horses. "I don't recognize
that black boy," he said. "I better go check up on him."

Hewey spoke quickly. "He's with us."

"What's his name?"

"Gabe."

"Ain't he got any other name?"

"He ain't mentioned it, and we ain't asked him."

The sheriff growled, "Well, you better keep him out
of trouble. Folks here can be touchy. Sooner you get
him away from town, the better."

"That depends on what we find out from Mr. Padgett."

The jail walls were every bit as thick as Hewey had thought them to be. The door was heavy enough that it groaned against the hinges. The jailer sat napping, his straight chair leaning back, his feet propped on an old desk. The sheriff threw his hat, striking him in the face. The young man awakened with a cry of alarm. The front legs of his chair struck hard against the floor.

Quincy's voice crackled. "Damn you, Willy, you're paid to watch the jail. If every prisoner in the place was to bust out, you'd sleep right through it."

Defensively the jailer said, "We ain't got but one prisoner, Uncle Quincy, and he ain't goin' nowhere."

If the jailer was the sheriff's nephew, Hewey thought, he was in little danger of losing his job no matter how sound a sleeper he might be.

Quincy said, "Get your keys. These two cowpunchers want to talk to Jerome. They'll have to do it from the hallway. We ain't lettin' them into his cell."

Willy nodded and took a ring of heavy keys from the desk. He said, "About time for the widder Simpson to bring supper, ain't it? She's been mighty prompt since you've had Padgett in here."

"Never mind about Miz Ellie, or supper, either. You ain't missed many meals." Quincy explained to Hewey and Walter, "Ellie Simpson runs an eatin' joint across the street. She's got a contract to feed prisoners when we have any."

Hewey said, "Maybe we'll go there for supper."

"You'll have to leave that black boy behind or else feed him on the back step. There was a time when his kind wasn't even allowed here after sundown."

Hewey had never spent much time thinking about the plight of black people, mainly because he had not been around many. No Calloway could ever afford to hire one to work, much less to own a slave in the times before the War of Yankee Aggression.

Walter mused, "Gabe can't help bein' the way he was born. That was the Lord's doin'."

Quincy grunted. "I wish the Lord had seen fit to leave them where they was in the first place. I hope the first white men that brought them to this country are roastin' in hell. There ain't no tellin' how much their cheap labor has cost us."

Hewey and Walter followed Quincy to the dark cells, where Hewey saw the shadowy form of a man lying on a cot, hands behind his head.

Quincy barked, "Rouse yourself, Jerome. You got company."

From the gloom a brusque voice answered, "If they're kinfolks, I don't want to see them. If they ain't, I don't want to see them, either."

Quincy said to Hewey, "You won't do any good tryin' to talk to that old rascal. He's spent his whole life with horses and cattle. He don't know how to act around human people."

The voice said sharply, "I'd know how to act if ever I caught you in some other county, without your badge on."

Quincy said, "That's the attitude that got him in here in the first place."

Hewey said, "Mr. Padgett, we came here for C. C. Tarpley."

"I wish he'd come himself, and bring money to bail me out. I know he's got it. Trouble is, he never wants to spend any of it."

"Maybe there's somethin' we can do to help."

"With Quincy runnin' the county courthouse? You'd just as well go back to C.C. and tell him the deal is off. I'll be in here a right good while."

Quincy nodded in the affirmative. "That's the truth if he ever told it."

Hewey asked, "What about bail?"

Quincy said, "That'd be up to the judge. He always does what I suggest when it comes to prisoners. I don't see Jerome gettin' out before the snow flies. And it don't fly often around here."

Hewey turned to Walter for advice, but Walter had none. "Looks like we're leavin' with an empty sack."

Hewey was not ready to give up, not after their long trip from the Pecos. "Look, Mr. Padgett, tell us where the cattle are at. Me and Walter can go ahead and make the deal for them, and we'll pay you a commission just like if you'd done it yourself. I believe that'd set all right with C.C."

Padgett swung his legs over the edge of the cot. He was barefoot, his high-topped boots and his socks lying on the floor. As he stood, Hewey saw that he was a lean, angular man. His hair was gray, his face deeply lined. His mustache showed signs of careful trimming in the past, though it had been neglected recently. He limped as he made his way across the narrow cell.

Been thrown off of too many horses, Hewey thought.

Gripping the bars with arthritis-knotted hands, Padgett asked, "How bad do you boys want them cattle?"

Hewey said, "Bad enough. C.C.'s countin' on us."

"What C. C. Tarpley wants don't bother me a particle. What *I* want, though, is another matter. I want out of this jail. You boys find some way to fix it, and I'll take you to the cattle. If you don't, them cattle stay right where they're at."

Hewey said, "We're liable to get fired."

"In this world, every man has got to take care of hisself. Ain't nobody else goin' to do it."

Hewey said, "Maybe if we talk to that judge . . ."

The sheriff put in, "Like I told you, the judge leaves things of this sort up to me. If you go botherin' him, I'm liable to have to lock you up for disturbin' the peace. Then you can sit behind these bars and play checkers with Jerome."

Damn stubborn people! Hewey thought. It was bad enough confronting them one at a time. Now he faced two. He turned to Walter. "Let's go outside and talk this over."

Quincy said, "Ain't nothin' to talk over, boys. Jerome stays right here till I'm ready to let him go."

The jailer poked his head through the door. "The widder Simpson's comin' with Jerome's supper."

Testily the sheriff said, "Well, don't stand there like a cigar-store Indian. Show her in."

A middle-aged woman entered as the jailer stepped out of the way. She carried a tray covered with a white cloth. Hewey caught the aroma of warm food and coffee. She paid no attention at first to the men standing outside the cell. She said, "Here you are, Jerome. Fried chicken and gravy and hot biscuits. Got to get your strength up so you can take me dancin' when Quincy makes up his mind to turn you loose."

She was forty years old if she was a day, but Hewey thought her an attractive woman, for her age. Her hair was a light brown with a few early signs of gray that were somehow becoming to her.

He caught a jealous look in the sheriff's eyes. Quincy said, "Maybe I better look under that cloth, Ellie, just to make sure nothin's there that oughtn't to be."

She made a show of indignation. "You know I wouldn't smuggle in a file, much less a six-shooter. You used to act like a gentleman. Now you're gettin' to be as cross as an old bear."

"Who wouldn't be cross, with you makin' a fuss over this worn-out old brush popper?"

"He's a cowboy. It's an honest profession."

Quincy motioned for the jailer to open the cell door. He reached for the tray. "I'll take it to him."

Mrs. Simpson spoke past him to Padgett. "You'll find an extra-big slice of chocolate cake there, Jerome. I know that's your favorite."

Quincy grumbled under his breath. Hewey thought he heard him say he hoped Padgett would choke on it.

The widow acknowledged Hewey's and Walter's presence for the first time. "Are you boys friends of Jerome's?"

Hewey said, "We'd like to be. We came a long way to do business with him, but it looks like there's no chance. He can't get out."

"Too bad. Well, if you-all come over to my restaurant for supper, I'll fix you somethin' nice."

"You can figure on it, ma'am."

She glanced at the sheriff. "I expect you'll be over after a while too, Quincy? Unless you're ready to poison yourself on your own cookin'."

His reply was curt. "I'll be along."

As she turned to leave, she shouted over her shoulder, "Eat hearty, Jerome. I'll see you at breakfast time."

Padgett answered, "Sure. I ain't goin' nowhere."

When she was gone he sat on the cot with the tray on his lap and dug into the fried chicken. Quincy gave him a look of resentment and turned away. Gruffly he said to Hewey, "You boys had just as well move on. Ain't nothin' more for you here."

Hewey admitted, "I reckon not." He hesitated. "Sheriff, supposin' we could raise money for his bail, how much would it be?"

"More than you cowpunchers can get ahold of."

"What did he do to get himself in so much trouble?"

The sheriff extended the fingers of his left hand and

began counting them. "There was drunk and disorderly. There was destruction of property and cussin' in public. There was disrespect to an officer of the law. There was assault on an officer of the law. There was resistance to arrest. Then there was just bein' Jerome. That in itself is good for thirty days."

"In other words, you just plain don't like him."

"Now, where would you get an idea like that?"

Hewey and Walter walked across the courthouse square to where Gabe and Fat were waiting. Hewey said, "The lady that runs the restaurant asked us over for supper. At least the day ain't a total failure."

Gabe asked, "Does that include me?"

"We'll find out."

The restaurant was simple, four tables and a counter with a few stools. A large iron range stood along the back wall, and to the left of it a set of shelves on which plates, saucers, and porcelain cups were stacked. A closed door indicated that another room or two existed beyond that, possibly a pantry and living quarters.

Mrs. Simpson smiled as the four entered. "Welcome, boys. You-all set yourselves down at a table." The smile faltered as she noticed Gabe.

He caught her reaction and said, "You got a place somewhere for me, ma'am?"

She thought about it. "Right now I've got no other customers. Sit with your friends if you want to. If somebody comes in, you can move back into the kitchen."

Hewey failed to see the difference. Her kitchen was separated from the rest of the room only by the short counter. But that was the way things were, and he saw no gain in starting another Civil War he was certain to lose. He said, "Ma'am, we appreciated your invitation, but we expect to pay."

"And I expect you to. A woman's got to live, and

there ain't too many ways for a respectable widow to do it these days." She shoved a couple of sticks of wood into the stove. "I took the last of my chicken to Jerome. Beefsteak suit you? It's cheaper than chicken anyhow."

"Beef sounds just fine." Eli Jessup's beef had always tasted good on the Two Cs table, dinner, supper, and sometimes for breakfast. There were usually enough J Bar strays that Tarpley's own beef was seldom needed. Even when it was, nobody told Tarpley.

She dipped the steaks in flour, then dropped them into sizzling lard in a deep cast-iron skillet. After they were fried she made gravy with flour and part of the leftover grease. She brought it out in four plates, following up with coffee.

Hewey asked her, "You known the sheriff long?"

"Long enough."

"He's got us in an awful bind. Is there a soft side to him anywhere?"

She stared out the window toward the courthouse. "He's a better man than most folks know, only he's kin to a Missouri mule. Everything has got to be his own idea or it's no good. What's your trouble with him?"

Hewey explained about their need to get Jerome Padgett out of jail. She listened thoughtfully, then said, "By rights Jerome ought not to be there. It was all on account of Quincy bein' jealous that he got in trouble. Some of the fault is mine."

"How do you figure that?"

She pulled up a chair and sat at a corner of the table. "You might think me and Quincy are too old for romance, but that's not so. He's been about halfway courtin' me for a couple of years now. The trouble is, he starts shyin' away whenever it looks like we're fixin' to get serious. Every time I think I'm gettin' him in a marryin' notion, he draws back. Jerome showed up here and acted like he was takin' a shine to me. So I started tryin' to make Quincy think I was interested."

"Was you?"

"Not really, and I don't think Jerome was, either. I was just tryin' to build a fire under Quincy. Guess I overdid it a little. He picked a fight with Jerome, a real head and knuckle buster. Quincy filed charges, and the judge ordered Jerome to jail. I feel bad about it because it wasn't none of Jerome's fault. It was mine. But he's the one payin' for it."

Hewey grimaced. "And us. Without him, we're rim-fired."

"I wish I could help you. I've tried tellin' Quincy that Jerome doesn't mean anything to me. It's like he's gone deaf in both ears."

Hewey found a piece of gristle in his steak. Grass beef was sometimes tough, but it could be chewed if one was determined. Most other problems could be worked out too if one chewed on them hard enough, he thought. He had run into what looked like a stone wall with Appleby in San Antonio, but that had been re-solved. Appleby was happy to tell him how to find Pad-gett once he realized this cattle venture would take the old cowman away for a while.

He said, "Maybe we've been goin' about this back-wards. We tried to get the sheriff to sympathize with us, and there ain't much sympathy in him. But if he was to realize we'd be takin' Padgett off to West Texas and out of his way, he might see things different."

The widow pursed her lips as she considered. "Might not work. I think it warms his heart to see Jerome be-hind those bars."

"But what if he decided it'd make his heart even warmer not to see him at all?"

"What would make him decide that?"

"Maybe the notion that feelin' sorry for Jerome was makin' you get more and more interested in him."

"I played that game already. You see what came of it."

"This time might be different. Maybe it hasn't soaked in on Quincy yet that as long as Jerome is in jail and you're feedin' him, you'll be seein' him three times a day."

Walter argued, "Hewey, I don't know where you got such a sneaky way of thinkin'."

"Bein' straightforward hasn't got us anywhere. It's time to try a little innocent dishonesty."

The widow brought the steaming coffeepot to refill the cups. "I don't guess things could get much worse. With Quincy, though, you've got to haze him along careful and make him believe it's his own idea."

Hewey looked out the window. "Now's a good time to start. I see him comin'."

Gabe got up from the table and carried his supper behind the counter, near the big range.

Quincy entered, speaking first to Mrs. Simpson. "Howdy, Ellie. Got anything left?"

"Not much. I gave the best to Jerome. Looked to me like he deserved it."

"He don't deserve nothin'." The sheriff turned his attention to the three cowboys at the table. "When are you-all leavin'?" It sounded like an invitation to go, and soon.

Hewey said, "We need to rest our horses a day or two before we head back to the Pecos. It's a long ways."

"How long?"

"It'll take us a couple of weeks if we don't want to wear down the horses. It'd take a lot longer if we was drivin' cattle. Might take a month on account of the calves."

Mrs. Simpson said, "I for one am glad Jerome won't

be makin' such a long trip at his age. I enjoy feedin' a man that likes my cookin' the way he does."

The sheriff growled, "He likes it too much. You're spoilin' him."

"Where's the harm in that? Maybe it'll fatten him up a bit. I like to see a man with some flesh on his bones."

"Have you looked at him real good? He's as ugly as an old rail fence."

"You're not seein' him with a woman's eyes. A woman looks past the outside. She sees what's in his heart."

She brought the sheriff a fried steak with potatoes, biscuits, and coffee. "Sorry I don't have any cake left for you. I gave the last of it to Jerome."

Quincy grumbled, "Looks to me like Jerome gets the best of everything."

"Just tryin' to keep him as happy as I can. My heart goes out to him, wastin' away in that awful jail."

Quincy picked at his food, showing no pleasure in it. Finally he dropped his fork. "Dammit, Ellie, I wish you'd quit comin' over there."

"A single woman has got to make a livin'. I have a contract with the county to feed the prisoners as long as there are any."

Quincy stared so hard at the three cowboys that Hewey began to fear he was about to arrest them for something. Being sheriff, he could always find a reason. "You say it'd take you a month or more to drive them cattle out to the Pecos?"

"Likely. And we'd have to buy and gather them first. That might take another week or two."

"Are you sure Jerome would be goin' with you?"

"That's the agreement he had with C. C. Tarpley."

Quincy glanced back and forth between Hewey and Ellie Simpson, his face in a twist. "I'll go talk to the judge. Might be he'd see his way clear to suspend Jerome's sentence. But he'd want to be promised that Jerome wouldn't be comin' back and causin' trouble anytime soon."

Hewey said, "He might even decide to stay out on the Pecos."

Quincy told Mrs. Simpson, "This means you'd lose a customer."

She feigned disappointment. "I'll sure miss him."

JEROME PADGETT LOOKED OVER his shoulder at the courthouse receding in the distance. "I don't know what you boys done to Quincy, but I'm almighty glad to be out in the fresh air and sunshine. A man can get moldy layin' around a stuffy old jailhouse."

Hewey said, "We just appealed to his good nature."

"I didn't know he had one." Padgett looked at the riders on either side of him. "Is this the crew C.C. sent?"

"All but Gabe. We picked him up on the trail."

"What does he know about cows?"

"He knows where the feed goes in and where it comes out. That's about all. But I'm bettin' he can learn."

"I've seen some black boys that was good hands. They can bring trouble to you, though. There's always people that don't like them."

"We've already found that out. But he's got no kin and no place in particular to go. We figure he can hold up his end of the work."

"It's up to you to see that he does. I ain't got the time or patience to be schoolin' any greenhorns."

As soon as they were clear of town, Padgett reached into his saddlebag and drew out a pint whiskey bottle less than half full. Hewey watched worriedly as Padgett flipped the cork out and let it fall to the ground, for he remembered Tarpley's warning. Padgett tilted the bottle up and did not lower it until it was empty. He coughed, wiped a sleeve across his mouth, then threw the bottle off to the side of the trail.

He cleared his throat with a mighty noise. "Had to get the taste of the jailhouse out of my mouth. That's my last drink till we deliver the herd." He made a crooked grin that exposed a gap in his teeth. "Bet Old Quincy told you I'm a hard-drinkin' man. I don't know where folks get such a notion. I only get drunk four or five times a year. Ain't never killed anybody, even when I felt like it."

Fat stared wistfully at the empty bottle, which cast a reflection in the sunlight. He complained, "Wouldn't have hurt him to share some of it."

Padgett heard. He said, "Fat boy, if you're goin' to bellyache through this whole trip, you'd better strike out for home right now. I don't tolerate malcontents when I boss an outfit."

Fat looked at the ground. "I didn't mean nothin'. Just a little thirsty, is all."

"Water and coffee'll have to do you. There's a time to drink and a time to work. They don't mix worth a damn." He turned to Gabe. "Are you a drinkin' man, boy?"

"Only when I can get it. That's been seldom."

"Let's keep it that way. If you've got any questions, ask Hewey or Walter. Don't come botherin' me with them. Do your job and I won't pay notice to what color you are."

"Does that mean I'm hired?"

"Four bits a day. Six when you show me you're a cowboy." Padgett asked Hewey, "You think that's all right with C.C.?"

Hewey nodded. "He's payin' me and Walter six."

"That ain't enough, but cowpunchers are in surplus supply. Cow*boys,* though, there ain't near enough of them."

"There's a difference between cowpunchers and cowboys?"

"There is. We'll find out pretty soon which one you are."

TWELVE

BECAUSE OF A LATE START IN LEAVING TOWN, THEY did not reach Karnes County until dusk the second day. Padgett did not remain with the wagon road. Knowing his way, he cut across the sandy grassland through mesquite and live oak.

He said, "Dark is fixin' to catch us. We'll make camp on a little creek up ahead. I'd rather approach Old Man Dodge in the daylight anyway. If we ride up on him in the dark, he's liable to shoot first and then ask us who we are."

Hewey said, "Nervous, is he?"

"Karnes County is a nervous locality. Been a good many men killed. Helena used to be the jumpin'-off place to the coast, as well as to Mexico. It was a hell-roarin' town till the railroad passed it by. It rolled over and died after that."

"Just because it didn't get the railroad?"

"It's happened to lots of places. Most of the business moved away. Folks called a new county-seat election.

Karnes City won, but it had to send an armed posse to steal the records out of the old Helena courthouse in the dead of night. You can still get killed if you cross the wrong people. Old Man Dodge has crossed a good many in his time."

Fat listened with growing apprehension. "I didn't figure on runnin' into any kind of danger."

"We won't run *from* any. A little danger flavors up your life, like salt flavors the beans. Just a pinch, though. Too much spoils the pot."

Hewey suspected Padgett was having a little fun at Fat's expense, but there was a chance he was serious. He said, "I'd better tell you now: if we run into trouble, I'm not a good shot."

"No matter. I'll do the shootin'. Me and the fat boy."

Fat looked as if he had swallowed a chew of tobacco.

Next morning they rode by several prosperous-looking farms and a small community with a steepled church. Padgett said, "There's good soil here. It doesn't always rain enough, but that's Texas for you. Before the war a bunch of Polanders came here from the old country. Poor as church mice they was. They come nigh starvin' the first winter till old Colonel Butler brought them a bunch of his own steers for beef. A good man, the colonel, if you was his friend. But you didn't want him for an enemy.

"That's the way with folks down here. They'll give you their last shirt if they see you need it, but they'll fight like bulldogs if somebody tries to take it away from them."

Hewey said, "Sounds like C. C. Tarpley and Eli Jessup."

"I bossed trail herds for them two mosshorns way back when they was partners. They was set in their ways like a pair of old maids. Quarreled like two snot-nose kids in a school yard. I had a gutful of it and quit."

Hewey said, "It hasn't got any better. I suspect that C.C. is havin' you buy these cattle just for spite. He's found some land for sale and wants to stock it before Jessup can beat him to it."

Padgett chewed on that a while. "This is the kind of childishness that made me quit them. I believe I'll make C.C. pay me an extra commission on this deal. He'll squeal like a stuck pig."

They left the farming community behind. Padgett pointed to an adobe house in the distance. "We're comin' up on Dodge's country now."

"Where's the fence?"

"He hasn't got one, except for a holdin' trap. Them's his cows yonder with the D Cross brand."

Hewey noted that they were in good flesh. He figured they were likely to lose some of that out on the Pecos, where they had to hunt harder to find grass. He asked, "How come Dodge is sellin' out? This looks like good cattle country."

"He's gettin' on in years, and stove up to where he can't take care of things like he wants to. He's got no kids, just a shiftless nephew he doesn't like much. He believes the boy would squander the whole shebang."

Walter declared, "If it was mine, I wouldn't squander it. When I get a place of my own I'll hold onto it, come hell or high water."

Hewey said, "With the money Dodge'll get for these cattle and the ranch, he could go to San Antonio and live high. I would if I was in his place."

Padgett said, "Dodge's not one for high livin'. All he needs is a good horse or two, a roof that don't leak, and a bed that won't make his bones ache. That'll keep him as content as a natural old grouch can ever be."

Nearing the adobe house, Hewey saw that it was but a crumbling shell, its roof gone, its windows and doors removed. At one corner stood a small round wall that he took to be the top of a cistern.

Fat exclaimed, "I'm thirsty enough to drink the whole thing dry."

Padgett made a wry smile as Fat loped ahead. "He's a little late. The cistern dried up years ago."

The windlass leaned a little. A short length of rotted rope still clung to it. Fat cursed a short complaint as he dismounted and peered over the edge. He said, "I can't see no water." He dropped a stone. Hewey heard it strike bottom. He heard no splash.

Padgett said, "Used to be a Mexican settler here. Dodge bought him out."

Hewey had heard stories about Americans driving the original owners away and taking over their land. "You sure he bought him out, or maybe he just run him off?"

"Old Dodge is rougher than a dry cob. He'll drive a hard bargain, but he wouldn't cheat anybody, not even a Mexican."

They came after a time to a fence. The barbed wire still had some of its original shine. Padgett said, "This is the holdin' trap. Dodge fenced it off for those times when he needs to keep stock gathered for a few days like for sellin' or for doctorin'. Keeps a few horses in it, too."

Rising dust drew Hewey's attention to a small gather of cattle moving up the fence toward him. A rider loped out in front and stepped down to open a wire gate. Padgett said, "Looks like they're throwin' them into the trap." He spurred up to help. Hewey and the others followed.

A Mexican lad in his teens gave them a civil nod, then turned his attention to pointing the cattle through the opening. Reed-thin, he was mounted on a sorrel bronc, using a hackamore instead of bridle and bits. The horse eyed the newcomers nervously, ears flicking back and forth as he searched for something to booger at.

The cattle, bearing the D Cross brand, filed through the open gate, followed by three Mexican riders. The young man beckoned Padgett and the others through the gate, then got down and closed it.

"Hola, Juanito," Padgett said. "We come to see your *patrón*." He turned to Hewey. "In this part of the country it helps if you can speak Spanish."

Juanito said, "Señor Padgett, you are many days late. The *patrón* has looked a long time for you."

"Had a little trouble. Where's the old man?"

"*A casa*. Yesterday he fall from his horse. Today he hurts much. We gather his cattle."

Hewey guessed four or five hundred head were confined within sight. He assumed there were more that he could not see. It would not take long for them to graze off whatever grass the small enclosure could provide.

Padgett said, "We'll ride on to the house and talk to him."

Juanito winced: "He has much to say to you, I think."

"What kind of humor is he in?"

"Same as every day. He has much anger."

"Nothin' new about that." Padgett jerked his head at Hewey and the others. "Come on, we'd just as well let him get the cussin' over with so we can settle down to business."

Hewey had built a pleasant mental image of what the Dodge homeplace should look like, perhaps a nice two-story frame house with a cupola and ornate gingerbread trim around the eaves. The first sight of it disillusioned him. He had seen spartan dwellings, including the one in which he and Walter had grown up, but the Dodge ranch headquarters was only a few notches better than a coyote den. The house was a small, squat adobe with much of its original plaster fallen away, leaving the mud walls exposed and gradually deteriorating. Standing in sharp contrast were a sturdy barn and an expansive set of solidly built corrals. Two windmills stood tall against the sky, their fans turning slowly. He could almost taste the water. It was clear that Dodge's first priority was business. Comfort came later, if at all.

Hewey said, "His stock lives better than he does. From the looks of this place, he doesn't have a woman naggin' at him for somethin' better." He aimed the remark more at Walter than at Padgett.

Walter made no response. Padgett said, "As far as I know he's been a bachelor all his life. When he was younger he would sometimes bring a sportin' woman down from San Antone, but they never stayed long."

Walter declared, "I can understand why. I'd want to give a woman somethin' better than what I see here."

Hewey frowned. "And she'd keep you broke. You're better off like you are. You don't have to worry about anybody but yourself."

"And you, Hewey. Sometimes you worry me half to death."

Hewey developed several different mental images of Dodge. They had one thing in common: eyes that flashed fire.

Padgett said to Fat and Gabe, "You boys tie your horses and rest yourselves in the shade. Mr. Dodge don't like too much company at once. Me and Hewey and Walter will go talk to him."

Fat seemed grateful for a chance to get out of the sun. He dismounted and handed his reins to Gabe, silently letting him know he expected Gabe to tie his horse for him. Hewey considered telling Fat to do it himself, but at the moment he had more pressing business.

If Gabe harbored any resentment, he did not betray it. He was probably used to being treated like a servant.

Padgett cautioned, "You-all better let me do the talkin'. Old Man Dodge is kind of peculiar."

More peculiar than you? Hewey wondered.

Padgett knocked on the doorframe because the door itself was open. From inside, Hewey heard a groan of protest, then the creaking of bedsprings. In a moment a bent-shouldered little man came to the door in his sock feet, limping heavily, grumbling with every step. He had shrunk considerably from Hewey's mental images.

The rancher blinked against the outdoor brightness, trying to see. "Who the hell is it, and what the hell do you want?"

Padgett said, "It's me, Mr. Dodge. Sorry if I got you up from bed."

Dodge mumbled, "Hell, if it wasn't you it'd be some other son of a bitch. Come on in." He squinted, still having trouble seeing. "Who's that with you? I don't invite just any damned Meskin into this house."

Hewey realized why Padgett had told Gabe to stay out in the shade. And he probably assumed Fat would have nothing constructive to add to the conversation.

Padgett said, "These boys are here representin' C. C. Tarpley. Hewey Calloway is C.C.'s top hand."

That was a shameless stretch of the truth, but Hewey liked the sound of it.

Dodge's flinty eyes were not ablaze, though otherwise they were much as Hewey had imagined them. They bored through him like a drill. Dodge said, "The hell. I've heard about Tarpley. He's too much of a tightwad to keep a top hand. These boys don't look very damned bright to me."

Hewey considered telling him he had been all the way through the fourth grade. He could even exaggerate a little and make it the fifth grade, but he decided Dodge wasn't interested in that much information. He said, "Me and Walter have been up the trail once."

Dodge was not impressed. "Hell, half the men in this county have been up the trail, and lots of them still don't know how to pour water out of a bucket."

Hewey couldn't come up with a good answer. Though he had run into cranky people all his life, Old Man Dodge might be the crankiest of them all. By all odds he was the most profane. The Calloway brothers would earn their wages, looked like, just putting up with his irascible nature for however long it would take to get the cattle gathered and onto the trail.

He wondered if he might have been better off waiting at the ranch and taking his chances with Smith or Trumble or whatever the cow thief's real name was.

Dodge motioned for the three to come all the way into the house. It was small, just one room with a stove, steel cot, table, and three well-aged hard wooden chairs. Shelves along one wall held dishes and canned foodstuff. Dodge braced himself on a chair, then sank with care onto the edge of the cot. He grunted painfully and pressed a hand against his hip.

Padgett mentioned that they had encountered the young vaquero Juanito turning cattle into the trap. "He told me you fell off of a horse."

Dodge loosed a short spurt of profanity. "Like hell. I ain't so old that I fall off of horses. I got throwed off fair and square. That boy talks too damned much."

Padgett quickly tried to cover. "Maybe he did say throwed off. Age has made me smarter, but it ain't helped my memory much."

Dodge ignored the explanation. "Where the hell have you been all this time? You was supposed to've got these cattle three weeks ago."

"Had a little run-in with a narrow-minded sheriff. I'd be in the hoosegow yet if it wasn't for these boys."

"You put me in a hell of a damned bind. I got to move all my cattle off of this property inside of three days. Me and my vaqueros been roundin' them up and throwin' them into the trap. Since you didn't show up, I figured I'd have to drive them to San Antone and take whatever the hell I can get for them."

"Why the big hurry?"

"Any remnants that's left here past the day after to-morrow will go to the new owner. I didn't figure on it takin' so long for you to get here."

It was common practice in ranch sales that ungath-ered remnants of cattle went to the buyer.

Padgett said, "It ain't your fault I got delayed. Looks like your buyer would give you some slack."

"Slack hell! You ever met Sid Slocum?"

"Seen him. Never cared to meet him."

"I shot better men than him in the border wars, and they wasn't even white. This'd be a better world if his mammy had stuffed him in a sack and drowned him the day he was born. Damned if I know how he's got by this long without somebody killin' him."

"The meek ain't inherited the earth yet. How come you sold to him in the first place?"

"I didn't." Dodge dropped his chin and turned his face to the wall. "I lied to you. I didn't exactly sell this place. I lost it to the bank, and they sold the paper to Slocum, the thievin' son of a bitch."

"I had no idea things was that tough."

"All I'll get out of it is what the cattle bring. They wasn't mortgaged."

"Why couldn't you have sold just enough cattle to pay off what you owed?"

"Too much debt and not enough cattle."

"Looks like the bank would accept what you could pay them and extend the note on the rest."

"The bank might've, but Slocum wouldn't. He demanded all of it in cash. He knowed I couldn't raise that much." Dodge's face was flushed with rage. "I wish I could set the whole damned place afire when I leave. Leave that bastard nothin' but a pile of ashes."

Hewey intruded. "Who is this Slocum?"

Dodge said, "He's a highbinder who got his start runnin' whiskey up in the Indian Nations. When he got chased out of there, he came down into this country and swindled poor Meskins out of their land. Now he's buyin' up mortgages and foreclosin' on them. A scavenger, is what he is."

Padgett said, "At least you'll have the cattle money. You can start over."

"At my age? Damn it to hell, why have we got to get old, anyway?"

"There's only one way to prevent it, and that's to die young. Me and you are already past that."

Dodge's anger subsided. "The way I figure it, we got just today and tomorrow to finish the gather, then push my cattle across the property line by the day after tomorrow. Any remnants we leave behind are Slocum's."

"Juanito and some of your Mexicans was pushin' cattle into the trap as we came along."

"They'll have time enough for one more sweep before sundown. We'll work the southeast corner tomorrow."

Hewey thought he was using the word *we* too loosely. Dodge appeared too stove up to get back on a horse.

Padgett said, "Me and these boys will throw in with you. We'll round up everything but the jackrabbits."

Dodge nodded. "I'll be able to ride tomorrow."

Hewey doubted that.

Dodge asked, "What kind of horse was Juanito ridin'?"

Padgett told him, "A sorrel bronc, with a hackamore."

"So I thought. He favors that colt and neglects the others he's supposed to break. I've got to give him a damned good bawlin' out."

Hewey suspected Dodge was handy at doing that.

Padgett observed, "Juanito seems like a good hand."

Dodge shook his head. "If arthritis didn't have such a choke hold on me, I'd be breakin' the horses myself instead of turnin' them over to a Meskin. That Juanito thinks he's *puro jiñete,* but he's got a hell of a lot to learn about bronc stompin'. How can you teach these Meskin boys anything when they're too dumb to know the American language?"

"He speaks American better than I speak Mexican."

"If they're goin' to live here, by God, they ought to learn to talk American. The Bible is in American. Ain't that good enough for them?"

Hewey caught a faint smile in Walter's eyes and hoped he was not going to try to educate Dodge on the history of the scriptures. The old man would probably chase both of them out of the house, and maybe off the ranch.

Dodge made an effort to get up from the edge of the cot but fell back, one hand pressed against his hip again. He seemed to pale.

Padgett took a quick step toward him. "Are you all right?"

Dodge waved him away. "Ain't nothin' wrong with me. Just sore as hell from that hard landin' yesterday."

Hewey suspected it was more than that, and Padgett's expression indicated that he had the same feeling. Padgett said, "We'll get out of the way and let you rest. If it's all right, we'll set up camp in your barn."

"Camp anywhere that suits you. Burn it down for all I care. It ain't mine for much longer anyway."

Dodge did not try again to get up as the three visitors went out the door. Walter said, "He looks like there might be more wrong with him than just fallin' off of a horse."

"He's wore out," Padgett said. "One of these old ranches'll do that to you."

Hewey agreed. "That's why I never want to have one. How many rich men did you ever see that looked happy? Soon as they get somethin', they start layin' awake at night afraid they'll lose it. Ownin' a lot of property makes a man grow old before his time."

Walter argued, "It hasn't hurt C. C. Tarpley."

"Don't get any notions about competin' with the likes of C.C. When a little fish tries to swim with the big fish, they turn around and eat him."

At the barn they found an elderly Mexican loading a wagon to which a chuckbox was attached.

Padgett said, "I suppose you're the *cocinero?*"

"The cook? *Sí, señor. Me llama Sixto.*"

"Well, Sixto, you got five more mouths to feed."

Hewey saw a horseman approaching the adobe house in an easy jog trot, his spine straight, his head back. He was Anglo, not Mexican, so he was no employee of Dodge's. His ruddy face was twisted as if he smelled a skunk.

Padgett clenched his fists. "Son of a bitch, that's Sid Slocum. Come to rub salt into Old Man Dodge's wounds, I expect. Stand by me, boys. We ain't lettin' him into the house." Padgett led Hewey and Walter back to the adobe. Gabe and Fat followed.

The closer Slocum came, the less Hewey liked his looks. He was already prejudiced by what Dodge had said, and the man's stiff-backed, arrogant way of sitting in the saddle indicated that he had appointed himself the cock of the walk. People like that made Hewey think of a bloated steer. The cure for those was a puncture in the side to let the air out.

Slocum glared down at the newcomers without making any move to dismount. "Who are you people, and what is your business here?"

Padgett set his feet apart in a challenging stance. "Ain't none of your business who comes here or what they do. This place ain't yours for a few more days."

"At midnight Wednesday, to be exact. I came to see if Dodge has moved his cattle yet."

"He's thrown most of them in a holdin' trap out yonder. You can't see but a few from here."

Slocum turned to look northward. A narrow neck of the trap ran up to the headquarters so that cattle could come in for water. A handful loafed around the water lot. The rest were grazing toward the trap's far end, out of sight.

Slocum declared, "They had better be gone on time, or they will be mine. The contract firmly states . . ."

Padgett stopped him with a gesture of dismissal. "I know all about your contract, and how you're drivin' an old man out of his home. You ain't wanted here while the place is still Mr. Dodge's. You'd better git before the sky clouds up and rains on you."

Slocum involuntarily looked up before he caught himself. Not a cloud was in sight. "I have come to talk to Dodge. I intend to do so."

"You can't. He's ailin'."

"He will ail more severely if he does not vacate this ranch. I'll be back Thursday to take possession." He scowled. "Your name is Padgett, is it not?"

Padgett gave him only a low grunt.

Slocum edged his horse closer to the house. Hewey

stepped in to block him. "Mr. Padgett says you ain't goin' in."

Slocum's scowl deepened. "Get out of the way, cowboy." He spoke the word *cowboy* as he might say *smallpox*.

For a moment Slocum appeared ready to try to ride over Hewey. Gabe grabbed Slocum's bridle reins just below the bits. Slocum said, "Turn loose, nigger." He roughly yanked the reins from Gabe's hand and jerked his horse around. He rode away, his chin high in anger.

Gabe rubbed his hand, for Slocum's leather reins had burned his fingers.

Walter said, "You've made an enemy of him, Hewey."

"He ain't anybody I'd want for a friend."

"From what I gather," Padgett said, "he doesn't have many of those anyway. But he's got money, and a man with plenty of money can rent friends when he needs them." He pointed at the barn. "Let's unload our stuff. Then we'll ride out and see if we can help Juanito pick up some more cattle."

He asked Gabe, "How's your hand?"

"Just smarts a little, is all."

"Rub some axle grease on it when we get back. Axle grease and Epsom salts will cure almost anything."

THIRTEEN

THEY GATHERED MORE THAN A HUNDRED HEAD THE next day and turned them into the small trap. Hewey noted that the grass was disappearing under the weight of heavy grazing. It would be high time to get these cattle on the move even if Dodge was not facing a short deadline.

Dodge had dragged himself from the house, ignoring Padgett's insistence that they could handle the job without him. By standing his horse next to a corral fence, he managed to climb up and force his aching body into the saddle. He turned away offers of help. "Dammit to hell, I can do this by myself," he declared, his face pinched in pain. "I ain't no damned cripple."

As the last small set of cows and calves passed through the wire gate and he finished counting, Dodge said grudgingly, "Altogether we're just about twenty short of seven hundred head. I hope whatever's left come down with the bloody scours." He reconsidered.

"Naw, I wouldn't wish that onto a bunch of poor dumb animals. I wish Slocum would get the scours instead."

Padgett said, "We'll have to commence movin' them in the mornin' to get across your property line by sundown."

"You can bet that graspin' son of a bitch will watch us all the way," Dodge grumbled.

Hewey could see a man on horseback, observing from a distance of several hundred yards. He said, "I believe he already is."

After supper the old man hobbled around the adobe house and made his slow way out to the barn, pausing often to stare at first one thing and then another. Walter told Hewey, "He's takin' a last look around. He hates leavin' here a lot worse than he lets on."

For a long while Dodge leaned against a corral fence, his gaze fixed far away in space, and perhaps also in time.

The young vaquero Juanito tentatively moved in Dodge's direction as if he sought to give him comfort. He stopped short and considered. He turned back reluctantly, leaving the old rancher's privacy undisturbed.

Walter said, "I reckon he sees Dodge as a substitute daddy."

Hewey said, "The old dickens doesn't treat him like a substitute son."

Padgett said, "To hear Dodge cuss you might think he's too tough for tears, but he's weepin' inside. He's put a big part of his life into this place, a lot of blood and sweat."

Hewey nodded toward Walter. "That's what bein' tied to a piece of property will do to you. I don't want to stay in one place so long that I grieve when I leave it. There's always somethin' better over the hill."

Walter said, "Even if there is, it won't mean as much if none of it belongs to you."

Watching the old man, Hewey felt a tightening in his throat. He thought it was probably something he ate for supper. Sixto's cooking had more pepper in it than he was used to.

Juanito and the other Mexican hands slept near the corrals in an adobe even smaller than Dodge's. Hewey awoke in the barn before good daylight, stirred out of sleep by excited voices speaking in Spanish. He laid his top blanket aside, putting on his hat and then his boots. In his underwear, he walked out into the first light of a pink dawn to see Juanito on the night horse, galloping toward Dodge's house.

Hewey shouted, "What's the matter? Who's dead?"

Juanito shouted back, "Most of the cattle, they are gone."

The youngster jumped to the ground, dropped the reins, and raced into Dodge's house. Hewey reentered the barn and shouted, "Somethin's gone haywire. Everybody better get up."

He took time to put on his britches but was still buttoning his shirt when he went outside and headed down toward the house. Juanito hurried past him, leading the horse back to the corrals. With one boot on and one in his hand, Dodge stood on the front step trying to holler in a hoarse voice. "Saddle my old dun. I'll be there in a minute."

Hewey followed Juanito. The young Mexican said, "I go to rustle horses for work today, but I don't see many cattle. What I see is the fence down, and the cattle gone."

Hewey found himself talking like Dodge. "How in the hell could that happen?"

"I think it was Slocum."

The ranch horses were accustomed to a morning feed and had not gone away with the cattle. Juanito had brought them in. Hewey saddled and was following Juanito out into the trap before the other men began catching their mounts. As the sun broke over the horizon, Juanito stopped to look at the ground. "Many cattle tracks," he said.

Hewey saw horse tracks as well. "Them cattle didn't stray out by theirselves. Somebody drove them."

Juanito showed him where the fence was down at the back side of the trap, some distance from headquarters. The wires had been cut, then pulled free of the posts for most of fifty yards. The cattle had been pushed out through the wide opening and scattered. Hewey saw a few grazing in the morning's early light, for some would stop when they were no longer driven. There were nowhere near the seven hundred that had been in the trap.

He said, "Slocum's bunch did their dirty work far enough away that none of us would hear them. And we were supposed to get the cattle off of the property today."

The other men caught up to Hewey and Juanito. Fat Gervin, sleepy-eyed, brought up the rear.

Dodge's face was crimson. "That damned Slocum. I always knowed he was a rattlesnake, but I never would've thought of him doin' this."

Padgett said, "We'll get busy and bring back as many as we can."

Dodge cursed. "How many will that be? Everything we can't find today will be remnants tomorrow. They'll belong to that schemin' son of a bitch."

"We'll do our best and salvage all we can," Padgett said.

Fat complained that he hadn't had breakfast, but no one paid attention to him. Hewey struck out in a long trot toward the farthest group of cattle he could see. Walter followed. They gave the cows and calves a push back toward the trap, then set out to seek more. Gabe joined them. Juanito and the other hands set off in different directions. Hewey lost track of Dodge and Padgett.

By noon a rough count told him they had recovered more than four hundred. That was well short of the number originally confined in the trap.

Fat said, "Looks like that old man ain't goin' to have as much money as he figured on for his retirement." If he felt any sympathy, he did not show it.

Hewey said, "We ain't done yet. We'll go back and scout for some more."

Fat's shoulders drooped. "I wouldn't've taken this job if I'd known it'd starve me to death."

"Missin' a meal won't kill you. If they was to render you out they'd get a hundred pounds of pure lard."

By late afternoon the hands had gathered a couple of hundred more. Dodge counted them, too discouraged even to curse. "Close to a hundred short."

Padgett said, "We'd best settle for what we've got and start them to movin'."

Dodge's face was pinched. "Even if we push all night, I doubt we can make it across my line by mornin'."

Padgett said, "Let's try anyway. Slocum ain't gettin' this herd without he knows he's been in a horse race."

Hewey helped get the cattle started westward, then stopped. "I'm for goin' back to hunt some more."

Juanito said, "I go, too."

Padgett counseled against it. "We'll need all hands to hold what we've got and keep them movin' at a good clip." He glanced worriedly at Dodge. "I don't know how much longer he can hold on, the shape he's in."

Walter warned, "Our horses are about give out."

Padgett nodded at Juanito. "You'd best go back to headquarters and bring up the rest of the remuda. Take Fat with you. He won't hinder you too much. And tell

Sixto to load the chuckwagon with everything he can lay his hands on."

Fat was willing. He said, "Maybe then we can get somethin' to eat." He and Juanito rode off in a long trot.

Padgett looked toward the afternoon sun. "We've still got a couple hours of daylight. We'll keep pushin' after dark even if we lose a few." He rode over to talk to Dodge. Dodge still lamented leaving close to a hundred head for Slocum.

Padgett said, "You know the old Bible story about the man who went lookin' for one lost sheep and forgot about the other ninety and nine?"

Dodge said, "I never read it. And these ain't sheep."

Juanito and Fat brought up the remuda just before dark so all the riders could change to fresh mounts. Sixto took the wagon on ahead. Later he would stop to build a fire. He would reheat last night's beans and boil coffee to be ready when the herd reached him. Another vaquero took charge of the extra horses. By their nature they wanted to move faster than the cowherd. Some played, biting at one another and pitching, squealing, breaking wind.

Hewey speculated, "If we travel all night, maybe we'll be gone before Slocum knows we've trumped him."

Juanito's eyes were cold. "What I would like to do to the Slocum . . ." He slid a finger across his throat.

Hewey said, "There's probably some fool law against it."

The cattle were allowed to water in the creek while the men ate a quick supper of coffee, beans, and dutch oven bread that had not been given time to bake all the way through. Hewey looked at the rising moon. "Lucky for us it's full. At least we can see better what we're doin'."

The skimpy supper gave him fresh energy for a

while, but the effect began to wear off in the long hours after midnight. One of the Mexican hands went to sleep and fell out of the saddle. The cattle had slowed considerably despite the best efforts of the men at the rear to keep punching them up.

He did not know the country well enough to recognize landmarks even if he had seen them. He became aware that darkness was fading under a weak show of early light in the east. He made out the ruins of a house ahead. It was the old adobe with the dried-up cistern.

Dodge seemed enlivened. His back straighter, he rode alongside the strung-out herd, encouraging the men. "Keep them comin', compadres. We're damn near there. My property ends a mile or so past that old homestead."

Hewey rubbed his eyes. His tired body ached, and the lack of sleep made his stomach cramp. He knew that from a legal standpoint they were already past the contract time for Dodge's ranch to pass into Slocum's ownership, and with it any cattle remaining on the property. But possession still counted for something.

Not enough, though. Three men rode out from behind the adobe walls. Hewey's stomach cramped harder as he recognized Sid Slocum. Not until the three approached the herd did he see the badge on one rider's vest. He assumed the third man was either a deputy or a Slocum hired hand. Neither was good news.

Dodge slumped. Padgett rode up on one side of him, Juanito on the other, offering moral support. Hewey moved closer, his tired horse slow to respond to the light touch of his spurs.

Slocum wasted no time on talk. He declared, "Sheriff, you have a duty to perform. You had best be about it, wouldn't you say?"

The sheriff grumbled, "If I was to say what I'm

thinkin', it'd blister your ears." Reluctantly the lawman moved half a length ahead of Slocum, drawing a folded paper from inside his vest. "Mr. Dodge, I hate to do this."

Slocum said, "Get on with it."

The sheriff snapped back at him, "Don't be tellin' me what to do. I'm the law here."

"And I am a taxpaying citizen of this county."

"Be careful, or you may find yourself payin' a lot more. I'll remind you that I'm also the county tax assessor and collector." He crumpled the paper in his fist. "Mr. Dodge, this is an order to turn over your land and whatever's on it to Sidney Slocum as of midnight last night."

Dodge nodded dully.

The sheriff said, "As an officer of the law I've got no choice, even though I consider Mr. Slocum to be first cousin to a javelina hog." He gave Slocum a poisonous look and reined his horse around. "Let's travel, deputy."

Slocum cried out, "Wait. Where are you going?"

"Back to town. I've served your damned paper. The rest is up to you."

"But I'll need help."

"You're rich. Hire some."

Slocum's haughty manner left him. Apprehension took its place. "I forbid you to ride off and leave me here by myself."

"Adiós, Slocum."

"I will sue you for malfeasance of duty," Slocum yelled.

The sheriff and the deputy kept riding.

Hewey wondered what *malfeasance* meant. It sounded like some dread disease. He hoped Slocum would catch it.

In his view the sheriff had left an open invitation. He waited for a reaction from Dodge.

Slocum did not wait. He reached down to his hip and came up with a pistol. "Now be gone from here, all of you. Be gone before I start shooting."

Dodge's eyes turned dangerous. "You ain't got the guts of a turkey buzzard. You won't shoot a man who's lookin' you in the eye." He urged his horse forward.

He was wrong. The pistol fired. Dodge grabbed his arm and almost fell. With a cry of rage Juanito slammed his horse against Slocum's, almost knocking the man from the saddle. Slocum brought the pistol down against Juanito's head. Juanito went to the ground.

Slocum waved the gun wildly. "Everyone stay back!"

The sheriff and deputy returned in a gallop. The lawman demanded, "Slocum, you throw that pistol down."

Slocum hesitated. The sheriff wrenched the smoking weapon from his hand and hurled it away. He sucked air between his teeth and rubbed his hand where the hot barrel had burned it.

Padgett helped Dodge down from his horse. Dodge knelt by Juanito's side, ignoring the wound in his own arm to dab his neckerchief at blood running down the boy's face.

"You all right, *hijo?* Say somethin', boy."

The sheriff dismounted, looking at first one, then the other. He touched the old man's arm. "You're hit, Mr. Dodge."

Dodge waved him away. "A scratch is all. I've had mesquite thorns bite me deeper than that. But he didn't have to pistolwhip this boy."

Slocum complained, "I was under imminent threat."

Padgett said, "As you can see, sheriff, there ain't nobody packin' iron except Slocum."

Slocum argued, "I was compelled to defend myself."

The sheriff frowned. "Looks to me like you overdid it. You want me to send a doctor out, Mr. Dodge?"

Juanito blinked, trying to clear his eyes. Dodge sighed, relieved. "You'll be all right, boy. You just lay still a while." He looked up at the sheriff. "Don't send no doctor. We can take care of our own."

"How about charges?"

"No charges, either. You go on back to town and get your breakfast." He gave Slocum a hard look and repeated, "We can take care of our own."

The sheriff gripped the reins his deputy had been holding and got on his horse. *"Hasta luego."*

Padgett said, "Ain't you takin' Slocum with you?"

"He ain't charged with anything. He can find his own way home."

Slocum yelled after the sheriff but to no avail. He made a run for his horse. Hewey cut in front of him, waving his hat and shouting. Already nervous from the shot, the horse ran off, trailing the reins. Gabe followed in a long trot, pushing it farther away. Slocum ran after him, shouting, "You bring that horse back here, nigger."

Gabe returned, but without the horse.

Fear came into Slocum's eyes. His voice was shrill. "I am within my legal rights."

Padgett knotted his fists. "Sure you are. Was I you, I'd go catch my horse right now and start inspectin' your ranch way over on the far side. Else some of these boys may forget their gentle nature."

Slocum ran for his pistol, which lay where the sheriff had thrown it.

Padgett shouted, "Head him off. He'll shoot somebody else sure as hell."

With no time to think about it, Hewey spurred between Slocum and the pistol. He loosed the horn string and shook out his rope. He flipped the loop around Slocum and rode away, taking a quick wrap around the horn. The rope went taut and jerked Slocum off his feet. He landed hard. Hewey dragged him away from the pistol.

Slocum tried to worm his way out of the loop, but Hewey jerked it tight. Slocum fell again. He raised up on his hands and shouted for the sheriff to help him.

The wind was blowing. The sheriff did not seem to hear.

The shot had spooked the cattle into a trot. They slowed again but continued moving westward. Padgett turned to Walter and the others who had gathered around. "Long as they're bound to drift anyway, I don't see any reason to get in their way."

Gabe grinned. "We'll just foller to be sure they don't get lost."

"We got to be careful not to drive them, exactly," Padgett cautioned. "The sheriff might consider that cheatin'. Just kind of nudge them a little."

Fat complained, "We're fixin' to get in bad trouble."

Walter rode to Hewey's side. "How long you goin' to keep your rope on Mr. Slocum?"

"I don't see any hurry. His horse has run off. Looks like the poor feller has got to walk home."

Padgett said, "He might come back with some of his hired help. It'd be nice if he could be talked into stayin' right here for a while."

Hewey looked toward the old house. Perhaps he might find something to which he could tie Slocum. His gaze fell upon the cistern. As he remembered, it was at least twenty feet deep.

He said, "I'll entertain Mr. Slocum while you-all go see after the cattle. It'd be a shame if they was to stray across the property line."

Gabe's grin reached all the way across his dark face. His teeth shone white as ivory. "Sure would."

Walter helped the shaky Juanito back onto his horse. Dodge admonished, "You hold on tight, boy. Wouldn't want you to fall off and hurt yourself some more." The two rode away in the wake of the cattle.

Walter held back. "Hewey, I don't know what you're plannin' on, but you're fixin' to get in trouble. Again."

"You go on. They can't lay any blame on you if you ain't here."

Walter left, but he looked back a couple of times.

Slocum still sat on the ground. Hewey made two more wraps around his middle, pulling the rope tight. Slocum's mouth sagged open. "What are you going to do?"

"I'm still studyin' on it. Been lookin' at them mesquites yonder, but I ain't sure any of them are big enough to hold a man of your weight."

Slocum blustered, "You wouldn't hang me." He swallowed hard. "Would you?"

"The thing that troubles me is what will I do with you afterwards? The shovel is on the chuckwagon, and it's gone on ahead. Couldn't depend on the coyotes to clean everything up."

He retrieved Slocum's pistol. "Get up and start walkin'."

Slocum struggled to his feet. The morning was not yet warm, but he sweated heavily. He rasped, "Be careful. That pistol is still loaded."

Hewey made a show of examining it. "Sure enough." He let it point casually toward Slocum.

"Look, cowboy, I have money. I'll give you a hundred dollars. . . ."

Hewey snorted. "A hundred dollars? That ain't a month's pay, hardly." Actually, it was more than three months' pay, but details could be tiresome.

Slocum dragged his feet as Hewey pointed him toward the crumbling mud walls. He got as far as the cistern when Hewey said, "That'll do. Stop right there."

Sweat cut little trails down Slocum's dusty face. "My God. Surely you wouldn't shoot me and throw me down that well."

"It crossed my mind."

Slocum trembled. "I'll do anything you ask me to. I'll even sign the ranch back over to Dodge."

Hewey shook his head. "Can't trust you. Soon as you got free you'd welch on the deal. But tell you what I'll do: you climb over into that well and I won't shoot you. Maybe somebody'll come along and find you eventually."

"I might starve to death before that."

"A slim chance is better than no chance at all. Climb over." He waved the pistol.

Slocum put one leg across the cistern wall. "You won't let me drop, will you? I could break my back."

"I'll hold onto the rope. You go on down."

He dismounted and braced the rope against his hip, playing it out as Slocum descended. It slackened when the man reached the dry bottom. Hewey said, "I want my rope back. I'll leave it here so if somebody was to come by, they'll have somethin' to haul you out with."

"What if no one comes by?"

"Let's don't think about that. Any rattlesnakes down there?"

"Snakes? My God."

"Must not be any or they'd've let you know. But if any show up, they won't bite you. They recognize their kin."

He opened the cylinder and removed the cartridges that remained in Slocum's pistol. Tossing them away, he leaned over the well and said, "I don't want you claimin' I stole your pistol." He dropped it in. Slocum yelped as it bounced off of his shoulder.

Riding away, Hewey could hear Slocum shouting, but the sound was muffled. He rode out to where Slocum's horse was grazing and removed the saddle, blanket, and bridle. He flipped the leather reins gently across the horse's rump. "I reckon you can find your way home." He watched the horse trot away, then took his time catching up with the herd.

Walter rode out to meet him. "I hope you didn't do somethin' that'll get us all sent to the pen."

"Never touched a hair on his head."

"Where's he at?"

"I left him back yonder. He's takin' a long look at some of his property."

FOURTEEN

THE HERD WAS WELL BEYOND WHAT HAD BEEN Dodge's property line when Padgett rode back from the point and said, "We're comin' up on the San Antonio road."

Dodge was riding along with the drags and seemed to be having a hard time keeping up. The flesh wound he had suffered at Slocum's hands was evidently causing a little fever. Padgett said, "There's a ranch house up ahead. Why don't you stop off and rest awhile? You can catch up to us when you feel better."

Dodge waved him away. "I'm stayin' with you to San Antone."

"We're not so far from your place that we can't send back for anything you want to take along."

"What little I need is in Sixto's wagon. I can buy whatever I might want, and it'll be new, not junk like I'm leavin' for Slocum." He looked behind him. "Where *is* Slocum? I figured he'd've caught up and be raisin' hell with us again by now."

Hewey had not told anyone what he had done. If trouble should come of it, he wanted nobody else to be blamed.

Padgett said, "After shootin' you and pistol-whippin' Juanito, he's probably keepin' his head down."

Hewey said, "Way down."

Padgett pointed the cattle onto the trail, though most trudged along on either side of it. After a while Hewey became aware of a horseman catching up from behind. Recognizing the sheriff, he felt uneasy. Maybe he should have left the herd and made himself scarce for a while.

The sheriff was alone. He greeted Dodge first and inquired about his wound. Dodge muttered, "I've done forgot about it."

The lawman said, "I see that your cattle have strayed past your old property line."

Dodge admitted, "They wasn't past it at midnight. This is Thursday."

"As far as I'm concerned, this is Wednesday. I believe Slocum read his calendar wrong."

Dodge straightened his shoulders as he realized the sheriff was opening a door for him. "Might be he did."

The sheriff continued, "If he hollers, it'll be his word against ours. The way most folks feel about him, I doubt that any court around here would give him much of a show. You sure you're feelin' all right?"

"Like I was twenty years old."

The sheriff smiled. "Then take care of yourself, kid." He started to turn away.

Hewey called to him. "Sheriff, hold up a minute. I need to talk to you."

Walter gave him a questioning look, but Hewey motioned for him to go on. He waited until the others had passed beyond hearing before he said, "It's about Slocum."

The sheriff's eyebrows lifted. "I hope you've done no violence to him."

"No, he's safe and sound where I left him, but he ain't goin' noplace for a while. You know that old adobe ruin with the dry cistern?"

"I've been there."

"I was figurin' on goin' back and doin' it myself, but since you're here . . . you might ride by that cistern and take a look down inside. Not today though, maybe tomorrow. By then I expect Slocum will agree to anything that'll get him back up into the daylight."

"You dropped him down that well?"

"Didn't drop him, exactly. He climbed down of his own free will and accord. Somehow he took a silly notion I was fixin' to hang him."

The sheriff laughed. "I wonder who gave him such an idea? All right, I'll go by there tomorrow. The next day for sure."

"If any trouble comes of this, I done it all myself. Wasn't nobody else knew about it."

"I'm not sure I ever heard your name. How does Bill Jones suit you?"

Hewey nodded. "That'll do."

JUANITO RODE IN THE wagon the first day on the San Antonio trail. The second day he insisted upon riding his sorrel bronc again. Dodge warned him, "You'll work that pony into the ground."

Juanito said, "A bronc needs plenty work. Work is the best teacher."

Padgett called an early halt. Dodge argued, "There's still daylight left."

"But there's grass and water here. A man don't want to push cows and calves too hard."

Hewey suspected Padgett's real concern was not the herd. Dodge looked pale and drawn. Both men had counted the cattle and come to an agreement on the number. All that remained from a business standpoint was the writing of a draft on C. C. Tarpley's bank account. Dodge said he was in no hurry about that. He could not spend the money until he got to San Antonio anyway, and he did not want to risk losing it by carrying it around. "I got in trouble that way one time," he said. "Didn't bank my check for most of a month. By that time the old boy who wrote it had gone flat busted."

Hewey said, "You don't need to worry about C.C. I suspect he's still got the first dollar he ever made. He sure ain't spent it payin' wages."

"Cowboys don't need much anyway," Dodge said. "Money leaks through their fingers like sand through a sieve."

Dodge sat on his rolled blankets and stared into the dying embers of Sixto's cooking fire. "That ranch back yonder ain't the first place I ever lost. Every cowman I know has gone broke two or three times. I just wish somebody had got it besides Sid Slocum."

Padgett said, "At least you got away with most of the cattle. We've crossed the county line, so I don't think Slocum is apt to send the sheriff after you. We're out of his jurisdiction."

"He might send a pack of damned lawyers."

Hewey itched to tell what he had done to Slocum, but now and then he suffered a spasm of good judgment. He said, "The sheriff told me if it went to court he'd swear that Slocum was lookin' at last year's calendar and we got the cattle off on Wednesday."

"And after all," Padgett told Dodge, "the boundary wasn't fenced. Slocum would have to get it surveyed to prove exactly where it lays. By that time this herd would be all the way out to the Pecos River. He'd never find it unless you told him where it went."

"I wouldn't tell that damned skinflint where to find a water bucket if his britches was on fire."

Fat spoke up. "I'll bet you could hire some Mexican to kill him for fifty dollars. Maybe less."

Dodge seemed to savor the thought for just a minute. "Wouldn't do no good. Everything would go to his sorry kin, and I wouldn't be no better off."

Padgett studied the old man's face in the firelight. "I'm wonderin' how long you can idle around the San Antonio hotel lobbies before you start itchin' to get back in the cattle business."

"I don't know. I was chasin' mavericks and burnin' my own brand on them before the big war. I've rode the market up and down so many times I've lost count, and watched my cows starve through more damned droughts than I want to think about. But there's somethin' about it that gets in the blood, like other people take to drinkin' or gamblin'. I guess ranchers and dirt farmers are about the worst gamblers in the world. The deck is stacked against them most of the time, but they keep playin' the game as long as they've got a chip left."

ALMOST FROM THE FIRST, Hewey had his eye on a wily-eyed spotted cow that kept looking around, seeking an opening for escape. It seemed that no matter how docile a herd might be, one or two incorrigible bunch-quitters were always awaiting their chance. He had chased her down and turned her back into the herd three times. His first thought was that she might have left a calf behind, but her udder was not swollen. She was just unsociable. Exiling her to short grazing in the Pecos River country seemed a reasonable punishment for her errant behavior.

Between watching for the cow to break out again and watching the back trail for a sign of Sid Slocum and the law, his time was fully occupied.

Dodge was closest to the cow the next time she decided to return to familiar range. The old man spurred after the fugitive, roundly cursing her and all her antecedents. Hewey turned to help him but saw that Dodge had managed to get around her, waving a coiled rope and yelling. She started back toward the herd, her head high and tail curled in a clear message that she had lost the round but not the fight. She would try again.

Dodge gave her a final angry shout as she rejoined the drag, then he slumped suddenly, gasping, and dropped the rope. He leaned to one side, grabbing at the horn. He looked toward Hewey with wide eyes, then slid to the ground. His startled horse snorted and jumped sideways, ears pointed forward. For a few seconds Hewey feared Dodge's foot was caught in the stirrup. If the horse panicked, the old man could be dragged. But his foot fell free before Hewey could reach him.

Hewey was down and at Dodge's side before anyone else got there. The rancher's face was drained, his hands trembling. He wheezed, "Ought to've left the old bitch for Slocum."

Dodge was having a seizure of some kind, but Hewey did not know what to do about it. Dodge strained to get up. He lacked the strength. Hewey said, "Lay easy, Mr. Dodge. Somethin' has happened to you."

The reply was a forced whisper. "Damned horse throwed me off is what happened." Dodge clutched the front of his shirt in a knotted fist.

He had fallen off, but Hewey would not anger him by saying so. Being thrown off a horse was no disgrace, but only a town-raised pumpkin roller would admit to falling off.

Word passed quickly to the point. Juanito came first and anxiously jumped down to join Hewey. "Señor Dodge, you are all right?"

The answer was hard to hear. "I'm fine. Just fine."

Padgett galloped back and demanded, "Is he hurt?"

Hewey said, "It's his heart, I'm thinkin'."

Frowning darkly, Padgett leaned over the rancher. "I been arguin' with him to ride in the wagon. He's got no business tryin' to be a cowboy anymore."

Dodge struggled to bring out the words. "You callin' me old?"

Juanito looked ready to cry. Padgett told him, "Ride up and tell the hands to hold the herd. We'll make camp."

Dodge whispered, "It's too damned early."

"It may be later than you want to admit."

Reluctantly the boy rode off on the assigned mission. Padgett muttered, "Couldn't let him bust out bawlin'. Looked like he was fixin' to."

Dodge murmured, "If *he* don't cry for me, who will?"

Walter rode ahead to catch Sixto and tell him to bring the wagon back. Hewey and Padgett carried Dodge into the thin shade of a mesquite and smoothed out a place for him in the soft sand. The old man gradually recovered enough strength to rail at his luck. "I wonder if that damned Slocum hired some *brujo* to put a curse on me."

Padgett said, "You know you don't believe in witches. This has been sneakin' up on you. You just wouldn't let yourself see it comin'."

When the wagon arrived, Hewey and Walter stretched a tarp out from one side of it to make a shade.

Against Dodge's protest, Padgett dispatched a Mexican hand to the next town to fetch a doctor. Dodge argued, "Damned small-town pill pushers, the only thing they ever do is open up my purse."

Sixto had a bottle of dark patent medicine in the chuckbox. Hewey recognized the label. It was advertised to cure almost any ailment known to man, woman, child, or horse. When Sixto uncorked it, the smell was like that of an animal two weeks dead. He prevailed on Dodge to swallow a large spoonful. The rancher immediately spit it out. He said, "Dammit, Sixto, you tryin' to hurry me into my grave? I'll get there soon enough."

Dodge lapsed into sleep after a time. His breathing was irregular and so quiet that more than once Hewey feared he had slipped away. Just at dark the Mexican cowboy returned by himself, explaining that the town ahead had no doctor.

Padgett accepted the news with a fatalistic shrug. "I don't know if a doctor could do much for him anyway. I'm afraid he may've run out his string."

Dodge opened his eyes partway. He said, "I'm afraid you're right. Old Nick has got me caught by the hind foot."

Padgett said ruefully, "I didn't think you were awake."

"Awake and thinkin'. You ain't wrote me that draft yet for the cattle."

"I'll do it right now."

"No need to hurry. I don't think I'm goin' anyplace where I can spend it." Dodge coughed and clutched at his chest. He motioned for Padgett to bend closer. "If I cash in, I want you to pay my hands the wages they've got comin', and a little extry besides. They're a good bunch."

Padgett seemed resigned. "Whatever you say, Mr. Dodge."

"And that boy Juanito . . ." Dodge coughed again. "He's the nearest thing to a son that I ever had. Take him with you and watch over him."

"Don't you worry. I'll see to it."

Dodge took a long breath. "Whatever money is left, send it to my nephew."

"If that's what you want."

"He'll blow it all in, but I reckon that's what I was fixin' to do with it myself. Too damned old to do anything else."

Dodge drifted off to sleep. Hewey sat on the ground watching him in the dim light of the campfire. Life left the old man so gently that Hewey did not realize for a while that he was gone. Juanito reverently folded Dodge's arms and pulled the blanket over his face, then walked out into the darkness alone.

Hewey started to follow him, but Padgett said, "Leave him be. Some things a boy has to work through by himself. Once he does, he's not a boy anymore."

Hewey and the hands dug a grave a little way off of the trail. Padgett said, "He can hear the herds goin' past. I think he'll like that." Padgett placed a silver dollar in the rancher's gnarled hand. "He's been broke more than once in life, but he'll never be broke again."

Juanito sniffled while Sixto recited a prayer in Spanish and crossed himself. They filled in the grave and marked it temporarily with a board out of the chuckwagon's end gate. Padgett promised to send money to the sheriff for a proper stone.

Walter asked, "What do you reckon it ought to say?"

Hewey suggested, *"If I don't like it where I'm goin', I swear by damn I'm comin' back."*

* * *

LATE THE NEXT DAY a rider caught up to them from behind. Hewey recognized the deputy who had been with
the sheriff and Slocum. The man rode up to the drags
and said, "I'm lookin' for a feller the sheriff called Bill
Jones."

Walter said, "There's nobody here by that name."

Hewey broke in. "There might be. Depends on why
you're lookin' for him."

"The sheriff sent me to warn him that Sid Slocum is
comin' and bringin' a ranger with him. Said to tell Jones
he might want to take a *pasear* out to the west and enjoy
a change of scenery."

Walter asked, "What's this Jones feller done?"

"Seems he coaxed Sid Slocum down into a dry cistern and left him there. Mr. Slocum ain't happy."

Walter forced a frown at Hewey, but his eyes were
laughing. "It didn't really hurt him, did it?"

"Just left him a little drawed is all. But he was mad
enough to chew up horseshoes and spit them at somebody. Especially somebody named Jones." He gave
Hewey a slight grin that said he knew. "If you come
across anybody by that name, you might pass the word
on to him."

Hewey said, "We will, if we come across him. Tell
the sheriff we're sure Jones'll be much obliged."

The deputy declined an invitation to ride along and
take supper when Sixto made camp. "Got orders to
keep lookin' for Jones. I think I'll hunt around over
east."

When he was gone, Walter said, "Hewey, I don't
know how you'll ever make it to thirty without gettin'
shot or hung." He chuckled. "I wish I could've seen
Slocum's face. I'll bet he was a pretty sight."

Hewey had to grin. "I saw it, and there wasn't nothin' pretty about him."

"What'll you do now?"

"Like he said, mosey off to the west a little ways, just far enough that I can't hear the cattle bawl. When Slocum gives up, I'll come back."

"We're already out of that county sheriff's jurisdiction, but Slocum's got a ranger with him. The rangers can go anywhere."

Hewey loped up to the point of the herd to tell Padgett what he was going to do. Padgett chuckled as Hewey told him about Slocum and the cistern. He said, "I figured you must've done somethin' like that. I wish I'd thought of it."

"I'm kind of proud of it myself."

"Get some grub from Sixto. Keep track of us. When we get to the outskirts of San Antonio we'll turn west so we don't stir up more housewives and dogs than we have to."

"I'll find you." Hewey shook Padgett's hand.

HEWEY STOPPED IN A clump of brush before sunset and built a small fire to make coffee with water from a canteen. He ate a cold biscuit Sixto had given him and some hog meat left from the noon meal. When the coffee had boiled enough he kicked dirt over the fire to kill it. Otherwise the flames could be seen for a considerable distance after dark.

A feeling of loneliness came over him, for he had never spent much time by himself. Walter had always been around, and usually other people as well. He wondered if Slocum and the ranger had caught up with the herd. If they hadn't, they probably would by tomorrow.

He could visualize Slocum and the ranger questioning the crew. The hands would probably feign ignorance of the English language. Mexicans often employed that defense against those who tried to intimidate them. Walter would not lie. That was something he had never been able to do. He would simply avoid a direct answer.

Padgett would probably just tell them to go to hell.

The next day Hewey rode at about the pace he knew the herd would travel, covering seven or eight miles. By supper he had eaten all the bread Sixto had given him, but he still had bacon and coffee enough to get him by. He saw a ranch house to the west and considered riding there for a meal. It was ranch custom to feed solitary drifters so long as they did not stay too long and abuse the hospitality. He decided against it, for if the ranger was serious about looking for him, he would probably visit the ranch and ask questions.

By the following day he had finished the bacon, and the sack of coffee was almost empty. He drew close enough to the herd that he could recognize the riders. He saw no strangers among them. He decided it was worth the risk to circle around and visit Sixto's wagon. It was a mile or so ahead of the cattle.

Putting a line of brush between him and the drive, he loped ahead. He sat at the edge of a thicket, watching as Sixto approached.

He had found the Mexican interesting. Sixto, well into middle age, had whiskers black as pitch, belying his age. He minded his own business and rarely talked beyond whatever was absolutely necessary. His black eyes seemed to see everything but hid whatever was behind them. He seemed always to be thinking. Hewey wondered if he thought in Spanish, or if he thought in words at all. He suspected the cook had come out of Mexico rather than South Texas. He liked to think Sixto had been a revolutionary and had killed some brutal hacendado for revenge. More likely, though, he had simply been a bandit.

Hewey rode out to intercept him. "I'm out of grub," he said. "Seen anything of Slocum?"

Sixto stood up and looked back toward the cattle. "Sí, the Slocum and a *rinche*. They come to find you, but they don't find nothing. Nobody tells them nothing."

"Where are they at now?"

Sixto shrugged. "*Quién sabe?* They go away, but two times they come back. They think maybe they catch you."

"They ain't yet. Sack me up somethin' to eat, will you, and I'll skin out of here again."

Sixto quickly filled Hewey's sack. He cautioned, "Those *rinches,* they have extra eyes. This one talks much and looks dumb, but I think he sees everything."

"He'll have to get up early in the mornin' to see me."

"Maybe he don't sleep at all."

Hewey said, "Tell my brother I'm doin' fine," and rode off in a long trot.

He found a suitable campsite near a windmill several miles farther on. The place had once been a homestead. He napped in the shade of a chinaberry tree some settler had planted, then shed his clothes and took a leisurely bath in the mill's earthen tank. His stomach began to talk to him, and he decided it was time to fix supper. He climbed out of the tank and walked to where he had left his clothes hanging on the bottom brace of the windmill.

They were not there.

A voice behind him asked, "Are these what you're lookin' for?"

He turned quickly, holding his breath. A tall, lanky man stood there, a round badge prominently displayed on his shirt. Hewey's clothes lay at his feet. "I reckon you'd be Bill Jones?"

Hewey recognized Len Tanner's broad grin.

Stammering at first, Hewey got over his surprise enough to say, "Where did you come from?"

"From all directions. Us rangers are everywhere. I figured you'd show up at the wagon sooner or later. I trailed you from there. Better get your clothes on while I decide whether you're Hewey Calloway or Bill Jones. I've got a warrant for Bill Jones."

"I'm back to bein' Hewey Calloway."

"I knew it had to be you as soon as I seen your brother Walter with that cattle herd. Everything fit. Naturally we didn't find anybody who'd admit to ever knowin' Bill Jones. Slocum doesn't know your real name, and I didn't see any reason to educate him."

"Thanks, Len." Hewey began putting on his clothes, starting with his hat. "I heard that you got yourself shot up by that cattle thief, what's-his-name."

"Olin Trumble. He just creased my ribs, maybe cracked one a little. It grabs me now and again when I move wrong. I made out like it was a lot worse because I wanted him to think he'd put me out of the way for a while."

"What brought you to this part of the country?"

"Trumble's a native of these parts. I had myself assigned down here where I could watch his white-trash kinfolks. I think I've got a lead on him."

"I hope so. It's on account of him that I'm on this drive. He threatened to get me for testifyin' against him. Some people thought they saw him back on the Pecos, so it was a good idea for me to go away."

"He *was* out there a while back, but he didn't stay long. Normally I wouldn't figure him to risk his neck for revenge against you, but them kind of yahoos don't think like us normal people. They can hate awful hard." He grimaced. "Sid Slocum for an instance. He's foamin' at the mouth like a hydrophoby coyote. He wants Bill Jones sent to the pen for life or a hundred and fifty years, whichever takes the longest."

Hewey tried to calculate how old he would be in a hundred and fifty years. "All that on account of me pullin' a little joke on him?"

"Some folks ain't got much sense of humor."

"What do you reckon I'd better do?"

"Keep doin' what you're doin' now till he gives up the hunt. If I was you I'd ride on ahead, take roundance on San Antone, and pick up the herd somewhere to the west, like over in the German settlements."

"You're not goin' to arrest me?"

"I'm carryin' a warrant for Bill Jones. I don't see anybody here by that name."

Hewey started breaking camp. "I'm much obliged."

Len shrugged. "For nothin'. Sid Slocum is a brass-plated son of a bitch. I just hope he don't find out that Bill Jones and Hewey Calloway wear the same size britches."

"Who's goin' to tell him? Padgett and the others, they're honest men." He reconsidered. "All but maybe Fat Gervin."

He was tying his blankets behind the cantle of his saddle when he heard a gruff voice. "Well, ranger, I see you have apprehended the culprit."

Before he even turned, Hewey knew Sid Slocum had caught up with him.

FIFTEEN

L EN TURNED TOO QUICKLY AND GRABBED AT HIS SIDE. He winced in pain, then said, "Sure did, Mr. Slocum. Caught him fair and square."

Slocum glowered. "He has a lot to pay for, leaving me to die. It will be my great pleasure to see him locked in the meanest cell of the Karnes County jail."

Len pressed his hand against his ribs, which had not yet fully healed. He said, "I'm afraid it ain't goin' to be quite that way. You see, I recognized him. His real name ain't Jones at all. It's Atwater, and his crimes take up half a page in the Rangers' fugitive book. He's wanted out in San Angelo for killin' a whiskey drummer just to get his sample case. They want him at Menardville for bustin' a teamster's skull in with a singletree."

Slocum's jaw sagged. "He did all that?"

"Sure 'nuff. He's a desperate man. Be thankful he didn't decide to kill you."

Slocum paled as he contemplated his narrow escape.

Len said, "I'll have to deliver him to Ranger headquarters in San Antone. They'll decide who gets to hang him first."

Slocum looked as if he were about to be sick.

Len said, "But I'll put your name on the list. You'll get the use of him if there's anything left. Would you like to help me put the handcuffs on him?"

"I am not an officer. You'd better do that yourself."

Len locked the cuffs. He said, "You can tell the sheriff down there that Bill Jones has been took care of."

Slocum summoned up courage enough to say, "I should be entitled to strike him just once."

"It's contrary to regulations, but if he gives me any trouble I'll do it in your name."

Slocum mounted his horse. He said, "At least I shall have the pleasure of telling Jerome Padgett and his motley crowd that Bill Jones is getting what is coming to him."

"I wouldn't. They might do you some injury."

Slocum reconsidered. "You are probably right. I'll go around them." He took one more look at Hewey. "I hope they hang you so high that even the buzzards cannot find you."

Len promised, "He'll get his due."

When Slocum was well gone Len said, "I'd better leave the cuffs on you for a while. Slocum knows my ribs are still touchy, so he might circle back around to be sure you ain't taken advantage of my weakness. He threatened to get me fired if I didn't stop what I was doin' and hunt for you. His money gives him pull in high places."

"He's got a lot worse comin' to him than spendin' a night or two in the bottom of a cistern."

"Bad as they need it, sometimes you can't punish his kind. You have to leave them to heaven. He'll get his comeuppance someday, some way."

Hewey accepted it, though it was not good enough. "I'd better stay with you till Slocum has given up for sure."

"I'd be obliged for your company all the way to San Antone, but you'd better know that I'm goin' there after Olin Trumble. His mother-in-law tipped me that he's hangin' around a low dive with a woman friend. The old lady wants me to shoot him so her daughter can marry a better man."

"Are you plannin' to shoot him?"

"Naw, I'd like to wake up every mornin' for the next twenty years and know he was fixin' to spend the whole day bustin' rocks in the state pen. The daughter can get herself a *dee*vorce."

Hewey rode alongside the skinny Ranger, imagining how it would be to wear the handcuffs for real. Though as a boy he had sometimes fantasized about romance and adventure in an outlaw life, the cuffs were a sobering reality. He said, "You're a natural born liar, tellin' Slocum that big windy about me bein' called Atwater."

"Wasn't much lie to it. There really was a Bill Atwater, and he does have half a page in my fugitive book. He got his light snuffed out a while back in Galveston."

"Shot?"

"Nope. Choked to death on a fish bone. Like I said, sometimes you have to leave them to heaven."

ARRIVING AT THE SOUTHERN edge of San Antonio late in the afternoon, Len said, "I know you volunteered to go in with me, but are you still sure? I won't hold it against you if you decide to back out."

Hewey had begun to rethink the situation, but he had given Len a promise. He would swallow hard and keep it, the way Pa would have. "Just tell me what you want me to do."

"We'll stop here and wait till dark. Wouldn't want the quail to flush before the gun is loaded."

Hewey had no argument with that. A larger question nagged at him. Why in the hell had he given Len his word in the first place? He was no lawman. He wasn't even a top hand yet as a cowboy. He should be with Tarpley's herd, and he would be were it not for Sid Slocum.

He wished he were back on the Pecos. He would even settle for East Texas.

He said, "I'd better tell you, I'm real consistent with a pistol. I miss every time."

"I don't want you to carry one anyway. I'd sooner face a dozen Comanches than a well-meanin' cowboy with a gun in his hand."

Len untied his blanket roll and spread it in the shade of a tree. Though he moved carefully, he stirred up fresh pain and sucked in a sharp breath. He said, "I've got my ribs bound up tighter than the bark on a tree, but they can still hurt like hell."

"You oughtn't to be ridin'."

"You can't catch a fish if you don't keep your line in the water."

To Hewey's amazement, Len soon dropped off to sleep. He wondered how the ranger could do that with the hurting in his side and the knowledge that he might soon confront a wanted man who had already wounded him once. Hewey's stomach was in turmoil from just thinking about meeting up with Trumble. Sleep was out of the question. He would be lucky if he didn't toss up everything he had eaten the last two days. He thought of a dozen excuses for spurring away from San Antonio like a turpentined dog.

Pride made him stand hitched. He had walked away from fights, but he had never *run* away. Running was for cowards. Hewey was merely cautious.

When darkness came, Len awakened, yawned, then got up and rolled his blanket. "About suppertime. I know where there's a pretty good chili joint that don't try to get rich in one day."

"I don't think I could eat a thing."

"I've got a rule. Never get shot on an empty stomach if you can help it." He saw that Hewey took him seriously. "You ought to know I don't mean half of what I say. I just talk to keep the silence away."

Hewey tried to make sense of that, but he couldn't.

Len said, "Silence gives me the shivers. It's what it must be like when you're in your grave."

Len ate a hearty meal of tortillas, chili, and beans. Hewey sipped half a cup of coffee that kept churning after it went down. He said hopefully, "Maybe Trumble has gone someplace else."

"We'll find out directly. You ought to try some of this chili. It's hot enough to light a cigar without a match."

The thought of it brought the coffee halfway back up Hewey's throat.

Len stalled until his pocket watch told him it was nearly ten o'clock. "If he's goin' to be there at all, he ought to be there by now. You've still got time to back out."

Hewey felt that he had committed himself too deeply to back out. "I'll go." But his heart was not in it.

They tied their horses in front of a low stone building that had a sign reading EL GALLO ROJO.

Len said, "That means The Red Rooster. It's the kind of place where folks pick their teeth with a bowie knife."

"And we're goin' in?"

"Me through the back door, you through the front. I hope we don't set off a shootin' inside. Might hit some innocent party, if there's any innocent parties there."

"I'm an innocent party. What if he decides to shoot *me?*"

"I'm bettin' he'll want to sneak out without a ruckus. You go to the bar and order a whiskey. If you see Trumble, don't act like you recognize him. The main thing is for him to recognize *you*. I figure he'll head to the back door. I'll be waitin' there for him."

"What if he runs over me and goes out the front?"

"A fifty-fifty chance is about the best we get most of the time."

Len started around the building but turned for another word of advice. "Don't drink that whiskey. It's apt to burn a hole in your belly. In joints like this sometimes they sell it before the snake heads have dissolved."

"Thanks for worryin'."

"I ain't worried. This is what I do for a livin'. I don't like for life to get dull."

"Around you I doubt it ever does."

He watched Len turn the corner and disappear. He waited another minute or two, giving the ranger plenty of time to get in place. Putting down a strong urge to turn and run, he took a deep breath and stepped through the open door.

He wished his breath had been deeper, for the air inside was thick enough to slice. Whiskey, sweat, tobacco, and lamp smoke all mingled in a toxic mix that assaulted eyes, nose, and throat alike. He coughed and tried to blink away the sting.

Through the haze he saw that the cantina was crowded with men and women of many shades and hues. The aggregate noise of multiple conversations made it impossible to pick out any single voice. He worked his way to the bar and told the dark-complexioned bartender, "Whiskey."

The man waited, his brow furrowed expectantly. Hewey realized he wanted to see the money first. He dug a coin from his pocket. The man examined it distrustfully, then filled a clouded glass from a bottle beneath the bar. Hewey could not see the label, but it did not matter. The bottle had probably been refilled many times with something other than what the label claimed.

He pretended to taste the whiskey but remembered Len's admonition and barely let it touch his lips. He turned away from the bar and saw Trumble. His heart gave a jolt. He realized the cattle thief had seen him first, his eyes fixed on Hewey in sharp surprise. Hewey tried to pretend not to recognize him. He let his gaze sweep on past, but he continued to watch Trumble from the corner of his eye. The fugitive sat at a small table with a slender Mexican woman whose dark eyes had been accentuated with heavy black makeup, her cheeks crimson with an overdose of rouge.

Trumble pushed to his feet. He started to move toward the front door. Hewey forced himself to act casual, though his lungs felt about to explode with pent-up breath. He carried his drink toward a vacant small table and blocked Trumble's path. Trumble turned and started for the back door. He got there just in time to bump headlong into Len.

The ranger held a pistol, but the collision was violent enough to knock it out of his hand. He grappled with Trumble, then gasped and doubled over in pain. Trumble had somehow struck the sore ribs.

He was about to go out the door. Hewey had no time to think. He grabbed a chair out from under a patron. He threw it at Trumble, knocking him off his feet. The patron fell to the floor in front of Hewey, tripping him. Four were down in a tangle: Hewey, the protesting patron, Len, and the cattle thief.

Hewey was the first to his feet. Trumble struggled to his hands and knees, at the same time trying to draw a pistol from his waistband. Hewey managed to step on his fingers and then slide the weapon across the floor. He righted the chair and set it down so that its legs straddled Trumble. He seated himself in it and fought to regain his breath.

Trumble floundered and cursed, trying to free himself from the chair. He was pinned down by Hewey's weight.

When he gained enough voice to speak, Hewey said, "You all right, Len?"

Len sat up and saw that Trumble was helpless. He wheezed, "I think he rebusted my ribs. You sure you've got a tight hold on him?"

Trumble's woman companion recovered from her initial shock enough to fire off a tirade against Hewey and the ranger. Hewey recognized only a couple of words that he had heard the vaqueros use against the cattle. The tone told him she meant him no kindness.

He would not have been surprised if some of the bar patrons came to Trumble's aid, but none did except for the woman. Her opposition was entirely vocal. Word quickly went around the room that Len was a ranger. If Trumble had any friends here, their friendship was not strong enough to make them butt in. It was well known that trouble with one ranger meant trouble with all of them.

Nobody had touched Len's pistol. He got to his feet and retrieved it, holding a hand against his side. He said, "You've sat idle long enough, Hewey. Go out and get the handcuffs off of my saddle, would you?"

Len took Hewey's place on the chair that held Trumble down. He said, "Hold still. Faunchin' around like that is makin' my ribs hurt. Bartender, bring my prisoner a drink. Maybe it'll settle him down." He set the heel of his boot upon Trumble's hand and pretended not to hear the howl of protest.

Hewey leaned against Len's horse for a minute, trying to let his nerves settle. He found the handcuffs and took them back inside. Len arose and lifted the chair from his prisoner. He pulled Trumble's hands behind his back and locked the cuffs.

He said, "We'll take this gentleman down to the county jail till state headquarters decides what to do with him."

Hewey said, "We don't know if he's got a horse."

"He's got two good legs. A long walk will help him to think about the wages of sin."

Outside, Trumble stood with shoulders drooped as Len dropped a rope around his middle. Len swung up onto his horse. He said, "Well, Hewey, you won't have to worry about him anymore. You can go back to the Pecos River and not give him another thought."

Hewey shook his head. "I can't believe I let myself do what I just did. If I'd had time to think about it, I'd've lit out like a jackrabbit."

"You done fine, though. If you ever take a notion you want to be a peace officer, let me know. I'll put in a good word with the Rangers."

"Nobody can ever accuse me of bein' that foolish. I'll be happy if someday they can say I'm the best cowboy C. C. Tarpley has got, and maybe get raised to a dollar a day."

*   *   *

LEN AND HEWEY SPENT the night in the county jail, though with the cell doors open. Hewey was tired enough that the hard cot felt like a feather bed.

After breakfast he bade Len good-bye. He did not stop to speak to Olin Trumble, for everything worth saying to him had been said. He saddled his horse and headed south on the road toward Laredo, hoping to strike the trail of the Tarpley herd. He encountered a woman and two towheaded youngsters traveling toward town in a farm wagon.

He asked, "Ma'am, you seen anything of a cowherd passin' this way?"

The question roused the woman to immediate anger. "You're damned . . . you're dern right I did. A bunch of them cows trampled my garden. What little they left behind, the cowboys ruined tryin' to drive them out. I'm on my way now to find the sheriff. I think I've got damages comin'."

"Yes, ma'am."

"Do you know who they belong to?"

Hewey thought quickly. "A man named Eli Jessup, out by Upton City."

"Mr. Jessup has got a surprise comin' to him when my lawyer sends him the bill."

"Yes, ma'am. I expect he'll be real surprised."

A herd of that size was not difficult to trail. Hewey cut across their sign and turned westward. He found them at noon, some of the men eating at Sixto's wagon, the rest continuing to push the cattle at a slow pace that did not tax the smaller calves.

Padgett noted Hewey's arrival with a casual nod and hardly looked up from his coffee. "Thought maybe you'd quit us."

"I couldn't do that. Ain't been paid yet."

Walter walked up carrying a plate of beans and some kind of meat. Hewey saw the freshly cut carcass of a kid goat hanging from the wagon. Probably a stray and fair game for whoever came along. Walter asked, "Are you sure you left Sid Slocum behind?"

"Did better than that. I left Olin Trumble in the San Antone jailhouse." He explained how he and Len had caught the cattle thief. Noting the eager reception his account received from Walter, Padgett, and a couple of the Mexican cowboys, he saw no harm in embellishing his own part a bit. Len probably wouldn't mind. Anyway, he wasn't here.

Walter said, "Now you won't have to keep lookin' back over your shoulder. You've got nothin' to worry about."

Hewey nodded, though he knew that was not entirely true. He still had to worry about Walter. His brother had not mentioned Eve in a while, but Hewey had sensed that he still thought about her often. A faraway look would come into Walter's eyes, and not even a clap of thunder would bring him back before he was ready. Hewey would try to distract him by talking about dreams of his own, dreams of being free as a pair of eagles, roaming the West wherever they pleased, visiting the Rocky Mountains, perhaps even wading barefoot in the California surf. The whole world was open to a man who carried no responsibilities except to himself, no baggage to tote that he could not wear or tie to his saddle.

He said, "I been thinkin', Walter. When we get these cattle delivered and draw our pay from C.C., let's quit and go see somethin'. I hear they're startin' up some big ranches out in Arizona. Been lots of Texas cattle gone up to Montana and Wyomin', too. I'll bet they're payin' a lot better wages than C.C. ever would."

"I thought you said money doesn't mean anything to you."

"It ain't the money, it's the excitement. A man can get bogged down in one place and never know what all's out there that he's been missin'. Like C. C. Tarpley. He doesn't know but what the whole world starts and ends along the Pecos River."

Walter frowned. "A man can also miss a lot by bein' always on the go. There's much to be said for takin' root in one place, buildin' somethin' of your own, raisin' a family and watchin' them grow with the country. It's the kind of life Pa and Ma had. They seemed to like it."

"Pa never got out of East Texas except for the war. He was always one crop short at the bank, and he died a poor man."

"Broke yes, but he never was poor. *Broke* just means out of money. *Poor* is when you're down in your spirit. Pa was always happy right where he was, him and Ma."

"Ain't many women like Ma, and there's few men lucky enough to find one."

"I believe I already did."

Hewey ran out of argument for a while.

Why wasn't Eve born fat and ugly? he wondered.

The terrain west of San Antonio quickly became hilly and rough, the rock-strewn road occasionally a challenge for the wagon. Padgett followed the old military route that would lead through Friedrichsburg and Fort McKavett, then on to San Angelo at the confluence of the Conchos.

Gabe had fallen moody and quiet. It was as if he isolated himself from the other riders, immersed in his own meditations much like Walter. Hewey pulled up beside him, hoping to strike up a conversation. Gabe offered none.

Hewey asked, "What you studyin' on so hard?"

Gabe was slow to answer, as if it took a minute to break through the invisible wall that surrounded him. "Walter's been tellin' me about a woman out in Upton

City that he's took a shine to. Got me to thinkin' about the one we saw workin' for the old man who sold us that horse Belcher. What was his name?"

"It was Hickley, maybe, or Hickson. I believe it was Hickson."

"I keep studyin' about her. His cook's daughter, he said she was. Name of Belinda."

"You remember her name but you can't remember his?"

"She was a right smart the best lookin' of the two. Goin' by the landmarks, I think we'll be passin' that place again."

"Looks like it to me."

"Reckon it'd be all the same to Mr. Padgett if I was to stop off for a little visit?"

"I don't see how it could hurt, but he's bossin' this drive. You'll have to ask him. What's so special about that girl?"

"While you was out on the Pecos, did you see any women of my complexion?"

"I don't recall that I did."

Gabe nodded as if no more justification was needed.

Hewey said, "You and Walter have both got women on the brain. Women tie you down. They keep you from doin' all the things you want to do and goin' to the places you want to see."

Gabe shrugged. "It's different with you. You're white. You can go anywhere and be welcome. I can't. You've seen for yourself, there's places they won't even let me stay for a night. I've seen signs sayin' 'Nigger, don't let sundown catch you in this town.'"

"Matter of fact, I have, too."

"I'm out of work when this drive is over. That old man asked if any of us wanted a job. I'd like to see if he was just talkin' to you and Walter, or if he meant me, too."

"He'll have you wrestlin' with them goats."

"That's all right. Goats won't care what color I am."

Juanito rode close, bringing in a cow and a calf that had moved off to graze. Hewey asked, "How about you, Juanito? You thinkin' about leavin' us, too?"

Juanito seemed surprised by the question. "Mr. Dodge, he is dead. Mr. Slocum, he got his own vaqueros. I stay with Mr. Padgett."

Padgett was careful not to let the herd get close to Hickson's field. The goat man rode out and looked the cattle over, then pulled up beside Hewey and Gabe. "I'm glad they're yours and not mine. I can grab hold of a goat and throw it down. Can't do that with a cow."

Hewey said, "They're not exactly ours. They belong to Mr. C. C. Tarpley. We're deliverin' them to him."

"So you're all hired hands. I'm still lookin' for help. Anybody interested?"

Gabe tried to be casual, but his eagerness showed through. "I might be."

Hickson stared at him as if appraising a horse. "Are you a workin' hand or a smart hand? I've had some smart hands."

"I'm a workin' fool."

"I believe in payin' a man what he's worth. How about six bits a day?"

That was as much as Hewey was making, and Gabe didn't know anything about goats. Sometimes life was not fair.

Gabe asked Hickson, "Is your cook really good?"

Hickson rubbed his stomach. His belt was buckled at the last notch. "You can see for yourself. Her daughter is a pretty good hand in the kitchen, too."

"Then I ain't a cowboy no more."

SIXTEEN

PADGETT SKIRTED SOUTH OF SAN ANGELO AS HE HAD skirted past San Antonio to avoid angry confrontations over trampled gardens and broken fences. He followed Dove and Spring Creeks past a village called Knickerbocker and a town known as Sherwood before bearing a little to the north and striking the Middle Concho.

He said, "I hope it's rained enough to fill up some water holes. Otherwise it's apt to be a dry drive from the head of the Middle Concho to the Pecos. Charlie Goodnight was one of the first to drive cattle this way, more than twenty years ago. He had all kinds of hell."

Hewey assured him, "There was water enough when we came this way, me and Walter. Even a few windmills that's been put up since the last time you were out here."

"Good. I was afraid I'd have to earn that extra commission I'm fixin' to charge C.C."

"What do you figure on doin' after we get these cattle delivered? You goin' to work for C.C.?"

"For that tight-twisted old hellion? No, I think I'll go on out to Pecos City and sign on with one of the big outfits. I'll take the Mexican hands with me. That way I can offer somebody a whole crew."

"Juanito, too?"

"I made Dodge a promise. I'll look after him till he's mature enough to look out for hisself."

That eased one of Hewey's concerns. He doubted that Tarpley would be hiring extra hands, and he had feared that Juanito might be left at loose ends. "You're good-hearted, Mr. Padgett."

Padgett seemed embarrassed. "Ain't nothin' good-hearted about it. It's just business. I'll be needin' Juanito and these other boys as bad as they may need me."

"How about Sixto?"

"There's times when cowboys are in surplus supply, but there ain't ever too many good cooks. Damn right I'm takin' him with me."

Hewey had been seeing travelers along the trail, so he paid little attention to a horseman coming from the west until he was close enough to recognize.

"Looky yonder, Walter," he said, "it's Snort Yarnell."

Snort stopped to talk to Padgett at the point of the herd. Hewey and Walter left the drags to Juanito and another hand and loped up to greet Snort. The gangly cowboy slouched in the saddle, his gold tooth gleaming in a foolish-looking grin that slanted across his homely face.

"Howdy, Hewey. How do, Walter."

Even before he was close enough to smell Snort's breath, Hewey knew he had been drinking. "Where you headed, Snort?"

Snort pointed in a vague easterly direction. "San Angelo. Thought it was about time I had me a good old-fashioned drinkin' spree and did somethin' I'll worry about from now till winter. I kind of dread it, though. I know how bad I'll feel when it's over."

Walter asked, "Why don't you quit it?"

"Can't. Got too much invested in it already." Snort reached inside his shirt and pulled out a half-empty bottle. "Drink, anybody?"

Padgett said, "Not till the drive is over."

Snort tipped the bottle, then stuck it back in his shirt. "It might be over sooner than you figured on. There's been hell to pay in Upton City."

Hewey pressed, "What're you talkin' about?"

"It's C. C. Tarpley and Eli Jessup. Them old jugheads got into a big cuss fight. Might've led to a shootin' if they'd been packin' iron, and there's liable to be a shootin' yet. I'd rather be someplace else for a while."

Hewey asked, "Aren't you workin' for Jessup?"

"Was. He fired me again. I figure by the time I've spent my wages he'll hire me back . . . if he's still alive."

Hewey remembered Tarpley's insistence upon secrecy about these cattle. "Were they fightin' about these cows?"

"The cows are part of it. Seems like there was a parcel of land the other side of the river that both of them wanted. Eli tried to buy it, but he was too chinchy to bid enough. So C.C. snuck in behind him and offered what the owner asked for. I gather he figured to stock the place with these cattle."

"That means we may be ridin' into a fight."

"You are if you keep goin' the direction you're pointed. You'll have to cross some of Eli's land to get to C.C.'s. Eli don't figure on lettin' you do it."

Padgett said, "The land's not fenced. I don't know where the boundaries are."

Snort considered. "Hewey and Walter can show you

how to go around. It's an extra long way, but it'd be the safest thing to do." He touched fingers to the brim of his hat. "Adiós, fellers. I got friends workin' for both outfits. I ain't stayin' around to see them get hurt. Or me neither."

The cattle had not stopped moving. Padgett touched spurs to his horse to keep up with the leaders. He said, "This ain't a fightin' outfit. There ain't but one or two guns in the whole shebang. I reckon we'd better turn them. But whichaway?"

Hewey watched Snort leave and for a moment wished he were going, too. "South. We may've already crossed Jessup's line. I see a windmill off yonder that I think is one of his."

He was fairly sure it was the mill where he and Walter had shared coffee with Jessup their first night on the trip.

Padgett said, "I remember a time when the Comanches came close to takin' C.C.'s hair. I almost wish they had. It ain't right, them two drawin' their men into a private squabble . . . gettin' them hurt, maybe killed. At cowboy wages, it ain't worth it."

Especially on what we're making, Hewey thought.

Padgett added, "But as long as you ride for a brand, you ought to be willin' to fight for it."

Hewey and Walter helped Padgett turn the leaders southward. The cattle had been traveling west so long that they resisted. Hewey explained the reason for the change to the rest of the hands.

Fat took it like a death notice. He said, "I ain't bein' paid enough for this. I'll send for my wages." He put his horse into a trot back the way they had come.

Hewey shouted after him, "What about C.C.'s daughter?"

"There ain't no woman worth it," Fat shouted back.

Juanito asked, "What do we do now?"

"Just what we've been doin'. Keep drivin' these cattle. Except now we go south."

Hewey loped off to catch Sixto and turn the wagon.

Sixto pulled on the reins. "There is trouble?"

"There could be. We're changin' direction to try and go around it."

The cook reached into a canvas bag beneath the wagon seat and brought out the biggest pistol Hewey had ever seen. It was of an old cap and ball design and probably as old as Sixto.

Hewey whistled. "Was that cannon made in Mexico?"

"Sí, but it can kill anywhere. Many times it has done so."

"Better put it back in the bag. We're tryin' to go around a fight."

"Maybe the fight is already come." Sixto pointed westward.

Hewey saw eight or ten horsemen approaching. His mouth went dry. He said, "We can't afford to start anything. There ain't enough of us to finish it."

Sixto handed him the pistol. Hewey tried to give it back to him. He said, "I couldn't hit anything noway."

Sixto would not take the weapon. "Then better you give this to Padgett. I think he will need it."

Hewey loped back to join Padgett and Walter. They had already seen the riders. Padgett said, "Looks like your friend Yarnell didn't come soon enough."

Hewey gave him the pistol. "Sixto thought you ought to have this, just in case."

Padgett's eyes widened as he examined it. "This thing could kill an elephant." He checked to be certain it was loaded. "I hope I don't need to use this." He shoved it into his right boot.

Walter squinted, watching the oncoming horsemen.

"That's C.C. and the boys, but I don't know whether to breathe easier or not."

Tarpley spurred out into the lead, slowing the last fifty yards to prevent frightening the cattle. He stood in his stirrups as if that would make up for his lack of size. He yelled, "Where the hell do you-all think you're goin'?" He pointed westward. "That's the way."

Padgett waited for Tarpley to come close enough that he did not have to shout. He said, "Howdy, C.C." His tone was civil but did not glow with friendship.

Tarpley grunted and turned angry eyes on Hewey. "You've worked for me long enough to know this ain't the shortest way to my ranch."

Hewey tried to keep his composure as Grady Welch and others of the Two Cs crew gathered around him. They were all armed. He said, "We figured it was the safest. We just found out that Eli Jessup intends to stop us from crossin' his country."

"I don't give a goddamn in hell what Eli Jessup intends. We ain't walkin' these cows two or three extra days just to suit him. Turn them."

Padgett flared. "You're the same blockheaded old fool I used to know, C.C. You're liable to get these cattle scattered and some good men hurt."

Tarpley flared back. "You've done your job, Jerome. I can do without your services from here on. I'll meet you in town and pay what I owe you after we get these cows settled where they belong."

Padgett did not retreat. "My job was to get these cattle bought for you and delivered onto your ranch. We ain't there yet. Till we get there and I get paid, I'm the boss of this drive."

Hewey had been in lightning and thunder storms when he could feel electricity crackling around him. He felt it now as the two men glared at one another. He looked at Walter but found no answers in his brother's worried countenance.

A distant movement caught his attention. He wiped a sleeve across his face and blinked away sweat that had rolled into his eyes.

He said, "You-all better come to a decision pretty quick. We got company comin'."

He saw at least a dozen horsemen, riding in a cluster. He knew they must belong to Jessup, for Tarpley had most of his crew here.

Tarpley looked at the men he had brought. "You boys check your guns. Make sure they're loaded."

Padgett exploded. "Now you *are* fixin' to get somebody killed. I thought when a man got older he was supposed to get smarter. You ain't learned a damned thing since the last time I saw you."

Tarpley gave no sign that he heard. "Get this herd movin'," he ordered. "Don't stop for nothin'."

The cattle had bunched up during the attempted turn southward and had not yet begun to string out again. Jessup and his men came on in a long trot, circling around them. Jessup drew rein with his horse and Tarpley's almost touching heads. His heavy mustache twitched like an angry black squirrel. He said, "You're on my land, C.C. Turn back, or we'll run them over you."

Tarpley's jaw jutted like a desert mountain rimrock. "This is a public road."

"The ruts are public, but the ground on either side of them ain't."

"These cows can't damage your land any. It's too sorry to hurt."

"If one of your cows travels a step farther west, I'll shoot her. And then I may decide to shoot *you*."

Tarpley leaned toward Jessup, eyes flashing defiance.

"You won't get the chance. You'll be dead before you can pull the trigger a second time." Both men dropped their hands to the butts of their pistols.

Hewey felt a prickling up and down his spine. Looking anxiously at the J Bar cowboys, he suspected they felt the same way. Jessup's foreman Mitch was tense, his right hand frozen halfway between the reins and his pistol. Hewey sensed that the men on both sides wanted more than anything to turn around and ride away. They were held in check by the crackling animosity between the two older men.

Padgett drew Sixto's pistol from his boot and pushed his horse between the two men. He pointed the muzzle first at Jessup, then at Tarpley. "There ain't nobody shootin' anybody unless I do it myself. You two heathens get your hands up away from them guns."

Both ranchers cursed him roundly. Padgett waited until they had run down, then said, "Both of you drop them pistols to the ground." Neither man moved. Padgett quickly lifted Tarpley's pistol from its holster, then Jessup's. He tossed them away.

He said, "You've both been spoilin' for a fight, but you've always wanted somebody else to do it for you. Get down off of them horses." He poked the pistol toward Tarpley. The skinny rancher dismounted stiffly, his face flushed in indignation. Padgett turned to Jessup. "Now you, Eli."

Jessup defied him for a moment, but he could not hold out in the face of that formidable weapon. He said, "Padgett, you're as crazy as a bedbug."

Padgett said, "Crazy enough to shoot one of you. Maybe both. Now, damn you, fight." When they did not, he shouted, "Fight, I said." He fired the pistol, which made a report like a cannon. The slug flung up dust between their feet. It started the cattle to moving away.

Jessup struck the first blow. It glanced off Tarpley's chin and made his head jerk back. With a roar of fury Tarpley tore into Jessup. Though Jessup was a considerably heavier man, Tarpley's anger gave him strength. His fists sent Jessup staggering.

Mitch made a move as if to interfere. Hewey told him, "Best leave them be. War would be a lot less bloody if they made the generals fight it theirselves."

For two men past their youthful prime, the two ranchers managed to inflict considerable damage on each other. They cursed and grunted and groaned, alternately grappling, then stepping apart and swinging their fists. They gradually slowed, gasping for breath, wiping sweat and blood from their faces onto torn sleeves.

Jessup was the first to go to his knees and stay there. Tarpley swayed over him, clenching blood-smeared fists but barely able to raise his weary arms. His wiriness had won out over Jessup's bulk.

Padgett's anger eased a little. He shoved Sixto's pistol back into his boot. He said, "I hope you two get so sore you can't move for a week. Maybe next time you feel like a fight you'll remember this. Now we're takin' these cattle south. If we have to cross some of Eli's land to get there, so be it."

One of Jessup's eyes was beginning to swell. He pushed to his knees but had to lean on his horse for support. His other eye narrowed in resentment as he faced his men. "You-all just sat there and did nothin'. Every last one of you is fired."

"Everybody was more scared of Padgett than of you two," Hewey said. "Some people think he's crazy."

Tarpley retrieved his pistol. He tried twice to get back on his horse, but his legs were too wobbly. Hewey attempted to help. Tarpley blistered him with a curse.

"Back away. I can do it myself." His third try put him up into the saddle.

"I still say we're takin' these cattle west." Tarpley looked toward his crew and shouted, "Stampede them, boys!" He ran his horse into the herd and fired his pistol into the air. The cattle shied away from him. A second shot put them into a run.

Tarpley kept firing until the pistol was empty. He commanded his men to do the same, but none did. The cattle were in full stampede.

Jessup shouted to his men, "Turn them. Get around them, dammit. Head them off." He spurred away in the wake of the fleeing herd.

Hewey lost track of other riders during the melee. Two Cs hands and J Bar punchers alike went after the cattle in a hard run, trying to move in front of them. They shouted and slapped coiled ropes against their leather chaps, trying to get them moving in a circle.

The run continued for the better part of a mile before the cowboys got the herd to milling. Jessup hollered, "Turn them south." Tarpley shouted, "Take them west."

Fuming, Padgett yelled, "Go to hell, the both of you."

Hewey was closest to him. Padgett said, "Better see if we got anybody hurt. It'll be the wonder of the world if we didn't."

Hewey immediately looked for Walter. He did not see him. He trotted up to Grady Welch and said anxiously, "Seen anything of Walter?"

Grady pointed. "He was over yonder way before I lost sight of him. I'm afraid his horse may have went down."

Hewey saw two horses limping with no riders on them. One was Walter's. The saddle was turned under its belly. Hewey's heart skipped. "Grady, help me find him."

The first man they found was Jessup's foreman, Mitch. He sat on the ground, one leg stretched crookedly in front of him. His face was pale in shock. Hewey said, "Grady, you better see what you can do for Mitch. I'll keep lookin' for Walter."

Grady dismounted, cursing. "Damned old rascals sure made a mess of it this time."

Hewey found Walter a little farther on. The first sight of him made Hewey's heart skip again. Walter lay on his side, one hand pressed against the other. Blood oozed out between his fingers. Hewey jumped to the ground, dropping the reins. He knelt beside his brother.

"Where are you hurt?"

Walter struggled to speak. "Horse fell. Then a cow ran a horn into me. Bleedin' like a stuck pig."

Hewey ripped Walter's shirt open. The wound still bled. Hewey could not tell how deep it was. He took a handkerchief from his pocket, wadded it, and pushed it partway into the hole.

Walter ground his teeth together. "If the puncture don't kill me, that handkerchief will."

"It's all I got." Walter's face was drained in shock, as Mitch's had been. Hewey looked up to see several riders coming to help him. He yelled, "Go get the wagon. We've got two men hurt."

Juanito wheeled around and loped off toward Sixto's chuckwagon. Two cowboys got down to see if they could help. Hewey recognized them as J Bar hands. In this emergency it did not matter which ranch they represented. They were cowboys together, the feuding owners be damned.

One of the men felt Walter's legs. "Don't seem to be broken," he said. "Looks like he got tromped on pretty good, though. He's probably bruised all to hell. Maybe got some hoof cuts."

Hewey told them about Mitch. One quickly rode off in Mitch's direction. The other declared, "They ought not to've stopped with a fistfight. I wish them two knotheads had shot one another."

Padgett rode up after a bit, his expression dark. He got down to examine Walter. He said, "As far as I can tell, there ain't but two men bad hurt."

Hewey said, "Two's more than enough." He saw Sixto's wagon coming. "We'll have to throw a lot of stuff off to make room for Walter and Mitch."

"Do it. If C.C. wants to bitch about it, let him. Right now I don't give a damn."

Tarpley rode up just before the wagon. Blood and sweat and dirt were smeared across his face. He launched an angry tirade against Padgett. "Them cattle are scattered all to hell, and you ain't doin' nothin' about it."

Padgett answered in kind. "And you can go to hell with them. Don't you see you've got a man hurt? And there's another one over yonder."

"That one's a J Bar man." Tarpley's tone indicated that Mitch was not his concern.

Hewey thought, *Some people learn awful slow.*

Sixto arrived with the wagon. He and Hewey and Juanito began throwing off bedrolls, dutch ovens, canned goods, and sacks to make room for the injured men. Tarpley shouted, "Wait a minute. Ain't that stuff mine?"

Padgett punched Tarpley's chest with the point of his finger. "If you ain't goin' to help, then get out of the way. Else I'm liable to forget that you're an older man than I am and finish what Eli started."

Sixto and Juanito spread a couple of blanket rolls while Hewey and Padgett gently lifted Walter into the wagon. Hewey told Sixto, "Mitch is layin' over yonder. We need to pick him up, too."

"We get him."

"What about them cattle?" Tarpley demanded.

Padgett said, "Let them graze Jessup's grass for a while. I'll take the boys and gather them when I get damned good and ready, only I ain't ready yet. Right now it's a good thing I've got no whiskey, or I'd get fallin'-down drunk."

SEVENTEEN

WALTER WAS RUNNING A STRONG FEVER BEFORE THE wagon reached Upton City. He seemed to drift in and out of consciousness. Mitch was awake, his teeth gritted so he would not cry out in pain. Grady and a J Bar cowboy had improvised crude splints out of mesquite limbs and had set the broken bone the best they could.

Hewey and Grady rode alongside the wagon. The J Bar cowboys trailed behind it. Jessup had fired them but later had harangued them to stay and see the cattle driven off of his grass. They had all left him anyway. He sat on his horse, a man alone, hunched in misery from the beating he had taken. Tarpley had persuaded his own crew to remain and help the South Texans gather the herd.

The doctor decided that Walter was in the most immediate need of attention. He told Hewey, "Your brother may appear unconscious, but he's likely to thrash around when I start working on that wound. You'd better hold onto him."

Grady joined Hewey in holding Walter's shoulders and arms. Walter groaned and struggled as the doctor cleared dirt and shredded grass out of the hole in his side.

The doctor said, "I'm afraid he has a couple of broken ribs, too. It's lucky they didn't punch a hole in his lung."

Walter sank into deep unconsciousness. The doctor closed and stitched the wound. "I'll bandage him in a little while. Right now I'd best see to the other one. I'll have to reset that bone."

Hewey had made a strong effort to keep his nerves under control while Walter was being treated. He almost lost his hold when Mitch cried out. Mitch's face glistened with cold sweat after the doctor straightened the leg.

As the doctor applied splints and wrapped Mitch's leg, he said, "You waddies need to learn that those cow brutes aren't house pets. They outweigh you by four to one."

Hewey was in no mood for small talk. "What about Walter? Is he goin' to be all right?"

"I have sewed him up. That's about all I can do for him at the moment. The worry now is blood poisoning. I need to watch him for several days. But as you can see, this house is hardly a hospital. It has little room."

Grady suggested, "We can take him over to Mrs. Pearson's boardin'house."

"That would be a splendid idea," the doctor agreed.

Grady placed a heavy hand on Hewey's shoulder. "You stay here with him. I'll go talk to Mrs. Pearson."

"She'll need to make a place for Mitch, too," Hewey said.

"We may have to pay for this out of our own pockets. You know C.C."

"Who cares? Money's not good for nothin' except to spend."

Grady said, "While I'm at it, I'll take our horses over to Brandon's stable and wagonyard."

"Brandon? I thought the owner's name was Sandy."

"It was, but he got caught on Alvin Lawdermilk's place with a hot runnin' iron. He ought to've known that a careful rancher like Alvin knows all his cows by name. You remember the calves we found with hair brands on them?"

"Yeah. We branded them over without lettin' C.C. and Eli get wise."

"Turned out Sandy was the one who sleepered those calves. Alvin caught him red-handed. On account of him bein' a family man, the sheriff gave him a chance to quit the country. He left last Saturday for California."

Hewey looked at his unconscious brother. "Just goes to show what too much ambition can do to a man. And all the time I suspicioned Alvin."

Grady had not been gone twenty minutes before Eve rushed into the doctor's house. Mrs. Pearson huffed along fifty feet behind her.

Eve demanded, "Where's Walter? How bad is he hurt?"

Hewey said, "The doctor can't say yet."

She accused him with her eyes. "Was this some of your doin', Hewey Calloway?"

He raised his hands as if to defend himself. "No, it was them two hardheaded old codgers, C.C. and Eli."

"I want to see him."

"He's in that room yonder asleep, or maybe unconscious. It's hard to tell the difference. But you'll be seein' a right smart of him for a while. If it's all right with Mrs. Pearson, we're fixin' to take him over to her place."

All the accusation had not left her eyes. "I think it was your doin' that he went on that drive."

She had him there. He did not try to deny it. He said, "I never figured on anything like this happenin'."

"I gather that you don't figure ahead about much of anything."

"No, ma'am, I reckon not."

"Well, I'm goin' to take good care of him even if you don't. Is that your wagon outside?"

"I reckon it belongs to C.C., along with the cattle."

Her voice was crisp. "We'll haul him over there in it, him and Mitch. You go out and see that it's ready."

Hewey's face warmed. He was not used to being ordered around by a woman, especially one he barely knew.

God help Walter, he thought.

WALTER'S FEVER GRADUALLY SUBSIDED. Eve hovered over him, fetching for him, holding his hands when she was not needed in the kitchen or dining room. Hewey watched the two with deep misgivings.

Padgett showed up after a few days to inquire about Walter's progress. His red eyes and flushed face indicated he was suffering through a hangover.

Hewey said, "I suppose you got the cows delivered?"

"Yep, but I thought I was goin' to have to whip C.C. myself, all over again. It's a good thing he finally came to see things my way. I hated to hurt a skinny wart like him after Eli had already scarred him up so."

"Their fight has been buildin' for a long time, like a boil on the butt."

"Maybe they got it out of their system."

"I doubt it," Hewey said. "When the fight was over they were still the same two old hardheads they were before."

"At least maybe they'll call a truce till the sores heal up."

Hewey nodded. "I hope so. If it wasn't for you they would've got somebody killed, more than likely. What do you figure on doin' now that the drive is over?"

"Got a line on a job out in the Davis Mountains. They need a crew, so I'll take the South Texas boys with me. There's a good many Mexicans workin' out there. My bunch will fit right in."

"Takin' Juanito, too?"

"Sure. I promised Dodge. Anyway, the kid's got the makin's of a top hand."

Padgett walked to the door of Walter's room and looked in. Eve sat in a chair beside the bed, holding Walter's hand.

He asked, "Is that the girl Walter was talkin' about?"

"Yep. I don't know what I'm goin' to do about it."

"Why do anything? If Walter's found what he wants, you ought to holler hooray and get out of the road."

"It just ain't what I planned on. I thought me and Walter would see the country together, travel when the mood struck us, and light wherever we felt like."

"Maybe that ain't what *he* planned on."

"I fixed it for Walter to go with me to South Texas so he'd get away from her a while. I hoped he'd have time to get over this foolishness about bein' in love. Looks like things turned out just backwards from what I figured on."

"What *you* figured on? That's where you went wrong. Bein' brothers doesn't make you the same. You wanted to do the figurin' for both of you, but Walter has got a mind of his own. You were only thinkin' about what you wanted."

"It's just that we've always done everything together."

"But Walter is old enough to be weaned. You'd best cut him loose, or you'll eventually be just two grouchy old dried-up bachelors, like me and Dodge."

Hewey glanced toward the door to Walter's room. He could hear Eve's soft voice, though he could not make out what she was saying.

He said, "Looks like it's been done for me."

Mitch frustrated the doctor by getting up on a set of crutches much too soon. Eli Jessup came to the boarding-house to visit him. His face was cut and bruised, one eye still swollen. He wasted no time on sympathy. He demanded, "How long are you goin' to lay there? Work's fallin' behind out at the ranch."

Mitch said, "You fired me, remember? You fired everybody."

"You'll be hired again when you can get back in the saddle. Till then you can understand why I can't afford to pay you for doin' nothin'."

Mitch's voice was bitter. "I understand real well."

Hewey bit his tongue and managed not to say anything, but he thought, *Even C.C. has got more human kindness in him than that.*

After Jessup left, Mitch said, "Padgett told me about findin' work out in the mountains. When I get up from here I think I'll go see for myself."

Tarpley came the same day, though fortunately not at the same time as Jessup. He, too, was bruised and battered, but he offered Walter more understanding than Eli had shown to Mitch. He said, "Don't you worry, you're still on the payroll just the same as if you was out there workin'. By the way, how long before you *will* be back out there workin'?"

Walter said, "Doctor tells me I can go to the ranch in a few more days. May be a while before I can ride."

Hewey told Tarpley, "We heard you got those cows delivered to your new ranch all right."

"Yes, but I damn near had to whip Jerome Padgett. He said he was in charge till we turned them loose and I wrote him a check. I didn't want a fight, so I finally let him have his way just to be shed of him."

Padgett would have made short work of Tarpley, but

Hewey said, "It's a good thing you-all didn't tangle. You might've hurt him."

"That's what I was afraid of. I didn't want an old man like that on my conscience."

Tarpley turned back to Walter. "I'll need to put a camp man out at my new place to watch over them cows. It's got an adobe house. Would you be interested in the job?"

Walter perked up. "I might be. Is the house fit to bring a woman to?"

Tarpley blinked, confused. "The roof might need a little work. Women can be fussy about such as that. But where are you goin' to find a woman?"

"I've already found her. Just ain't asked her yet."

Hewey followed Tarpley out of the room and down the hall toward the front door. Tarpley shook his head. "A woman? The boy must still be runnin' a fever."

Hewey said glumly, "I'm afraid he is."

On the porch Hewey said, "After Walter goes to that camp job, you'll be shorthanded at headquarters."

"I figured I could pick up one or two of the J Bar hands that Eli fired and ain't unfired yet."

"If Walter gets married, he'll need a raise."

Tarpley considered. "I suppose a camp job does justify a little extra. Reckon he'd be satisfied with thirty a month?"

"*I* would. I'm only gettin' six bits a day."

Tarpley untied his horse from a post in front of the boarding house. He said, "I'll raise you someday when you're a cow*boy*. Right now you're still just a cow*hand*."

Hewey sat on the step and whittled a stick of wood into slivers while he watched Tarpley disappear on the road that led to the Two Cs.

Oh well, he thought, *money ain't everything. Look at the fun I'm having.*

Look for

RANGER'S LAW

(0-765-31519-X)

BY ELMER KELTON

Available November 2006 in hardcover
from Tom Doherty Associates